IN WHICH A CAMEL

Wellington managed to grab Eliza ahead of a camel bolting for the main gate. Astride it was a lean young man, working the skirmish saddlebags with both hands. Gatling guns on each side of the camel twirled and snarled at the gate. The wood surrendered to the assault, and when the doors collapsed to the sand with a groan, the camel and its rider galloped out into the night. Without so much as a "thank you" Eliza dashed for the camel enclosure, swearing loudly. Apparently her disdain for the ships of the desert was not feigned. Wellington and Rateb ran after her.

"Those coins are deadly," Eliza said, grabbing hold of the bridle of the nearest, outraged camel. "Imagine what the House of Usher could do with them!"

Rateb tapped Wellington on the soldier. "Give me the coins you found. Showing them to Donohue might inspire him to rouse Agent Noujaim and the local authorities."

"Donohue can find us using the ETS rings," he said, handing the cinched kerchief to Rateb.

It took Wellington a moment to remember how; but with the right manipulation of the bridle, he managed to get his chosen mount to flop down on its knees. The skirmish harness each of the brigade camels wore was kept fastened on five camels just in case of raids from the desert tribes. It made the camels harder to handle than usual though.

Eliza let out a little yell as the camel lurched up. "Finishing school never really prepared me for this sort of sport," she said, running her hands over the controls of the saddle's guns. It was a poor joke, since he'd studied her record and Finishing schools had been spared the delight of educating Agent Braun.

"You're never too old for new experiences," Wellington quipped as he mounted the camel and ascended upward.

"I'm liking this side of you, Books, you know that?"

"Yes, and that scares me a bit," and with a cry, Wellington drove his camel into the night with Eliza right behind.

Other Books from The Ministry of Peculiar Occurrences

Featuring Agents Books & Braun

Phoenix Rising

The Janus Affair

Dawn's Early Light

The Diamond Conspiracy

Operation: Endgame

Featuring Verity Fizroy & the Ministry Seven

The Curse of the Silver Pharaoh

The Mystery of Emerald Flame

The Secret of the Monkey God

Anthologies

Ministry Protocol: Thrilling Tales of the Ministry of Peculiar Occurrences

The Books & Braun Dossier

Pip Ballantine & Tee Morris

Imagine That! Studios, Copyright 2018, 2020
All rights reserved.

Cover Design by Designed by OliviaPro
Interior Layout by Imagine That! Studios

No part of this publication may be reproduced, stored in or introduced into a retrieval system, or transmitted, in any form, or by any means whatsoever without the prior written permission except in the case of brief quotations embodied in critical articles and reviews.

This book is a work of fiction. Any resemblance to any person, living or dead is purely coincidental. Any actual places, products or events mentioned are used in a purely fictitious manner.

www.ministryofpeculiaroccurrences.com

For all our loyal podcast listeners

Case Files

A Nocturne for Alexandrina 1

Tangi a te Ruru / The Cry of the Morepork 17

The Touch of Hine-nui-te-po 27

Sins of the Father 46

The Precarious Child 57

Merry Christmas, Verity Fitzroy 71

Positively Shocking 81

Darkest Before Darkwater 97

A Christmas to Die for 112

The Fawlt in Our Stars 128

In the Spirit of Christmas 147

Silver Linings 154

Home Alone for the Holidays 173

The Evil that Befell Sampson 187

A Very Southern Christmas 200

A Nocturne for Alexandrina

By Tee Morris

London, England
Buckingham Palace
1839

For the first time since becoming queen, Victoria—unequivocally—was not amused.

Today was just one of those days where being queen really was more trouble than the title warranted, and certainly there was a lot of trouble to being queen of the British Empire. First, you needed to look like a queen. That went without saying. Getting up early enough to dress the part. Then there was the pomp and circumstance on the tiniest of life's most mundane details. Just making it to the table to enjoy a hearty breakfast with her beloved betrothed, Albert, practically demanded an act from Parliament. Then came the maintenance of the Empire itself. Petition upon petition from her overseas representatives, all imploring the crown for more money. Many of these "imperative missives" from ambassadors were about as dodgy and as superfluous as a man trying to sell high quality sand to a Persian desert gypsy. This, however, did not try her patience so much when compared to the explorers wanting to "expand the Empire" with her financial help.

Antarctica? Really? Why in the name of God would anyone wish to claim any part of that frozen wasteland?

She then felt a light trickle against the back of her neck. *I'm the Queen of the British Empire*, she seethed, *and with all this technology in my realm* they can't keep this palace cool in the summer? It's not even two years old! Bloody hell.

Suddenly conquering Antarctica struck her as a good idea. A summer retreat there sounded quite nice. Perhaps this was the price of being "the first" of anything—a sacrifice of creature comforts.

What gave Victoria a real chill of dismay was that she had only been queen for just over two years. And this miserable, droll routine would be her life for the next few decades. No, becoming queen had not come as a complete shock to her. Victoria's entire life and training had been leading to this, but certainly this predestination did not make the transition any earlier. Good Lord, just the news reaching her had hardly been an easy process. She could still remember that night involving a rather delightful dream of a Scotsman from good breeding, fine manners, and the kind of calf muscles, just visible from his kilt, that promised thighs and accompanying backsides a woman would take great delight in having within reach. She was enjoying a day's riding and then a lovely tea—and that was when she knew it was a dream, of course, as a Scotsman, no matter how fine the breeding, would not enjoy a tea, nor describe an Assam as delightful. He was about to become quite forward when she was awakened at the break of dawn by Mamma, informing her that the Archbishop of Canterbury and Lord Conyngham were in her sitting room, awaiting an audience.

How disappointing. She would have preferred to return to her rather saucy dream, but instead she was to accept the charge of Queen of the British Empire.

Now, Alexandrina Victoria, crowned Queen Victoria, merely tightened her smile and gave the most imperceptible of sighs through her nose. Yes, even queens woke up on the wrong side of beds, even ones as plush and as comfortable as the ones in Buckingham Palace. She had to find a silver lining to this day, or remain trapped in this rut. For the rest of her life. She was queen; but she was human, too. Currently, she was bored and frustrated to the point of tears.

"Finally," spoke her Lord Chamberlain, "we have a request for an audience."

Then he paused. Queen Victoria crooked an eyebrow, inclining her head to the Lord Chamberlain. Yes. Yes. Out with it.

"This request is — well..." He went to speak again, but his words appeared replaced by a clumsy silence. "He wants permission to establish a new branch of Her Majesty's government."

"I see," Victoria acknowledged with a nod. Let's see, she thought, suppressing a wry grin as she dreamt up new ministries. We are in need of a Ministry of Truly Appalling Pub Songs. We have no Ministry of Tweed. I think there are some patterns that are in desperate need of regulation. And then of course there is the priority to establish a Ministry of Silly Wal—

"Your Majesty," the Lord Chamberlain spoke, his voice shattering her witticism. "This branch he proposes would cover the entire Empire. It would be a global entity."

That caught her full attention.

"Does this petitioner have a name?"

"Professor Culpepper Source." The Lord Chamberlain paused to look over the papers in his hands, and then added, "He's a scientist."

"Is his name registered or recognised in any of our Royal Societies?"

"No, Your Majesty."

She turned to look at him. "And the reasons behind how he made it this far in the petition process and why I am seeing him this afternoon?"

"It is the evidence he has presented to his patrons and, in particular, to me personally."

"Are you saying you yourself have entertained this Professor Source?"

The man's complexion blanched as he spoke. He looked so pale in that moment that Victoria believed he would succumb to the vapours. "I cannot impress upon you the importance of seeing this man."

Perhaps Victoria's silver lining was at hand. "We shall see this man straight away then."

She was a tad disappointed at catching a glimpse of the petitioner when he came around the corner. The closer he drew, the fatter he became. He was a portly gentleman, with a rather bushy moustache that in some odd manner flattered him. The receding hairline, however, she found slightly irritating. Perhaps with a full head of hair, she would have found him quite dashing. In a rather plump sort of way. The suit seemed common enough. Not of any fashion she recognised, but of a tweed that did not speak of any fortune or elevated station.

A scientist. That is exactly what he looked like. A kindly scientist.

On this deduction, she gave a long, low sigh. *This day, I fear,* she grumbled inwardly, *is not going to get any better.*

"Your Majesty," he announced, giving a deep bow. When he came up, he paused, taking in a deep breath.

"Something amiss, Professor Source?"

He blinked. "Beg your pardon, mum?"

Mum?! Victoria asked, her back straightening slightly. *Did he just call me 'Mum'?!*

She began to worry about her appearance; she was only twenty, after all!

The man then released a little cough as he began what appeared to be a case of some sort. "Do forgive my impertinence, Your Majesty. I'm just a bit nervous, is all. I did not expect to see you upon such short notice."

On that, Victoria softened. An honest man. What a refreshing change. "Well, professor, it would seem that Fortune favours you as we are having a rather slow day here at the palace. Still, our time for an audience with you is fleeting."

"That it is, Your Majesty, so let us not bandy about." He clapped his hands together and then motioned to her. "I desire your company tonight, and yours alone."

That gave the collected court quite a shock. Victoria, on the other hand, raised an eyebrow. A bit bumbling. Sincere. Mindful of manners. And now, forward. With her.

This ought to be fun.

"This is a bold request you make of your Queen."

"Yes. So bold that you may wish to have me thrown in irons, but what I wish to bring to your attention—more importantly, what I have to show you—are matters pertaining to you and only you."

"Are these matters pertaining to the preservation of the Empire?"

The odd man nodded, his two chins jiggling as he did. "Of course."

"Then why not share these matters with my Privy Council, with those whom I trust with my life and with the direction of the Empire?"

"With all due respect and honours, Your Majesty," Source began, "you may trust them. I, however, do not."

Her Lord Chancellor stepped forward, and Victoria started at the deep hue of red his face had turned. "How dare you, sir! You did not tell me of this outlandish—"

Professor Source spoke over his tirade. "Sir, may I remind you of our previous luncheon, or should I reveal those daguerreotypes shared in confidence?"

That stopped the Lord Chancellor. Quickly. His red blush quickly receded to a ghostly pale wash. He swallowed, glanced towards Victoria, and then took a few steps back.

"Is this true?" Victoria asked the scientist.

"Did I lie to your Lord Chancellor, Your Majesty? No. I am no cad. Did I withhold a few details in my petition?" His eyes twinkled. "Yes. I am a bit of a rogue, on occasion I am afraid."

She had worn a smile often in court, but this one was the first in a long time that was truly sincere.

"And why should we trust you?"

"Because I am the only one you can trust concerning the darkness that threatens your empire." He gave his odd cravat a slight adjustment and then tipped his head back proudly. "I have been witness to things unparalleled and unexplainable, and while some of these revelations are fantastic and inspiring, there are phantasms and evil forces beyond our collected comprehensions that counter their purity and benevolence."

Victoria felt herself shift from intrigued to positively enthralled.

"You are a most peculiar man." She rose from her throne, and gestured him closer to her, though her guards flanked them as they walked. "You also have conviction."

"Shall I expect for your company then upon the hour of nine?" He reached into his pocket and checked the time. "That should give you ample time to dress in something appropriate. Something that would allow for movement and—considering who you are—anonymity." He then paused, as if a thought suddenly came to him. "Dress warm."

She crooked an eyebrow at that. "Warm? But it's summer."

"I know," he said with a nod. "Trust me. Dress warm."

Victoria pursed her lips, looked to either of her guards, then leaned in and whispered, "Outdoors, are we?"

"Avebury Circle."

"At night?" She glanced over to one of her guards. He looked poised and ready for an order. She leaned forward to make certain her guard couldn't hear her reply to the odd man with "Sounds like a lovely evening."

The professor reached into his coat, and produced a small folded parchment held between two fingers. "I will be by the fire, waiting for your arrival, Your Majesty." His eyes darted to the present gentry, and then he whispered, "Alone."

"We can make no promises."

"Nor do I expect you to." He gave a wink, extending the parchment to her. "I could be mad. Or an anarchist. Or both."

"Doubtful," she retorted, taking the paper from between his fingers. "You are far too clever."

He beamed in reply, stepped back from the Queen, and spoke to her again in a full, proper voice. "Your Majesty, my gratitude to you and your devoted court for your time." He took up the small case by his feet, and then with a few more steps back, his body remaining in a slight bow, the man turned on his heels and walked out.

"Your Majesty?" the Lord Chancellor spoke finally, causing her to start. "Your Majesty, I am sorry, I had no idea—"

"He shared something with you?" Victoria asked. "Exactly what, may I ask?"

His complexion paled even further. "Documents."

"Really?" She felt her twin shadows follow her up to the man. He flinched as she leaned into him, his eyes seeming to bore into the floor underfoot. "These documents must have some hold upon you."

"Your Majesty," he spoke, his voice hard and brittle. "What I saw..."

Tears welled in the man's eyes, and Victoria stepped back. Now she was to be the one stunned to silence. She was the queen of the most powerful nation in the world; yet an odd man armed only with a large suitcase, it would seem, could win himself a private audience.

She opened her eyes, read the time and place on the parchment, and then folded it back up neatly.

Yes, a bit of intrigue was in order. Things were getting unbearably dull in court. Now free of Mamma's influence and ruler of the British Empire, it was high time for her to stretch her legs and have a bit of fun.

⋄⇌⇋⋄

No one paid her a second glance once she walked into the humble tavern just outside the stones of Avebury Circle. The hearth was modest but managed to give a hint of warmth in this quiet corner of her empire. Just as promised, Doctor Culpepper Source sat in a lovely, high-backed chair, and he stoked coals in the fireplace. Victoria tugged the lapels of her black coat tighter and walked across smooth, worn planks that groaned lightly as she closed on him. She did not concern herself with stealth or with grace. Her attendants were all enjoying a lovely deep sleep thanks to a delightful laudanum concoction that her Mamma used on Victoria when she was younger. She was as he wished her to be—alone, which could have been an invitation for the downfall of the crown. Only two years into her reign as queen and to be kidnapped or worse, assassinated, and the British Empire would be thrown into chaos. And yet, here she was, the Queen of the Empire, in The Red Lion, unattended, meeting what her attendants in court—all save for her Lord Chancellor—believed was a madman.

How thrilling, she thought with a delightful rush.

He placed the poker back into its holder and then sat back into a reclining position. "I would stand upon ceremony," he spoke over his shoulder softly, "but even with the collected subjects here, few as they are, that is attention neither of us desire, now is it?"

She gave a giggle and took the seat opposite of him. Victoria crossed her legs, taking a moment to enjoy the outrageous outfit she currently wore. The thigh-high boots, even with their dull finish, caught the light of the tiny fire as did the leather trousers she wore. The clothes would have appeared more appropriate for riding, had she decided that black suddenly suited her as a colour. He looked at her and smiled approvingly. No doubt, he found the cleavage she was sporting with her cinched corset and waistcoat most unexpected as well as most appreciated.

"I took you on your word," Victoria purred, her breath appearing for just a moment before disappearing as wisps of æther, "and dressed appropriately."

"Indeed. You look hardly ladylike or appropriate." His eyes sparkled in the firelight. "I approve."

Victoria gave her lapels another tug and looked around her. "And thank you for advising me on dressing warmly. I had no idea—"

"The chill you are feeling has nothing to do with the weather or even an odd day of the season." He looked over his shoulder, fixing his eyes on the publican for a moment, and then glanced around at those sitting at tables, many of them enjoying a soup or a pint. When Source spoke to her, his voice had dropped to nearly a whisper. "Your Majesty, what I have to show you tonight are those responsible for the anomaly."

"Those responsible?" Victoria considered that turn of phrase, and then asked, "You're saying this cold is the work of man, not God?"

Source went to answer but paused as if remembering something important. He pulled out his pocket watch and clicked his tongue lightly. "Actually, Your Majesty, it would be easier if I got on with it and showed you." He stood, and then slipped a large haversack across his shoulder. He patted it for good measure, and motioned for the door. "Shall we?"

Victoria looked at the door of the Red Lion and felt something in her slowly recoil, much like a cat feeling growing danger and slinking back into a corner. Stepping through that door carried a cost, something akin to that fateful night when she was first addressed as Queen of England. She knew following Professor Culpepper Source would completely change everything.

Source was standing there at the door. He was far from the hearth, but his eyes still twinkled.

Victoria placed her palms gently on her hips, feeling the two concealed Derringers that the Lord Chancellor insisted she have upon her person. Instinct told her she would be using them tonight, but that same instinct told her she would not need them against the professor.

When she reached the door, he handed her a pair of Starlight goggles, leaned in, and stated quite plainly, "Do not leave my side, no matter what this evening offers. I wish to return you to the throne in one piece, and cannot guarantee as much if you gallivant off without me."

What cheek! Whatever made Source think he could address her in such a fashion?

She would have voiced her outrage, had it not been for the look in his eyes.

Victoria nodded, slipping the goggles around her neck and giving him a reassuring "Very well."

The affirmation, however, did not sound all too convincing to her.

At first, there seemed to be no need for the Starlight goggles. They kept to the path defined by the outer circle's larger stones. While still visible under the light of the full moon, the Red Lion was growing farther and farther off. As clouds began to block out the moonlight, however, the quaint pub seemed to wink out of existence.

When her Starlights revealed the thick darkness, it dawned on her that it had been a crystal clear night moments before. A full moon. No sign of any cloud in the sky. Now, they were both plunged into a thick darkness where even the goggles were struggling to grant her vision. She looked up to see a rippled, tumultuous cover suspended above her. Not a single ray from the pale goddess of night pierced the heavy sky now over them.

"Victoria," came a whisper.

Hearing such presumption ripped her gaze from the obscured heavens back to a pair of Starlights looking at her.

"All will be made clear to you," he whispered. "Just stay close and not a word until we are well-hidden."

Well-hidden? Calling the queen of the empire by her Christian name? And a cloud cover that appeared from nowhere?

This intrigue was more and more exciting with each passing moment.

The stone they crouched behind widened at its base, and it was here that Professor Source seemed to be settling in. Taking her gingerly by the wrist, he guided her to a tree growing just at the top of a deep ditch. He checked his watch, and then adjusted the goggles as he studied the clearing before them. He freed from his pocket a small flask and took a quick sip.

"Care for a nip?" he asked Victoria pleasantly.

When in Rome. "C'est bon," and she took a swig.

Whatever was in the flash tasted of nuts, burned a bit when it hit her throat, and gave her body a delightful warmth a few moments later.

"Direct your eyes to this open field before us," he whispered, slipping the flask back into his coat pocket. "The party I wish for you to see should be appearing momentarily."

A deep rumble sounded in her ears, but instead of casting a glance to the far-off thunder, she concentrated on where Source assured her "all will be revealed."

Wind rustled through the nearby grove. Again came a threatening rumble of rain. Why was it so bloody cold? She dared to look back up for that full moon she remembered shining over the Red Lion when something caught her attention. Something in the forest. Running. Drawing closer, fast.

Whatever they were, the beasts were about to emerge from the wood just off to their right.

The shadows leapt across the ditch to land softly in the clearing, but the creatures stepping into her enhanced sight were not what she expected. They were human. Women, it seemed, by their gait. Three of them.

She could hear another pattering of feet and then the noise ceased. Coming to meet them from the opposite direction, also dressed in some odd cloak, was a man.

"Professor, they seem to be talking to one another."

"Yes, yes," he muttered, and then offered her what appeared to be a palm-sized suction cup. "Place that on your ear, if you please."

When she did as told, a woman's voice could be heard as if Victoria stood next to her. She followed the cable connected to the earcup, and it ended at what appeared to be a small gramophone, except that its bell pointed in the direction of the gathered in the clearing.

"What is that?" she asked.

"What I sincerely hope will become a tool of the trade," he whispered, placing a similar cup to his own ear. "But please, Your Majesty, we must be quiet."

She turned her Starlights back to the clearing, and now saw a woman closing on the man. "Are you certain it is to be this way, Matthew?"

"It must be," he told her in reply. "The only alternative we have is to live in hiding, and I have grown tired of it. We strike, and we strike now. The patronage of the House of Usher will give us everything we need."

"We have never needed the help of those outside our coven," the woman in the middle protested.

"It is a new world, Evanna," Matthew conceded. "The Industrial Age is bringing upon us changes that we must understand, that we must exploit, before society does so. Then can we return to the true power we once held in this land."

Victoria felt herself bristle at that. "Not very pleasant people, are they, Professor?"

"Your Majesty, please," he whispered before placing a pudgy finger to his lips.

Her mouth opened with a reminder to whom he addressed, but the words caught in her throat on hearing the third woman in the clearing ask, "Did you hear that?"

The four faces turned in their direction, motionless save for the wind that tousled their cloaks. Victoria felt something in her stomach roil. Outlandish as it was, some instinct whispered to her that these four could hear her heartbeat.

It was Matthew that finally broke the silence, turning to the elder woman and assuring her, "Merely the Goddess, Miriam, whispering her approval through the trees. Nothing more."

Victoria finally released the breath trapped inside and her muscles relaxed.

The chill suddenly kissed the back of her neck, raising goose flesh on the nape of it and down along her arms. The professor's hand gently touched hers, and she saw him staring at her through his own goggles.

"The wind," he whispered.

In her Starlights, the one called Miriam snapped her head back in their direction. She was sniffing the air.

"A man. And a woman. Over there. And…" Her voice trailed off. "Something metallic. I smell grease."

"Right then," Source muttered. "Time to leave."

"Not just yet," Victoria whispered. "You should give my guard a moment to intervene."

"Your what?" And both the Professor and she returned their gaze to the four treasonous strangers.

Behind them, the shadows were taking forms of featureless grey men. The closer they drew, the more details appeared in their Starlights.

"You really didn't think the Queen of England would go unattended to Avebury Circle in the middle of the night?" Victoria said with a toss of her head. "If you did, you really are mad."

The four of them turned to the advancing soldiers. They had only taken three steps when the Queen's guard stopped, shouldering their rifles, calling out, "Halt in the name of Queen Victoria!"

The four traitors kept walking. In the Starlights, Victoria watched them slip free of their robes, their pale skin giving them semblances of phantoms closing in on her loyal subjects.

"I command you to ha—"

That was the last utterance from the soldier as the man named Matthew disappeared, his form moulting, pieces of flesh peeling away from him as he walked, revealing something like a dog, or something that could have passed for a dog had it not sprouted bat-like wings and borne the posture of a small bear. The enormous size of the beast did not hinder its movement as it was on the soldier a moment later. There was no shot in defence, nor was there a scream.

It was all over in seconds.

"Your Majesty," the professor said, tightening the strap of his Starlights, "whatever I tell you to do, do not question it. You must trust me. Secure your goggles. You will need them."

Victoria gave her own straps a few sharp tugs, feeling the goggles press deeper into her face. They were going to make a run for it, a tactic she would be hard pressed to hold in question as she watched the three women shimmer in the same grotesque manner Matthew had. With their massive wings cutting through the air, the four creatures made quick work of Victoria's elite, then looked back where they hid. Through her goggles she could see small voids, where, no doubt, amber eyes would have stared back at her, narrow on her. Around their monstrous snouts were dark patches of what Victoria deduced was fresh blood and gore, now smeared into their own sheer pelts. Their heads jerk upward ever so slightly, nostrils flaring as the wind carried her fear to them.

"Follow me. Stay close."

Professor Source leapt free of their hiding place, running towards the beasts, setting quite the pace for such a rotund gentleman.

"Bloody hell," Victoria hissed as she bounded into the night on the Professor's heels.

The queen could hear their footsteps pounding against the grass, but her eyes were focused in front of them on the four beasts, muscles underneath their smooth, shiny pelts bending and rippling underneath folded wings as they closed the distance. In her Starlights, she watched details emerge with each step. The beasts' breath appearing for only a moment before the night's chill claimed its warmth. Long, thin mouths that could not completely conceal such protruding curved teeth.

Closer.

Closer.

The alpha male, Matthew, leapt upward, his wingspan extending fully to catch an invisible wind, causing his fantastic form to reach vertically into the night.

Victoria felt Source take her by the arm. He called out, "Slide."

On feeling him tug, she followed his lead, repeating his command to herself as she tucked one leg underneath her and reached forward with the other. Their momentum and the evening's moisture underfoot carried them onward, sending them underneath the flying monster and between those flanking him. Over the shrill, squeaking sounds of their bodies sliding on the wet grass, Victoria could also hear the dark beasts slipping and stumbling over themselves. Whatever precious seconds they had would be enough to stay ahead of them.

His grip tightened on her arm as they stood.

"Professor?" No need to whisper now. They were completely in sight.

"Your Majesty, you must trust me," he said, pulling a small rod from his coat pocket. His other hand snaked inside his coat's outer pocket, but his eyes never left the pack of four creatures regrouping before them. "Look above us—are the clouds parting?"

She looked behind them, and up. Much like a curtain rising to reveal Macready's boy-king overlooking the field of Agincourt, the blanket of clouds were thinning, and suddenly they were awash in moonlight. She squinted from behind the Starlights, and then removed them all together. Victoria could now see the four beasts pacing slowly, sizing up their prey for a final attack, only a pale illumination cutting them free of the night's canvas. She swallowed, and flinched at how dry and grating her throat felt.

"Yes," she whispered.

"Hold your ground with me," Professor Source spoke over the packs' low, undulating growl. He still kept his eyes on them, even as he affixed a perfectly clear crystal onto the end of what now Victoria could make out in his hand to be something like a brass spike.

The pack leader—Matthew, Victoria had no doubt—did not look to either of the three she-beasts. He did not bark a command, or even paw at the ground. He gave a snort, conjuring a veil of breath that concealed his head for a heartbeat. When the warm mist dissipated, Matthew leapt forward, his only sound being his panting. Even. Rhythmic. Controlled.

With a tiny click, the crystal locked into place.

Victoria could hear a quick, soft snarl accompanying each breath now. The creature's eyes flared crimson in the full moonlight.

Then came the small explosion of steam from Professor Source. His hand was pressing a small button in the brass rod, and now the rod extended to the length of a quarterstaff. Source reared back, and drove the metal staff into the ground.

On entering the grass and earth underfoot, Victoria watched the other three beasts flinch and melt quickly back to their human forms, their naked bodies pale and ghostly under the moonlight. They were now on their knees, grabbing at their stomachs and chests, wailing in pain.

Matthew appeared far too determined to slow down, even though his growl told Victoria he had been struck hard by something. It pushed on through whatever pain had stricken his followers, threatening to overtake them in a moment.

Victoria started back when the beam appeared. It was as brilliant as a noonday sun, only pure white in its colour. The blast lifted Matthew off the grass and held him in the air, suspending him in time and space. She was not certain how long the winged creature remained frozen above the ground; and in this grandeur, Victoria became aware of Matthew's nightmarish form. He had still not reverted to a human shape like his companions. She watched him fall, but his body never hit the ground. The beam exploded out from its back, splitting in three to strike each of the wailing women. As it had been with Matthew, the women swayed back in a slow, languid manner, defying the natural way of things before winking out of existence with a sudden crack of thunder.

From above Victoria's head, something popped and sizzled. She looked up to see the quartz obelisk at the tip of the staff emitting light wisps of smoke. It seemed to be glowing faintly, its colour reflecting the moon high above it.

His eyes betrayed nothing. The skin around them tightened for a moment, the only indication that he himself had not been frozen by whatever force he had conjured mere moments ago. A mist appeared under his flaring nostrils, and his grip on the brass staff in his hand tightened.

Victoria looked around her. Only mist and moonlight touched the grass of Avebury Circle. The stones remained standing as silent sentinel in the night.

"Your Majesty," Professor Source spoke gently, "I believe we should return to the pub. Warm ourselves by the fire. And," he chortled, managing a friendly grin, "perhaps indulge with a wee drop of sherry."

Flames danced merrily in the hearth. Pint glasses of stout, ale, and bitter mimicked the overflowing conversation, a delightful mingling of mirth and laughter. From the kitchen came sweet, succulent smells of dishes far heartier than anything found in her royal kitchens. Victoria thought absently that perhaps, on nights when she craved something simpler, she should request from her cook a Shepard's Pie. Any chef worth their salt would have a good recipe for Shepard's Pie.

The diminutive glass of sherry was placed ever so gently before her. Two fingers then slid it closer to her hand. She picked it up, and that was when she noticed the tremble. She was no longer cold, but still shaking.

Victoria downed the sherry in one gulp, and groaned as the liquid burned its way down her throat. She much preferred her sherry sweet. She kept staring into the fire. She would not cry. She would not scream. She was Queen of the Empire, and would not falter.

The second sherry was placed next to her empty glass. "Do have a care, Victoria, and make this one last. I would loathe to have someone of your station in a state when I escort you home."

"You are far too familiar, Professor," Victoria seethed.

"Due to the rather crowded nature of the pub, I'm afraid necessity will out." The professor settled back into the high back chair in front of her, interlacing his pudgy fingers across his rotund belly. His once hard, cold eyes now seemed to glow with warmth. "So, your questions?"

"Who were those—" She meant to say "people" but that was not quite right, was it? They were completely and utterly horrific. "—things?"

"Hellhounds," he said quite factually. "Or I should say, a small coven of necromancers that, through some dark sorcery, possessed the ability to change themselves into hellhounds. I have been tracking them since stumbling on one of their ceremonies in West Yorkshire where I was on the trail of a cursed talisman, completely unrelated to them, I should add."

"West Yorkshire? A far cry from Avebury Circle," she chortled.

"I am tenacious in some things," Source quipped. "Matters such as this, I hold as high priorities."

"Matters?" Victoria asked. "You mean, there are more of those abominations out there?"

The professor smiled, the corners of his eyes crinkling as the firelight softened his plump features. "Have another sip of sherry." She did so, but her eyes never left him as he spoke. "This coven was, perhaps, one of a more darker nature. Wiccans prefer a more peaceful life, as would a Christian, a Hindu, or any other follower of a faith." Source gave a slight sigh as he glanced out of the window, as if he were returning to the circle of stones just outside. "As it is in any faith, there are some that are forward thinking in their manifestos. They wish to enact peace by their religion through violence. A Holy War, as contradictory as the term Civil War." He produced the quartz that had come to their aid, and placed it before her. "Another coven offered me this as a weapon against Matthew's black magic. They call this Luna's Prism. They entrusted me with it much in the same way you will, following this evening, entrust me with the means and resources to preserve the empire."

Victoria knotted her brow at that bold conclusion. His smile never faltered.

"The coven who held on to Luna's Prism, were in need of a special branch of Her Majesty's Empire. They trusted me as I assured them such matters would no longer be dismissed by either Palace or Parliament after tonight."

"And how were you so sure?"

Professor Source took a sip of his own sherry before motioning to the barkeep. The man gave a nod and produced from around his neck, a key. He disappeared for a moment in what could have been a corridor to the kitchens, or perhaps storage, Victoria could not be certain; but she concluded it was a private room of some sort when the publican emerged from the back of the pub again, the key was no longer in sight and the small case that the professor had upon his person at their palace appointment was now in the publican's hands. Placing it at Source's feet, he gave them both a tip of the hat and then returned to the bar.

There was still a good amount of conversation and din around them, but she started at the sound of the clasps flipping open. The professor slid the box closer to her and motioned to it. "If you would indulge me, Alexandrina."

Feeling that it would be needed, Victoria took a long sip of her sherry, savouring it before she bent down and opened the box in front of her. Her eyes went wide for a moment, and then jumped back to the mysterious man opposite her. "Is this—?"

"If you have to ask me, then you already know the answer, don't you?"

She shook her head, but it was no illusion. No mirage. It was real, and her fingertips resting gently on it, only confirmed as much. "How is this possible?"

"There are more things in heaven and earth than are dreamt of in your philosophies," he quoted. "When these things call for the attention of the Crown or threaten the preservation of the Empire, this is where and when your new ministry will step in and intervene." From his coat's inside pocket, he produced what appeared to be a modest proposal, perhaps five pages or so, folded neatly and held together by a deep blue ribbon. "A clandestine organization specialising in that which defies explanation. We will employ the brightest and most resourceful men and women representing every corner of the realm, dedicated to the preservation of the Queen, Her country, and the Empire."

The queen looked up from the bound decree, whatever shock, fear, or confusion she felt festering within her now gone. "Just like that?"

Source cast his eyes to the open case, then back to the queen. "Do you need more proof?"

She hooked her foot under one of the case's open lids and flipped it up. Both lids closed like a small creature clamping its leather-encased mouth around a snack. She gave the case a slight push and slid the box back over to Source.

"Yes, I could have simply presented this evidence to you in court, but I needed to know if you were the monarch that would undertake such a venture; and you did." His eyes narrowed as he continued, "There are dark forces at play, and I will not rest until I return these villains to the shadows from where they were spawned."

Victoria looked down to the proposal still unopened in her hand, then back to the professor. "I barely know you, sir, but I believe you will." She raised her sherry glass. "As decreed by Her Majesty, Queen Victoria of England and the British Empire, I raise a glass to your new charge…"

And then she paused. Her silence became a small chuckle of delight, and she raised her glass a fraction higher.

"A toast, to the Ministry of Peculiar Occurrences."

On their glasses touching, just over the chatter and jocularity of their pub, a lone dog cried out in the night.

Tangi a te Ruru / The Cry of the Morepork

By Pip Ballantine

The man lying face up in the rain at the bottom of the gorge looked surprised. Agent Aroha Murphy, looking down at his broken body, shared that very emotion, though hers was tinged with the bitterness of disappointment. The cloak of thick bush around them and the rush of the Manawatu River made it seem like a far too pretty place for the man to have breathed his last—even in the pouring rain. Allen Henderson was a liar, a thief, and should have been dead years ago. However, it should have been at Aroha's hand. As water filled his damnable eyes, she ground her teeth to hold back a scream of outrage at the unfairness of fate. She had been hunting Henderson for years after the attack on the farmhouse that had ended with her sister, Emma dead, and her mother quite lost to her senses. *Perhaps I should feel more relieved*, she thought to herself, *but damn it, I wanted to end him.*

After a long few minutes, James Childs, the constable at her side, cleared his throat. He was trying to gallantly hold the umbrella over her head, but he was having some difficulty keeping his footing in the growing mud of the riverbank.

"Agent Murphy?" he asked softly, and that was enough to snap Aroha out of her contemplation.

She was here, she recalled, not as a wronged party, but as an agent of the Ministry of Peculiar Occurrences, and she had a job to do.

Aroha poked Henderson with her foot, rolling him over onto his face, and then bent down to examine his back.

"I can't see any wounds apart from that from the fall," she commented, pursing her lips. "I couldn't think of a man less likely to commit suicide than Henderson." She pointed up the hill to the path where carts and carriages made their perilous way along the side of the mountain between Ashhurst and Woodville. Her Maori kin had named the gorge Te Apiti, the Narrow Passage, and it was well deserved, for at any time a landslide could take out the fragile road. It was, however, not the cause of Henderson's plunge down to the river because the road was intact.

She looked up, her brown eyes focusing on Constable Childs. "You say this isn't the only one last night?"

The young man ran his fingers through his ginger hair and glanced at his damp regulation issue notebook. "Indeed, Marie Lafayette, Tommy Ring, Hemi Hudson, and two others that we don't know of down by where the river exits the gorge."

"And the moon last night was full?"

Childs nodded. "A huge one."

"Not all of them could have accidentally walked off the road on the same night," Aroha muttered to herself. She already knew she was on the right track, so she just had to find the culprit. That task sat poorly with her though, given the identity of one of the 'victims'.

"It's very strange," Childs replied, "but it was lucky you were in the area, Agent Murphy."

"Yes," she said examining the towering hills and bush around them. "Lucky indeed." She didn't dare tell him the Ministry had sent her chasing after a string of similar suicides up and down the North Island. The Ministry of Peculiar Occurrences did not have a large office in New Zealand, so resources were spread very thin, and she was pretty much it for the lower half of the North Island.

The wars with the Maori were still fresh in people's minds, and the Imperial forces had only left the shores of Aotearoa. Still, because of her heritage, Aroha could move more easily around the countryside than most agents.

However, it was probably her dark skin and strange dress that had this young local policeman nervous. He was about to get a lot more so in a moment. She was sick of explaining herself to the locals. Lately she had given up telling them all about her airship captain Ngati Toa father, and her Italian mother, so she let her outfit speak for itself. Aroha might wear *pakeha* male clothing for ease of use, but she also had draped over her shoulder her father's *kahu huruhuru*. She had received the highly valued cloak, which contained the highly sought-after kereru feathers, as some kind of recompense from him for not taking her into the tribe. He already had a fine Ngati Toa wife and children, after all.

She wore the cloak not because it was his, but because it came from her ancestors, and that still meant a great deal to her.

Swinging down her backpack and placing it carefully on the ground, Aroha began to pull out the equipment she'd been hauling around since she'd left Rotorua three weeks ago.

She extracted a small brass box, attached to it a needle-thin rod, and to that a white sail-like shape about the size of her spread hand.

Constable Childs couldn't help leaning down to see what she was doing. "That looks…"

"…delicate," Aroha interrupted, worried the enthusiastic policeman might start poking at it in the way of men.

"What is it?"

She let out a sigh. "It's an aether tracker. A brand new device just shipped in from the London office last month."

Childs nodded as if he had a clue what she was talking about, and now she knew his eyes were fixed on the *moko kauae* that was carved proudly on her chin. The marks made her lips a dark blue, and decorated her chin with the curves and spirals she was entitled to. It was a declaration of her mana, her rank, and her past. She was proud of it, but she knew many others just didn't understand why she would mark her face.

The policeman was earnest but clueless, so Aroha smiled at him as she explained something he might be able to grasp. "The tracker is an extension of what my ancestors were very good at, but instead of following tracks in the bush we can follow the emissions of anything beyond the normal."

"You mean ghosts?" Childs whispered, going even paler.

That such things existed had always been accepted by her father's people, but pakeha tended to become a little unhinged if they came near to the truth.

"No," she said, as she began to turn the small crank on the side of the tracker, "ghosts do not exist Constable Childs…" she added under her breath, "…at least not here."

The small receiver on the top flicked back and forth, and narrow tape of paper chugged out from the side. After examining it, Aroha let out an exasperated breath. "The signal is too weak. Show me where you think the body fell."

Constable Childs gestured to two local men who were waiting some distance away from them, and they hustled down to carry Henderson away before he spoiled the beauty of the spot with his rotting corpse.

Aroha watched dispassionately as they did their work. It felt odd to know someone else had stolen her vengeance. Her father's ancestors believed firmly in *utu*, the concept that all must be kept in balance with kindness or vengeance depending on the action. Her mother's ancestors had also believed in an eye for an eye. Apparently both sets of ancestors would not be satisfied this day.

Still, it was a new world with new rules.

Aroha packed up the tracker, and then together she and Constable Childs climbed up the slippy, narrow track to the road. The wet bush dripped on her head, and the occasional fern slapped her in the face. New Zealand bush was thick and dense, unlike forests in the old world, and Aroha wondered if it concealed at this very moment an attacker.

"If Henderson didn't kill himself," Childs asked, holding back some *horoeka* saplings from her path, "and he didn't accidentally walk off the road, then what do you think happened to him, Agent Murphy?"

Holding her *kahu* around her tightly, Aroha considered how much to tell him. It looked like the local constable had nothing better to do than follow her around, and she couldn't really order him away; these were his locals that had died.

"I am not sure," she said finally, "but I am determined that we find out."

They were nearing the top when Childs finally asked the question she had been waiting for. "So…Murphy isn't much of a native name? Was your mother Maori?"

Half-caste girl they had called her when she was a child, and other less kindly words.

Aroha answered as reasonably as she could manage. "My father is Ngati Toa, an airship captain, but he and mother were never married. He went on his way when I was small, and she married an Irishman." She locked eyes with Childs. "I just found it easier to use my stepfather's name, but that is all I took from him."

The constable looked away, his face flushing red. He probably wouldn't have been so probing if she'd been a pakeha girl, but Aroha had nothing to be ashamed of, and she'd always found lies more trouble than they were worth.

They reached the roadway, which wasn't much more than the track they had just left, except it wound its way parallel with the river down below.

Aroha wordlessly set up the tracker on the edge of the roadway and cranked it to life while Childs watched. The tiny device began to spit out the long white tape, and this time the pattern of dots indicated a stronger reading.

"This is definitely where the event occurred," Aroha muttered, tucking her dark hair behind her ear. "There is a disturbance in the…"

The tracker resting just under her fingertips exploded. For a moment she wondered if she had done something terribly wrong, but then she realized that her ears were ringing from the retort of a very close gunshot.

She spun about, pulling the two-foot staff from under her cloak, and Childs had his pistol out, but neither of them could see where the attack had come from. Before she could say anything, Childs had grabbed her under the arm and dragged her back so that they had the cover of the downhill slope away from the road.

The constable's breath sounded very loud in her ear, but then her own heart was racing in time with his breathing.

"That," she whispered to Childs, "was either a very good shot, or a very poor one."

"Whichever," he replied, "they are prowling on the Queen's road, risking killing people. We have to stop them, but…" he paused. "Your device is all broken, how are we going to find them now?"

With a slight tap on his arm, Aroha grinned. "You pakeha—so married to your technology. We will do this the old fashioned way. Now, how do we get to the other side of the road?"

He jerked his head to the right. "There are the drainage pipes running under the road, otherwise it would get swept away every winter."

Together they slipped and slid sideways until they found one. Luckily it was a rather large size, and agent and constable were able to navigate through it hunched over. They emerged on the other side a little dirty, and Aroha led them back towards where they had been shot at. For a pakeha, Childs was actually rather quiet.

As they drew near he did whisper in her ear, however, "Do you have a gun by any chance, Agent Murphy?"

She smiled at him and shook his head. "But I am armed, never fear."

Working their way up the hillside, Aroha easily found the place where their attacker had shot at them. "Maori," she said after examining the spot. When Childs frowned in confusion, she pointed to the impression in the mud. "Do you know many pakeha that wander through the bush barefoot, constable?"

She led the way, following the trail of partial footprints, and broken undergrowth further up the hill. They were nearing the edge of the bush trail when Aroha heard the sound of something she had never imagined hearing in such a place.

It was a flute, or rather the *kōauau*, the Maori instrument that she still recalled her father playing to her as a child. Yet this was something more than mere music.

Aroha did not need an aether tracker to feel the pull of it. Suddenly, the music was all that mattered. Nothing else was of any consequence. Constable Childs turned to her, his face split with a huge, ridiculous grin. "You are a true Aphrodite of the South Pacific, Agent Murphy." His voice was slurred as he reached out to grab her, and for a brief moment Aroha leaned into his embrace. She wanted contact. She needed him. Then the ghost of her mother's experience reached her and gave her a jolt of much needed reality.

Henderson had captured her mother, drawn her into a web, and then killed her with it. Aroha had sworn never to allow that to happen to her.

So she evaded the constable's clumsy attempt at a clinch, grabbed his arm, dragged it behind him, and then used it to push him away. In the slippery, wet conditions of the hillside, it didn't take much. With a surprised yelp, Childs slid down the hill into the embrace of the bush itself. Within a few feet he was lost to her sight, but she could hear his cries of sorrow. Perhaps some time in the mud and rain would cool the unnatural ardour the music was pushing onto him.

Aroha didn't pause to see how far he slid; she was already climbing up the rest of the hill as quickly as possible. Luckily, she still had some Ministry technology at her disposal.

It wasn't the first time that the paranormal had tried to overcome the agents of the Ministry, and one of the standard issues were a tiny pair of plugs for her ears. She paused to wind the exquisite clockwork before jamming one in each ear. The random tickings were louder than the music that filtered through the bush, and as she climbed higher, Aroha was relieved to find that the compulsion to lie down was less.

When she crested the hill and saw the open sky, it was very welcome. Off in the distance she could see an airship with the Ngati Toa colors. It seemed strange that her *iwi* was so close, and yet perhaps not.

She turned and looked across the ridge and saw the musician standing against the horizon. He was only fifty feet away from where she was, but the ticking of the clockwork in her ears could not take away from the beauty of him.

He was only about her own age, with a kiwi feather cloak over one shoulder, and a *piupiu* around his lean hips. The flax skirt was seldom worn by itself anymore; in this day and age most Maori had adopted some type of pakeha clothing. This tall, dark skinned young man wore none of that. As he stood there, with the flute raised to his nose, playing the most haunting music she knew, it was like he had stepped out of another age.

For a long moment she quite forgot why she was there. She glanced over her shoulder and realized she was not imagining it; the Ngati Toa airship was getting closer, and she finally had confirmation that her *iwi* had something to do with this.

The player swayed slightly on the spot, but then his eyes locked on Aroha, and eventually he saw that she was not moved by the power of the flute. He lowered it from his lips.

"Aroha," the man called to her over the wind, "I hope you know this was for you."

Under her cloak, her hand closed on the shaft of her weapon. "*Do I know you?*" she asked, Maori feeling strange on her tongue after so long in the world of the Ministry.

"No," came the mild reply, "but I know you. I am Ruru."

It was the name of the owl in the dark, the one heard but seldom seen. It was very clever.

"And that," she said, inching her way closer, "is the instrument of Tutanekai." She had heard the stories, even though they were not ones of her tribe. Tutanekai had fallen in love with a beautiful maiden of another tribe, but they had been separated by a lake. When he had played the flute, the maiden Hinemoa had been so moved that she had dared the frigid waters of the lake to reach him.

Aroha swallowed as she heard the engines of the airship over the wind. "I thought it was a love story, but now it seems poor Hinemoa might not have had a choice. Where did you get it from?"

Ruru held the flute up, so she could see how small but intricately carved it was. "I found it," he said simply.

The instrument of the most famous love story in all of Aotearoa's history, and he held it like it was a weapon—which he had turned it into. Aroha suspected he must have found the burial site of the lovers, but did not belong to his *iwi*.

"That was made for love," Aroha said, pointing to the flute. "It wasn't meant for vengeance."

Ruru glanced up, behind her, to where the airship was drawing close and closer. "It depends on how you play it."

Aroha held out her hand towards him, trying to keep her voice unemotional. "Tutanekai's love and yearning shouldn't be used to kill. Let me return it to his people so it may be re-buried with him."

Now the airship engines were very loud. Aroha didn't know who was on it, but she understood that once it came close Ruru and the flute would disappear.

Ruru shook his head. "Utu was exacted for you, Aroha. Among others, but for you most of all. We have to use what we have, just as our people have always used what we have." He pointed to the airship. "Your own tribe know that."

Aroha could feel the tearing inside her; the two parts of her heritage pulling at her. What was left in the middle? Anything at all?

Both parts understand vengeance, but at the same time she remembered her role, the oath she had made to protect the people of this land from the strange, the unusual, the bizarre. Despite her own personal feelings, no one should have the power of Tutanekai.

"Give me the flute," she said, pulling her *taiaha*. The short three-foot tube extended out with a hiss.

Ruru's eyes widened when he saw her innovation up close, as she spun it around and directed it at him. He met her first attack with a parry of the rifle he quickly snatched up from against the rock.

Her *taiaha* hissed with its internal power, jetting steam into his face, and he backed away blinded for a moment. When he regained his vision, Ruru actually looked upset. "You are attacking your own people? I am setting wrongs right!"

"It is a different age," Aroha said, as she swung her *taiaha* for his legs. "You cannot be judge of all things. None of us can."

A ladder unfurled from the airship above them. Ruru glanced up at it for just a heartbeat, and Aroha knew that she had only that moment. Distracted as he was, she could have had the killing blow, but instead levelled a strike for his head. When he jerked out of the way, she quickly stepped in and snatched the flute from the waistband of his *piupiu*.

Their brown eyes locked as her fingers tightened around the delicate piece of bone. "You have had enough utu," she shouted to him over the roar of the airship engines. "Tell my father, so has he. We are done."

Ruru let out a laugh at that, and then turned and leapt for the ladder just as it pulled it away. His fingers locked on the rungs, and then he climbed up and away.

Aroha did not look up as the airship moved away. She had not seen her father in years, but he had his life in the clouds, and she had one on the ground. Just like Rangi and Papatunuku, the sky father and the earth mother. Somewhere in between was a place for her to stand, but she just had to find it.

It took Aroha a couple of weeks to return to Wellington and the district headquarters of the Ministry. It was the fault of a rather roundabout trip she took. She knew she was a mess of mud and stank sorely, but the idea that had begun worming its way into her head would not be put off by even the few minutes needed to wash up.

Miss Tuppence let her into the Regional Director's office, with only the slightest of winces at her appearance, so perhaps it was not that bad.

Anderson looked up from his desk, his bright blue eyes roaming over her condition, while his wrinkled face folded in an expression of vague disgust. "Agent Murphy, I see things must be urgent with you. I take it your mission was successful?"

This was going to be the hard bit. "Yes, sir. It turned out that a Maori nose flute with unusual properties was being used to extract utu on some rather nasty people."

He placed his pen carefully down on his desk and steepled his fingers. "And I take it you apprehended the suspect and got hold of this flute?"

She looked him directly in the eye. "Actually Regional Director, the perpetrator escaped, but I did manage to make sure he no longer had the flute in his possession."

Anderson waited for her explanation in a way that was rather unnerving.

"Unfortunately," she said with the steadiest of voices she could manage, "the artefact was smashed into pieces in the process." She did not tell him that it had been returned to Tutanekai's *iwi*, to be buried with honour. As far as his ancestor's knew the flute was merely a *tapu* item, sacred but with no mysterious powers. She had not enlightened them on that, just as she was not enlightening her superior.

"Well, that is a shame," the Regional Director said, picking up his pen.

Aroha did not move.

"Is there something else, Agent Murphy?"

She swallowed hard, thinking of her torment at taking such a sacred object, and how she was stuck between the worlds of her parents—but perhaps that could be put to advantage.

She stood a little straighter, resting her hand on her taiaha under her cloak, gaining strength from that touchstone of tradition. "Director Anderson, in all my travels, I have noticed that there is something missing from the Ministry."

Her superior's dark eyebrows pressed together. "You have had a sudden dose of insight. Do tell, Agent Murphy."

"I believe there is a better way to handle the acquisition of dangerous objects." Her fingers rested on the breast of her coat where the flute had so recently ridden. "Rather than barging in and snatching away objects, might a softer, gentler approach be not the best way, with a position made especially for it?"

He leaned back in his chair and tapped his fingers on the desk between them. Morning sun spilled over the pile of papers and gleamed on signet ring on his finger. "And what would you call this position?"

Aroha smiled. "I believe we could begin by creating a liaison agent. Someone who could be a bridge between the Queen's Ministry and the tribes of Aotearoa."

"And that," he said with a tilt of his head, "I presume would be you?"

Aroha raised her chin just a fraction, feeling the pride of her ancestors' whisper in the back of her head. "Yes, sir, that would be me."

For a long moment she feared the Regional Director would brush off her suggestion. However, finally he let out a sigh. "We are a long way from Headquarters, Agent Murphy, but I will take your suggestion under serious consideration." His gaze focused on her. "I can see that you have the particular…experience and qualifications for such a role. I will give the HQ Director my recommendation. I don't think they comprehend our ways are different down here."

She smiled at that. Perhaps there was hope, if they could understand each other just a little.

"Thank you, sir," she said. "I believe I can make a difference."

He dismissed her, and as she turned to go, she thought of Ruru and the Ngati Toa airship, and wondered what the days ahead would bring.

The Touch of Hine-nui-te-po

By Pip Ballantine

**Auckland, New Zealand
1878**

The Angel of Death Strikes Again

    The citizens of Howick are once again locked in their homes after the second visit from the so-called Angel of Death.
    Mr Cornelius Hart is the latest victim of the murderer in the quiet suburb. Despite locked doors and windows, Mr Hart was found this morning by his daughter, dead on the floor of his home. The terrible condition of the body was just like the others, resembling nothing so much as some strange ancient mummy that had been left to the predations of the sun. The neighbours of the deceased say they saw a winged figure ascend to the heavens sometime around midnight.
    The city is awash with rumour and fear, as honest citizens lock themselves in every evening and pray to see morning without a visit from the Angel of Death.

Aroha Murphy folded up the newspaper and put it on the table before her with a soft sigh. She had been hoping to investigate this peculiar occurrence in quiet without the glare of the public's attention, but somehow the newspapers had not been silenced as was protocol. It had to be the local constabularies' fault, since it wasn't the first time.

She spared a glance around the pub and could immediately tell that such a bold headline had caught everyone's attention.

It took a lot to shake up the salty and street-wise regulars at the *Powder Keg*, but these series of murders had certainly done so. Two sailors were shaking their heads, while one read the headline aloud to perhaps his illiterate friends. A couple of street walkers, taking a moment to rest their feet after the long night's work, were talking in hushed tones. Perhaps they were surprised that for once they were not the target of a mad killer. Aroha could only imagine what it would be like in the genteel parlours of the city's ladies.

Not that she saw very much of those in her line of work. Being an agent of the Ministry of Peculiar Occurrences—in New Zealand at least—took her to many wild and dangerous places, but not so often into high society. That was quite alright by her, and when she visited Auckland, Aroha always made the public house down by the docks her first stop.

It was one of the few places where her mixed race and similar mixed attire would not be commented on. The curling marks tattooed on her chin, the *moko kauae*, were not unfamiliar that they would be stared at as they often were in higher echelons of society. Sailors, travellers, near do wells, and even the odd Australian air pirate stopped at the *Powder Keg*, to fill up on excellent beer and gossip. Yet it was also a place where no one would make unwelcome advances or unwanted introductions. She did not care for such familiarity, used as she was to the backblocks of New Zealand. Cities, with all their milling crowds, were not Miss Murphy's favourite haunts.

Aroha raised a hand towards the bar where Mr Braun was talking to a couple of old soldiers, but he was so intent on the conversation that he didn't notice her gesture. Instead, it was his competent wife that bustled over with a jug of ale and a mug to go with it.

"There you are, Miss Murphy," Julia said, placing it at her customer's elbow without having to be asked. "Will there be anything else?"

Mrs Braun was—as always—observant. She might not have the gregarious nature of her German husband, but she was a most excellent listener. Which was the second reason Aroha always stopped into the *Powder Keg*. Aroha moved her taiha and rucksack from the chair next to her, and patted it with the palm of her hand. "A moment of your time, and you needn't be so formal either. Remember that I asked you last time to call me Aroha."

Sometimes pasting on the social graces was a great trial to her, but at this moment it was genuine enough gesture.

The tavern lady raised her eyebrow, glanced around the room to judge the quietness of their establishment, and then settled on the seat. Aroha had never divulged her employment with the Ministry of Peculiar Occurrences, but Julia was astute and familiar with the more covert people of Auckland. She probably suspected Aroha was a private detective of some kind, or perhaps had connections with the *Tangata te Rangi,* the hapu of the Ngati Toa that had taken to living and fighting from airships. They were indeed Aroha's family, but only through the father that had abandoned her soon after her birth to her Italian mother.

If Julia had known more of Maori ways, she would have been able to guess the connection by reading Aroha's tattooed chin. It was lucky for her that most people did not examine her moko kauae closely, or with any real knowledge.

The agent slid the paper across the table, and tapped the headline with one finger. "I presume you've heard about this...do you think this is all some tall tale or could there be truth in it?"

Julia didn't even need to glance down at it; she simply shrugged. "There is always some truth in tall tales. The papers are calling it an Angel of Death because some drunk on his way home saw wings, but whispers are that it was *Hine-nui-te-pō* come to cast judgement on the old bastard."

The goddess of death. Aroha sat back in her chair and shared a steady look with Julia. She knew the rumours about Mr Braun's wife; that she was the great-granddaughter of the first white man to marry a Maori woman. She was also whispered to be friends with the rebels of the Tangata te Rangi who had taken to the air. Life on an airship, travelling from town to town, being beholden to no one had tempted Aroha—especially since her father had a high standing with them. However, she had still to forgive him.

Aroha trusted Julia's judgement more than most, so calling Mr Hart a bastard made as much of an impact as her mention of the goddess of death. The gleam in the tavern lady's eye was one made of *kōhatu,* the black stone of glass that cuts.

"You knew him, then?" Aroha asked, softly so that no one in the bar would overhear them.

Julia glanced up, locking her green eyes with her patron's brown. "I knew of him. His wife used to come in here, all battered and bruised...before her death that is." Her jaw clenched, and it took her a moment before she was able to go on. "At first, I told her to go to the police, file charges, but he was a copper, and that was never going to work. So instead, I suggested she leave him, get out, but I guess he got wind of it..."

"No one ever charged him with her murder though?" Aroha had to ask, though she suspected the answer.

Julia shook her head and then shrugged. "He claimed she had run off with some other nameless man, but Annie would have never left those two children with him. Never. I hope Hart's murder was as painful as they said it was..."

"Mum?" A childish voice rang out from the backroom, and a girl of about ten with brown plaited hair that gleamed red in the sun appeared in the doorway with a sheepish look on her face.

Julia immediately got to her feet with a sigh. "What is it now, Eliza? Please don't tell me you've been fighting with those boys again."

Her daughter stared at her feet and mumbled, "Herbert is stuck in the attic, I think he might have fallen through the rafters just a bit, he was following me and..."

Julia Braun shook her head, and flicked her fingers at her daughter. "Go and help him there, I'll fetch the ladder." She turned back to Aroha. "That girl is always up to something—but I'm lucky; Annie didn't get the chance to enjoy her children's antics. If you want my opinion, if you're looking into Cornelius' murder at all, then perhaps you shouldn't be looking too hard." With that she bustled off to find out what mischief her brood had wrought.

Children, Aroha thought, the Hart's had children, and children had eyes, but no one had reported what they had seen in the paper. Leaving payment on the table, she gave Samuel Braun a slight wave, and exited the *Powder Keg*.

Outside Auckland was baking in unseasonable heat, but the city was still bustling. Wharfies were hard at work swinging down precious cargo off ships from around the world, a few urchins looked to have escaped school, and the sun was gleaming off the harbor; in other words it was a beautiful day to be investigating a murder.

Hitching her taiha and her rucksack over her shoulder, she began to walk to the bus station. Sometimes being an agent of the Ministry was glamorous, sometimes it was just hard slog. Aroha had spent the last year acting as liaison with the Maori tribes, but she had thought that she's been assigned this case because of another substantial lack of staff. The New Zealand office of the Ministry of Peculiar Occurrences was very small, and due to the somewhat dangerous conditions they sometimes had vacancies they couldn't fill. This wouldn't have been the first time Aroha had been asked to step in after a mishap with a colleague.

However, after finding out about Hine-nui-te-pō she wondered if her superiors had concerns that this might overlap into tribal affairs. The fact that Hart had lived in Howick, one of the fencible settlements, where old soldiers had been given land for their service might also stray into that terriotory.

The green bus picked her up from Queen Street, and she took a seat near the driver. A young fashionably dressed woman, and a workmen with his lunchpail on his lap were already on board, and gave her the usual strange glances. It shouldn't have bothered Aroha, because it happened every single time. It was not just her combination of Maori and pakeha clothing that drew the curious and the judgemental, but also her face. She wore the heritage of her Italian mother and her Maori father everywhere she went. When she'd been a child it had been a millstone around her neck, but she had since grown into it.

Now it made her sit taller in her seat, and stick out her chin defiantly. The moko carved there was her badge of honor. Not everyone was entitled to wear the tattoo, it had to be earned, and by God she had—many times over.

So as the bus jerked and rolled its way out of the city, leaving a trail of steam behind it, she endured the stares with pride. The Ministry had taught her being different was also being unique. Sometimes she didn't just investigate the peculiar occurence—sometimes she *was* the peculiar occurrence.

By the time they reached Howick, she was the only passenger remaining on the bus.

"Last stop!" The driver said, huffing almost as much as his vehicle. He glanced at Aroha out of the corner of his eye. "You sure this is where you want to get off?"

She glanced out the window at the row of small whitewashed buildings surrounded by picket fences. "Yes, don't worry. I think the natives are friendly."

She didn't look back to see what his reaction was, but she hoped it was outrage. The newspaper had not mentioned which house was the Harts, but it was easy enough to pick out, because of all the women gathered around it.

Cautious not to disturb the flock, Aroha walked slowly up, and was able to catch the trailing edge of the conversation of the ladies of the neighbourhood.

"Justice," one was just finishing saying, "yes, definately justice..." She held her fruit cake aloft. "Those poor children are finally free."

Aroha moved in swiftly, and snatched the baked goods from her hands. When the woman whirled around, Aroha smiled brightly. "Friend of the family, I'll take this in," and then she turned to walk up the small path to the door. For the umpteenth time today she was the recipient of a stunned stare. Yet it was not the place of a good Christian woman to make conversation with a native, even if said native had just stolen her cake.

By the time Aroha had knocked on the door, she'd already forgotten the concerns of the neighbours. Maybe they were righteous now, but from the little bit that Julia had told her, they had not prevented the death of one of their own in their small, tidy community.

A little boy answered the door. He was tidily enough dressed, but his eyes were shadowed, but still, when he saw the cake his face lit up.

Before Aroha could say anything though, an older girl of perhaps seventeen appeared behind him, her hands going protectively onto his shoulders. "Who are you?" she demanded, her voice rough with suspicion. Aroha had the feeling that it was a tone she was familar with.

She held out the cake. "I'm from the newspaper, and I'm interested in your story about what happened last night."

The girl frowned, even as the little boy snatched the cake. "You don't look like a reporter..."

"Funny," Aroha said with a smile, "so many people say that, and here I am." Reaching into her rucksack, she fished out a notepad, and a fold of money. "Stories pay though, and I am guessing that might be what you need right now."

The little boy had already pulled out a handful of cake and stuffed it into his mouth with the rapidness of the truly hungry. The girl's eyes flicked down to him, and then she pulled him back to allow Aroha to enter.

Inside was surprisingly clean and well kept; Aroha would venture that was not because of Cornelius. After sliding her taiha from its place on her back, and placing it by the door, she sat down on the rocking chair by the window. Aroha watched the girl retrieve the cake from her brother, cut him a slice and let him sit on the bed to eat it.

Aroha held out her hand to the girl. "Aroha Murphy."

She took it in a firm grasp and gave it a shake. "Pearl Hart," she replied and suddenly the agent had no doubt this young woman might have been through pain, but she was not going to let it defeat her. Aroha had seen that same look in many of her fellow agent's eyes. It made her feel a little better about pressing the child for details on her father's death.

Aroha slipped the fold of money into Pearl's hand, even if it was customary to give payment after services rendered, because she wanted this young woman to know it was going to be alright.

"So," Aroha said, retrieving a pencil and flipping open the notebook, "tell me what you saw last night when you father was killed."

"Cornelius," Pearl said, folding her hands in front of her. "I never called him father because he never was one to us."

The girl was so matter-of-fact about it that Aroha realised she had stumbled on an excellent witness. She cleared her throat. "Cornelius then. Can you tell me what happened to him last night?"

Pearl's gaze narrowed, and she glanced over at her brother. "We were asleep when it happened...I only found him in the morning..." The girl was good at deception, perhaps she had a lifetime to perfect the craft, but the boy's eyes Aroha noticed had not left the window in all the time they had been in the house.

The agent got to her feet and went over to examine it. "Is this kept locked?" she asked, running her finger along the windowsill.

"Yes," Pearl replied, "Cornelius had been a soldier his whole life, he was parnoid about people slitting his throat."

The lock was a crude latch, but the little box underneath it was another story. "A McTighe alarm, I see your point. This is not a cheap device to have."

The girl's eyes darkened. "It was the only thing he spent any money on—except booze that is."

Aroha found her magnification spectacles in her rucksack and slipped them on. Under close examination the alarm had suffered considerable damage. All of the interior was blackened, and the gears twisted as if from some heat source. Leaning out the window, she examined the other side of the window frame. At the exact spot parallel to the device was a matching scorch mark. Some sort of excitation device had been used to disable Mr Hart's alarm.

"Most definately not an angel or Hine-nui-te-pō," she said to Pearl, who despite trying to show little interest had come up to see what the other woman was doing.

"Angel...angel!" The little boy crowed, as a wide smile cracked his up until then solemn face.

"Your brother does have quite the imagination though," Aroha said, turning back to the window frame. It still had one last secret to give up; a series of sharp, thin, parallel scrapes were on the top and both side pieces of wood that held the window in place.

Then glancing down at the floor she noticed a smudge of red dirt directly below the windowframe. Frowning, Aroha swiftly bent and brushed the strange dirt into a sample bag. Once she had it sealed and tucked in her rucksack, she rubbed her fingers together; it was curiously rough and sharp.

Whirling around, Aroha replaced her glasses in her rucksack, and picked up her taiha. "I suppose I should ask about your father's enemies... vI am guessing he had quite a few?"

Pearl let out a snort. "More than I can list, especially after he came out of prison."

"When was that?"

"Only about a month ago, he was in for theft." The girl bit her lip as if she was trying to keep back a bitter laugh. "Theft of all things—but they let him out, and we had to put up with him—" Now she stopped suddenly, and stared at Aroha. They both knew that what she'd just said could be construed as a motive for murder. Luckily, the agent was not a policeman, and not constrained by the narrowness of their vision. Besides, the evidence had already told her that this girl had not murdered her father—as much as she might have wanted to.

"Auckland prison I take it," she said to Pearl, not missing a beat. "Good, I know where to head next."

Spinning around on her heel, Aroha went for the door. Pearl's voice however made her stop, reminding her that the joy of the chase was not the only thing in this particular situation; there were human casualties apart from the late not-so-lamented Cornelius Hart.

"If you find them, whoever they are," Pearl said, drawing her brother in against her, "then thank them. Brian thinks they are an angel, and I do to." She tilted her head up defiantly.

Aroha wanted to give her the same argument she had last year, when confronted by a man using ancient magic to exert revenge from the world; that they were not the people to judge who lives and who dies. However, looking at their faces shadowed with events they would never be able to forget, even if they could get past them, she found she couldn't make that argument. Instead, Aroha gave them a nod and turned to the door once more.

She didn't look back, but she heard Pearl's words hit her like sharp stones just as she turned the doorknob.

"Oh and he's not my brother, he's my son." Her jaw tightened, and suddenly Aroha understood. No, her father had not been a father to her.

Auckland Prison looked exactly as it was meant to, foreboding and menacing. While Aroha knew that not everyone in this place deserved to be here, she was glad that at least Cornelius Hart had been forced to spend time here.

She showed her credentials to the guard and was admitted, though she had to surrender her taiha. Glaring at the guard, she did so with extreme reluctance, but social norms meant she held back from punching him in the face. Aroha was just in the process of explaining she wanted to meet the cellmates of Mr Hart, when a rather out of breath pale-face guard appeared, and hastily asked her to follow him to the warden's office.

Concealing her bewilderment as best she could, Aroha obediantly followed behind the man, wondering at the speed of the guard's awareness of her arrival. When she was shown into the office, it all started to make more sense.

The large room was half occupied by desk, half occupied by a collection of wires. This meant that the woman sitting behind the desk looked like a spider sitting in the middle of her impressive web.

The woman, whom Aroha could only presume was the warden, was a round, iron-haired older lady. She might have even been called cheery if she smiled, but she was most definately not smiling.

"It's about bloody time," she barked at Aroha, so loudly that the agent wished that she had her taiha in her possession. "Parker, you can wait outside!"

Aroha almost glanced behind her to see if the warden was talking to someone else, but her guide had promptly disappeared as soon as she had been delivered. The name place before her assailant said, *Mrs Jan Pollock, Warden*.

Once again, Aroha's appreciation of societal norms failed her. She said nothing, but stood her ground just in case there was an attack to follow.

"What sort of system are you Ministry folk running?" The warden leaned her fists on the desk, and glared at Aroha. The more agitated Mrs Pollock became, the stronger the Scottish accent became.

"I sent for some help weeks ago, and now is when you bloody choose to show up? I had to dispose of the corpses at night, and pay my guards a little extra to keep it quiet. I can't be held responsible for your cockups, and I sure as Hell want to be paid back!"

Aroha blinked at her, finally able to get a word in. "I assure you, the Regional Director only gave me this case two days ago, and—" She paused, tilted her head. "You aren't talking about the Hart case?"

Mrs Pollock stared back at her. "What bloody Hart case? I'm talking about the three bodies turned into damn mummies right in my prison."

"You don't happen to read the papers, do you Mrs Pollock?"

She waved her hands in the air. "When the bloody hell am I supposed to have time to do that? I have half the staff I need to control the most blood thirsty folk in the country, as well as a budget that I couldn't run a household on—let alone a prison." The warden gestured to the wires around her. "The only way I keep control is knowing what they are planning before they do it. I've stopped five escape attempts and three riots in the last year alone..."

Carefully, least the move be taken as some kind of threat, Aroha put the newspaper in front of Mrs Pollock. "Is this similar to what happened to the corpses in you found in your prison?"

It was obvious that though Mrs Pollock had plenty of experience with rough, deadly types, this came as quite a shock. "Indeed," now her voice had lowered to a whisper. "The very same."

"Excellent," Aroha said. "Can you tell me a bit about the circumstances of your deaths then? I am guessing that somewhere along the way your request to our Ministry got lost. Paperwork, it can by misplaced even by the best and brightest."

A scowl said exactly what Mrs Pollock thought of that. Aroha made mental note not to try any of her own poorly crafted jokes on this woman. The warden gestured over to a chair. "If this has spread out to the general population and all, we could be in for a Hell of a ride. From my end there isn't that much to tell. Rawlings, Daniels and Dawkins were in the army together, near as I can tell. Once shared a cell, but I had to separate them. That was when it happened. They were killed in their sleep, and not one of my guards saw who did it."

"Mummified just like Hart then." Aroha began to take notes. "Seems like your prison can't be blamed for this. This murderer is quite advanced."

The warden let out a *hurmpf* of annoyance. "I want it reported that we did try our best for Daniels. Once Rawlings and Dawkins were killed I made the connection, and we kept watch on Daniels; extra lighting, more guards."

"But it was obviously not enough. What happened?"

Now Mrs Pollock looked embarrassed. "The lights blew, and the guard...well he fell asleep."

"Odd behaviour." Aroha scribbled furiously in her notebook. "I would suspect he was more likely drugged than fell asleep."

"Daniels wasn't." Mrs Pollock pushed a file over the desk to Aroha. "Save yourself the writing, it's all in here. Daniels' screaming eventually brought the other guards to the scene."

Despite her lack of funding, apparently the prison had at least one camera. The images made even Aroha wince; desecrated faces, hands raised in a fruitless attempt at defence, lips pulled back from teeth, and skin like jerked beef.

"Can I see the cells where the men died?" she asked tersely sliding the images back to Mrs Pollock. The warden pushed a bell behind her desk and the first guard reappeared as if he'd been pressed against the door. "Parker, show Miss Murphy here to the cell where Daniels bought it."

As Aroha followed him out, Pollock called out one last thing. "Make sure you get all you need, don't want to see any more of you Ministry types around here for quite some time." The door slammed behind them without anyone touching it. Everyone was an inventor these days, Aroha thought. It made her work much that harder.

The cells in the prison were small, but surprisingly clean and tidy. Mrs Pollock ran her place like a ship it appeared, with everything Bristol fashion. The guard led her to the cell Daniels had occupied, and after some problems with his shaking hands and the keys, opened it for her.

Aroha slipped in, while he stayed outside, shifting from side to side. Parker would have bolted she was sure, but fear of his warden probably kept him in his place. Putting the guard out of her mind, Aroha set herself to examining the tiny space.

It contained a small bed, a tin pot, and that was it, so not much to investigate. "No one else has been in this cell since?" she asked over her shoulder.

The guard shook his head. "Mrs Pollock said no one should touch it."

"Good woman," the agent muttered under her breath, as she went to the window. It was immediately evident that this had not been tampered with like Hart's; there were no scratches, but there were three stout iron bars instead. Whoever had come in to kill Prisoner Daniels must have had to find another method of ingress.

Bending down, she did find something strange; once again that fine red, sharp dirt; definitely not something to be found in this part of Auckland. Carefully, she brushed it into another sample bag, and sealed it for later examination.

"Parker," she turned on the guard, "can you look at the records and find out how many visitors, Daniels, Dawkins and Rawlings had?"

"Don't have to," he said, staring down at his toes.

Aroha frowned. "I rather think you have to."

"No," he said, his shoulders jerking back, "sorry m'am, I didn't mean it that way. I mean the three of them never had any visitors—not even family. They were horrific men you see, child killers. We even had to keep them away from the other criminals. They were the worst of the worst, if you don't mind me saying..."

Aroha nodded, casting one last look around the cell. "So no one ever saw them?"

"Well, only us guards, and Nurse Lange," Parker admitted.

"Then I will need to talk to her," Aroha said, leaving the cell. "Immediately."

Parker shrugged. "Well, she isn't working here anymore." Aroha stared at him until he got the hint. "She...she's working in the public hospital I think. You can probably find her there."

The agent gave him a nod, and then turned on her heel, already dismissing the wildly youthful guard behind her.

The night was drawing in, so she decided to head back to the Ministry offices, and visit Nurse Lange in the morning. Besides she really wanted to identify the strange red soil she had found at both locations.

The New Zealand Regional Office was in Wellington, but the Ministry did maintain smaller offices in other towns. The Auckland office was above a stable just off Queen Street. Aroha entered through a back alley, inserted her clockwork key, and climbed the stairs to the offices.

She had the place all to herself, which was just how she wanted it to be. As darkness descended, she made herself comfortable at the bench by the window, flicked on the small arc light, and pulled the office microscope towards her.

Shaking out both samples onto separate slides, she slid them under the lense. Flicking open the *Soils of New Zealand*, she quickly identified them as volcanic and containing small amounts of scoria. By examining the weathering of the samples, there was only one place they could come from; the volcanic island of Rangitoto.

It was a mystery for sure, since the island was considered bad luck, and an unlikely holiday spot for either Hart or his prison friends.

Hopefully Nurse Lange could answer some questions about the three dead prisoners, and maybe how such distinctive soil ended up in that prison cell. Pillowing her head on her rucksack, Aroha curled up on the camp bed in the rear of the office, and got a few hours sleep.

Next morning she got up with the dawn, and after securing the office, made her way to the Auckland hospital in search of her nurse. The great stone edifice was the largest hospital in New Zealand, and quite new. It was also an audible assault on the senses.

Aroha stood in the waiting room and stared about her. It was full of crying children, howling injured, and the old grumbling that no one was seeing to them—which was true. For a long time she struggled to pick out the workers from the throngs of patients. Eventually, a tall Maori woman, with a white cap tied to her head, a brass watch pinned to chest above an apron and with a clipboard bustled past. Aroha had to grab hold of her arm to make her stop.

The look the nurse shot her could have killed, but Aroha had been in worse situations with only slightly more formidable opponents. "Yes?"

Quickly, to make sure it didn't come to that, Aroha blurted out, "I'm looking for Nurse Lange." She flashed her government identification just in time to avoid further conflict.

"Upstairs," the nurse said, already turning away, "the children's ward."

It got quieter the higher Aroha climbed, and that unnerved her. A plain black and white sign directed her to the west wing, and the ward where the children were treated. In the room itself some kind of order had obviously been laid down by better nurses than those downstairs. Wide-eyed children stared at her from orderly lines of beds, while three nurses slipped about silently checking on their charges.

Aroha noted that there was however a knot of people including three more nurses at the far end of the ward. When her enquires with the nearer ones did not find Nurse Lange, she made her way there.

Several of the people huddled around the bed were shaking their heads, and Aroha, her curiosity peaked, shouldered her way through to see what was happening. When people complained, she raised her badge defiantly, and eventually she reached the bed without incident.

A rosy-cheeked girl of about ten was sitting up in the bed, and the agent had never seen anyone who looked less in need of a lie down. The girl obviously felt the same because she was struggling with the nurse. "But I want to play," she said, wriggling mightily. "I don't like hospitals!"

"Not until the doctor sees you," the nurse said, her voice low and patient.

"It's a miracle!" Aroha's head came around as one of the bystanders whispered. The agent felt a chill go up her spine; first a horrific death, and now miracles.

"Clear the area," she snapped, and somehow the spectacle of a Maori woman with a taiha and a badge had soon sent the bystanders to the far end of the room. Only the nurse remained.

"Nurse Lange?"

The woman, who looked far too soft-faced to be an effective nurse, nodded, and her eyes were guarded.

"You used to work at the prison?" Another nod. Aroha jerked her head to the child who was already sliding out of the opposite side of the bed. "And now you preside over miracles?"

The nurse shrugged, but a man with a greying beard finally gathered enough courage to return to the bed. "They said to prepare a coffin." The man said, scooping the girl against him, as if he expected Aroha to snatch her away. "My grand-daughter should be dead, and she's not. That's a miracle."

An older lady, who had to be the grandmother scampered up, glaring at Aroha. "We brought her here because we heard of these miracles happening here, and look!"

The agent knew she could cause a scene at this moment, however her eye had lit on something, barely a smudge on the floor, but it was the red soil she had seen at the murders.

She looked up with a smile and replied, "So very glad to hear it." Then she turned and left. Nurse Lange and her miracles would have no more to tell her.

Murders and miraculously returned life. Her mind began to run through cases she had read, but she could not recall anything like this. She could put in a request with the archivist in head office in London, but with his record, she suspected it would be a month until she heard back.

Terrible things happened when agents were hasty, and Aroha knew harring off without informing her colleagues was a quick way to disaster. When she returned to the regional office, the prim Miss Farthing was there. The agent scribbled a quick note, and requisitioned a Ministry ornithopter as well as a few maps.

At least if she did not return that someone would come looking. By the time she'd done all that, evening was drawing on.

Miss Farthing glanced at the location, and raised one eyebrow. "Are you sure you don't want to wait until Agents Beckham and Lorde come back on assignment?"

Aroha shook her head. "I feel like this is best handled quickly. I'll be fine."

Agents were used to working alone, resources were stretched, and Miss Farthing knew better than to question Aroha further. She tapped the sheet of paper in front of her. "Then sign here for the ornithopter, and I'll log your destination."

Aroha climbed up to the roof and after strapping herself into one of the two ornithopters kept there, set off into the sky which was already turning bloody with the sunset. It was in keeping.

Her destination, the volcanic island of Rangitoto, meant 'bloody sky'. She could only hope her visit there would result in no such thing.

The island was hard to miss. Against the dying sun the wide island stood out clearly, and the cone of the slumbering volcano rose over eight hundred feet above it. As the sun slipped beneath the horizon, and the moon and stars took their place, Aroha slipped goggles of her own making on. They gave her a dim view of the world, but better than nothing.

There was a large volcanic field the wrapped around the top of the island, and below that was a cape of low shrubs and stunted trees. Certainly there were not a lot of places to hide. Experience with all kinds of villains made Aroha look deeper. She knew Rangitoto had its secrets, and though the ground was treacherous, its past had made some interesting locations.

Landing her ornithopter on the beach, she used the maps to locate the places she had thought of. Under her feet scoria crunched as if to tell her she was on the right track. Rangitoto was a young volcano, the youngest in the field of volcanoes which Auckland sat upon. The last eruption from this island had been only five hundred years before, and must have been quite a shock to the local Maori.

It had left behind a legacy of lava and ash that was far younger than the weathered locations of the other volcanoes in the area. The scoria that Aroha had examined under the microscope had none of the weathering, and that could only come from this location.

Lava had flowed down the sides of the island, and created a series of tubes that wound their way up the hillside. Amateur adventurers often took daytrips over to Rangitoto to explore them, but there were a series of hidden lava tubes, that Agent Moran, had found two years ago by falling through the bolt hole. At the time the human changes to the tubes had been unexplained, but now Aroha had her suppositions.

Using the map she found the hatch Moran had discovered, and to her practiced eye it looked well used. The hatch slid smoothly open, and she dropped down into it, taiha in hand.

Following the tunnels as far as the map went, she found another dead end. She pushed and felt around the edges of rock, but this genuinely seemed like the end of the tunnel. Just as she was about to turn to leave, her light flashed over the ground by the end of the tunnel. Hers were not the only boot-prints in the dirt; others were there too, small like her own, but they stopped in one spot.

Aroha drew out her taiha, and took a position in the same place. Nothing felt different, but when she experimentally rocked back and forward, she could have sworn she felt something move underneath her; something decidedly mechanical. Girding herself, she twisted a little bit, feeling the scoria grind under her feet. She waited one tense moment, and then heard another metallic click. Now there was definitely something moving under her feet, and it was carrying her down with it. Bracing herself as best she could, Aroha rode the platform down. When it finally came to a stop, she found herself in another tunnel. Holding the lantern before her, she followed it.

She knew immediately that she was entering a burial ground; the smell alone informed her of that. It was the odour of long ago death, not rancid, but more distant, like ancient books.

The lavatube opened into a wider section, and now the lamp was no longer necessary. Aroha slide the goggles off her head, and looked about.

The widened portion of the tube was lit by candles, large and dripping for sure, but still telling that someone took care of this place. Yet as she walked closer, Aroha was able to tell this was no normal tribal burial chamber. Hine-nui-te-pō could not have chosen a better spot.

For a start there were the daguerrotype images placed above a niche in the lava.

Young girls, three, dressed in a combination of Maori cloaks and wide pakeha dresses, stared back at her. They looked to be just blossoming into womanhood and beauty, but there was no explanation of who they were, so instead she examined the body beneath. It was desiccated, in a similar fashion to the men in prison, and the moko on her chin said she was a woman of some standing.

"I'd appreciate if you'd step away from Kiri." It was seldom that a person could seak up on Aroha, so as she turned about she expected a slight creature.

What she saw, filling the tube was far more bulky and menacing than she'd expected. A carved brass face stared back at her, while the rest of her was shrouded by a cape. However, over her shoulder, something gleamed in the candlelight. It was a backpack, and suddenly Aroha realised she could meet the same fate as the men in the prison and Mr Hart.

She angled herself with her back to the wall, knowing that the only way out was blocked. The taiha felt warm in her grasp, but the device in the new comers posession she feared might pack more of a bite.

"Kiri," Aroha said evenly, "a woman of strength, like yourself."

The eyes behind the mask flickered between Aroha and the corpse, and the agent got the impression the dead woman mattered to whoever wore the disguise. "You don't know anything, Kiri Hokopa was the greatest mind of New Zealand. She suffered greatly, but she took the power of Hine-nui-te-pō and made it a mission."

As the masked figure drew closer, Aroha got a better look at the device strapped to her back; it was bulky on the woman's back, and had a long tube running from it. The end of that tube made Aroha even more on guard. It was a long needle, like you might find on some foreign creature like a scorpion. She could only imagine that had been plunged into the prisoners to drain them of their vital energy.

"Hine-nui-te-pō," Aroha said softly, "so I see you are some kind of vendetta, some kind of revenge for—"

"Not revenge!" The masked woman screamed, "For justice. How is it right that so many good people are condemned to death, while terrible men like Cornelius Hart keep breathing? How is that right?"

Aroha paused to consider for a moment. She had seen many terrible things in her life, many wrongs committed, and many good people cut down for no reason.

"You see," the masked woman continued. "You know what I am talking about." She pointed to the corpse. "Kiri suffered. Her girls were killed by a mad soldier during the wars. He went on to live a good life on land he had stolen, and had children of his own."

The faces of the dead children seemed to sway in the candle light, and though she was not a superstitious person, Aroha thought she heard for a moment a whisper in the tunnels. Her hands clenched on her taiha.

"So what did she do?" Aroha asked, almost afraid of the reply.

"She found the heart of the mountain." The woman turned slightly, giving Aroha a better look at the device on her back. It was about the size of a valise, and with all the carvings and moving parts very beautiful. Between the gaps in the machinery, Aroha saw a deep red glow. Something in the middle of the machine was burning, giving the device an eldritch power.

"We call it the Touch of Hine-nui-te-pō," the woman whispered. She was only feet away now. "You can help you know. Kiri left the work in our hands, the hands of the daughters of Hine-nui-te-pō. We carry out her work, and I think you have seen enough of the death goddess to know her touch can be transferred."

The recollection of her mother's death was very close to Aroha. No one had been sweeter, kinder and less deserving of death than Mama. For a moment it was a beautiful idea, but she also knew as well as these things started, they always ended badly. The best intentions that these Daughters of Hine-nui-te-pō might have, soon enough they would begin letting their own biases in. They had begun with the worst, but the power of life and death would corrupt their good intentions.

"You're going to have to give me the device," she said softly. "It is not meant for mortals to wield power like this."

She knew that the charge would come, but she also knew something about these women, whoever they were—they were not warriors. They found people in their sleep. In one smooth movement and a press of a button she had extended her taiha. The Daughter lunged at her, and the agent stepped aside, catching the woman in the stomach with the end of the taiha.

She heard the breath go out of her, but she made another attempt the grab hold of Aroha. The agent stepped under her grasp, took hold of her hand and twisted in a lock behind her back. The Heart of the Mountain was hot against her torso, and she could almost feel it beat with an odd rythum. Whatever Kiri had discovered it felt wild and hungry. Now she was sure no woman, no matter how much she wanted to be Hine-nui-te-pō could bear this thing with impunity for long.

"Now," she whispered in a calm manner to the masked woman, "we can continue this dance, in this confined space, but the martial disciplines are not your strong suit. It will only end with me beating you soundly, and removing that mask. Neither of us want that, do we?"

The woman let out a long breath, and struggled for a moment, but Aroha held her soundly.

The agent continued. "It will take me a moment to cut these straps, by that time I imagine you will have escaped to that ornithopter you have on the surface. Your time as Hine-nui-te-pō has been short, but you have changed lives; that should comfort you in the future."

A tremble passed through the woman, even as Aroha released the knife from the sheath at her waist. With two sawing gestures, she cut the device from the masked woman's back.

She fled. Daughter of Hine-nui-te-pō no more. Perhaps deep down she had known her justice could not be sustained. Yet for Peal Hart, she had made a difference.

Aroha was left holding the device, with its depiction of the death goddess carved in the brass. It was warm and beautiful and just for a moment she considered what could be done with it. Those that deserved life could take it from those that did not. It was literally the power of a god she held in her hands.

Hine-nui-te-pō had once nearly been overcome by the Maori hero, Maui, and Aroha imagined herself taking that place. She would be feted around the world, famous and powerful.

Before she could go too far down that path, Aroha raised the machine on high, and smashed it against the rocks again and again, shattering the delicate device's interior. Then wrapping her hand in her jacket, she reached in among the remains, and took the heart of Rangitoto from where its creator had placed it. When it was tucked in her rucksack, she took the remains of the life giving over to where the corpse of its creator rested in the narrow niche. Murmering a little prayer, Aroha slid the remains of the device in with Kiri Hokopa. Without her, and without the Heart, Kiri's followers would not be able to replicate the wonder she had made.

She would not pursue them, she was no detective, and there would be no court case—there never could be. If it was Nurse Lange, Pearl Hart, Mrs Pollock, or even Julia Braun, that really didn't matter.

Hine-nui-te-pō was once again in control of her domain, and that was how it had to be.

Sins of the Father

by Tee Morris

Summer, 1888

The air never smelt right. It stopped smelling normal when the iron lung was installed. It tasted of metal and carbolic acid, and felt like it was burning its way down his throat.

Arthur didn't give a damn. He was alive. Regardless of the bellows that continued to feed him oxygen, the hiss of machinations that threatened to cocoon him, and the tinny, metallic voice that he now used to issue commands to his house staff, he was alive. He was still lord of the manor.

"Sir," the voice came from behind him.

His right index finger pressed the small white button he felt there, and the apparatus shuddered lightly as it turned him slowly to face his butler, Martins.

"Young Master Books has arrived, Sir," the servant spoke evenly.

"Show him in," Arthur hissed, returning his chair to the view he had grown so accustomed.

He had learned at an early age that a man was defined by his legacy; by the harvest one would leave their descendants. It should be a bountiful harvest, and his heart kicked harder in his chest as he looked across the grounds of his estate. Arthur's touch would be felt for ages to come; a new chapter in the great epic that was the British Empire.

Footsteps drew closer. One pair he recognised as his butler. The other pair were almost graceful. Arthur knew that second man could be as quiet as a breeze through the treetops.

The machine forced another breath into Arthur's body, and he coughed at the invasion. To distract himself he thought of something more pleasant than his current predicament. Perhaps later he would indulge himself and venture out to the courtyard, enjoy the warmer weather, and taste a hint of real, fresh country air.

"You can leave, Martins," he wheezed. "And you, Captain, please, have a seat."

The familiar steps of the butler receded into the depths of the mansion. Once he knew he and his visitor were alone, he tipped his head back, and allowed his mouth to stretch into a grin. "You made it out alive." He disliked how the words grated out of his broken body.

"I did." Another pause where the silence felt more heavy than peaceful. "As you trained me to do."

Turning his chair around, Arthur surveyed what he had created. Unconsciously his fingers curled into loose fists.

The result of over two decades of training, conditioning, and regimen now sat before him. Good breeding had undoubtedly been useful. Perhaps Lillian had not been so worthless as he had once thought.

The visitor's uniform was immaculate. His chest was adorned with honours, accomplishments, and victories that were just as much Arthur's own as they were the young captain's.

The lord of the manor's grin widened as he looked into the hard face that betrayed no emotion. The captain stared at something behind him, probably the corner of a painting or some small fixture in the wall.

"So the Prodigal Son returns," Arthur spoke, his artificial voice doing very little to ease the growing tension in the room.

"Did you expect any less, Father?" came the stunted reply.

"No, Wellington. In fact," Arthur began, shifting his motorchair, "if you had not, I would have berated your rotting corpse even if I had to dig it up myself."

The young captain nodded, his eyes darting down to the floor. "Then it is a pleasure to deprive you of that particular joy."

"Do not dare be impertinent with me, boy," he snapped, the loose fists now tightening as the bellows inflated full, stayed there for a moment, and then slowly deflated as he eased back into his iron lung's embrace. "I raised you better than that."

"I do forget myself," Wellington muttered, his gaze on the tips of his boots.

No apology? The army had indeed hardened him up.

Good.

"And how are things in the African wilderness?" Arthur asked.

"Quite manageable now," his son replied. Was that a slight tick he saw in his son's expression at the mention of Africa. "We avenged General Gordon, managed to airship Emin to safety, and effectively reclaimed several territories under hostile rule."

"I understand Emin was a bit difficult when you all finally met up in Mswa. Damn fool wanted to reclaim Equatoria, did he not?"

Arthur took a great amount of satisfaction when his son finally made eye contact with him. He knew what his son was thinking; how did he, the invalid, know that little mission detail? His son had never really understood the reach his father and the family name had over the Empire. Even thousands of miles away from his estate in God-forsaken, savage-infested country, Arthur Books still had an eye and an ear on his son, and on what those lurking above him were doing.

"The governor was a bit difficult once we made contact, but the Expedition—save for the failure of the Rear Column—met its objectives." Wellington cleared his throat. "According to Stanley, it was a rousing success. I believe as I was planning for my return journey, he was planning out his speaking engagement schedule."

"Is that a fact?" Arthur snorted. "Pompous Welshman."

Wellington's gaze shifted back to the corner of the room. "Of course, this is all after I left Banalya. The Congo is a large territory. Many things can happen."

"Indeed, they can." Arthur flexed his fingers open, then closed. "Sometimes, without outside influence." He cast his glance out over the grounds for a moment, feeling that pang again to smell the air as he once had. "And what of you? Are you planning your speaking engagements, or perhaps a publishing of your memoirs?"

His son was smiling now. Wellington's eyes were still looking deep into the shadows behind Arthur, but a strange smile was evident on his lips. It was curious that Wellington made no sign to even try and conceal it. "Not quite, Father."

He hated it when Wellington smiled. It was particularly at times like this—times he made sure were few and far between—when he resembled her. Lillian had betrayed him in her blatant rebellion. First, she would not listen to his reason. Then she refused to heed to his authority.

Yes, my darling Arthur, she purred in his ear, *you took care of me, didn't you? And you thought you could erase me from our son's memory? You underestimated him.*

Arthur shifted nervously in his seat. "And just what do you mean by that, boy?"

"Father, I have returned early from a successful mission in the Dark Continent so that I may end my military career with dignity and honour."

Arthur nodded, his smile returning once his son's faded. "End with a victory, with Her Majesty and those who tend to her every bunion and boil wanting more, eh?"

Wellington's smile had completely vanished on that. "Perhaps not my own words to describe it, but yes, something resembling that."

"This may surprise you, Wellington, but you have made me proud." The way his son started, Arthur would have thought the boy had pissed himself. He chortled. "Oh, but you have, my son. You left this estate as a product of training, conditioning, and discipline, in desperate need of refinement."

"I only reached captain, father," Wellington said, his jaw tightening.

"As I wished it to be," he stated, nodding slightly. Again, his son's gaze returning to meet his own was most satisfying. "Son, I wanted you to taste ambition, be it conscious or not. I made sure no matter how valiantly you fought or how brilliant your performance would be, you would never rise above the rank of captain." He gave another dry laugh that evolved into a cough. A metallic tang filled his nose as he breathed deep, and his voice returned in some small measure. "Afraid to disappoint me, you would only work harder to achieve promotion, hardening you, preparing you. Additionally, keeping you at the rank of captain, you would not soften in your resolve or skill." He settled in his chair and looked at his progeny, a warmth now building in his chest. "And now you have come home."

His pride was now an inferno, and it had been so long since Arthur felt anything in his body react to such primal urges. "Are you ready, son?"

"I am."

The warmth in his chest subsided as Wellington's smile returned.

"Are you?" Wellington asked.

Now the only part of him tingling was the fingertips resting gently on the red buttons built into his handrest. "Of course I'm ready. It is time for you—"

"To live my life, father," he interjected, "by my own morals and my own regimen. No longer yours."

A dryness now clutched at Arthur's throat, and tightened even in spite of the iron lung's efforts to keep him breathing comfortably. "I beg your pardon."

Wellington paused, narrowing his eyes on him. "You. Beg my pardon? Will wonders never cease?" He stood, without asking for leave, and held his eye contact. "I have come here, as a courtesy, to let you know that I have taken a position in Her Majesty's government. This position and its demands will probably limit our contact in the future." He gave a light chuckle. "Well, I was planning to limit our contact in the future, regardless. Better for both our sanity."

Arthur's fingertips itched. "Why was I not consulted about this?"

"Because it is not your concern," Wellington replied smartly.

"If you are involved," Arthur spoke, hating the slight waver the iron lung was giving his voice, "then it is very much my concern."

Wellington shrugged lightly, crossed over to the door, took off his uniform hat and set it on a small end table there. He returned to the seat before his father, glanced outside, then locked his eyes with Arthur's.

"When I was a child, yes, my concerns were yours. When I was a young man leaving school, yes, my concerns were still yours." He leaned forward, the creaking of his chair sounding far louder than Arthur knew it truly was. "The moment I fired my first bullet, the moment I took my first human life, the moment I felt a friend's blood run down my hands, my concerns became my own."

"You believe that, do you?"

"Most assuredly." Wellington tilted his head to one side, and that smile Arthur detested so much returned. "I have found employment on my own, and intend to pursue this career with great zeal and determination. I came here, as I said earlier, out of courtesy. You gave me a life," he said, motioning around the two of them, "if you can call it that much. At the very least, you have earned that."

"A position in Her Majesty's Government, you say?" Arthur's fingers slipped away from the two red buttons. He fought back a smile of his own. "So where have you placed yourself?"

"A clerical position."

Bellows rose and fell faster now as the lord of the manor's rage began to build. No, this wasn't happening. This little whelp would not betray him as well. "Clerical?" was the only thing he could manage to gasp out.

"Yes, clerical."

"But your skills, your abilities—"

"—are my concern now, not yours."

"Damn your eyes, I groomed you for better things!" His natural voice was ravaged and painful, even to his own ears. Its metallic assistant cut in-and-out as their coils and diaphragms were overwhelmed by Arthur's sudden outburst. He felt spittle cooling on his chin; and this was when he realized he was also leaning forward, and the brass tubes that were connected to his lungs were tugging painfully at him, silently beckoning him back into the motorchair.

He had to take in a few more deep breaths. A wave of nausea swelled inside his stomach as he eased back, but he fought the urge to vomit. After a moment, he lifted his head up and looked at his son; his ungrateful, treacherous son.

I'm so proud of him, Arthur, Lillian whispered in his mind.

"And how will you survive, boy?" Arthur hissed. "Live in the barracks or perhaps some halfway house for those who served Her Majesty's army? Hardly the lifestyle you are accustomed." He let that sink in for a moment with him. "I'll disinherit you."

"Father, there were two mistakes you made in raising me all on your own." Wellington stood. Arthur immediately recognized the gaze in his son's eyes, and he felt another wild rage blossom in his chest. "One of those mistakes was grossly underestimating mother."

"You will not mention that harlot in this household," he wheezed. "Not while I am still master of it."

Wellington nodded. "Of course not, but still you did underestimate her. She left me a bit of property in…" He paused, and shook his head. "No, I prefer you didn't know about it. Instead, I will simply assure you that you will never find it and have no hold on it whatsoever. The property is in the name of her side of the family, not yours."

"I will destroy you, boy."

"And destroy what has been your crowning achievement, Arthur Books? Your legacy? If you truly wanted me dead, I would be." He held out his arms, mimicking the crucifix on the mantle just above the room's fireplace. "Go on."

Yes, Arthur, Lillian's ghost implored, *please. I've missed him so. Reunite us.*

Wellington's arms lowered, and again, pity welled in the young gentleman's eyes. "As I thought."

He crossed over to the end table. Arthur could see Wellington in the corner of his eye replacing the officer's hat on his head, and checking it in the mirror as he spoke. "There is no need to make inquiries of where I will be, father, as this organization is quite secretive. In fact, I was sought out by its director. He was most impressed by my performance in logistics, and remained quite adamant in drafting me for this position.

"Before I go, Father, and before I become nothing more than a memory to Martins, unless of course you have him removed as well, I do have one request to ask of you."

Arthur turned the chair to face Wellington. He had the audacity to ask of something from him? He thought he had purged that bitch's influence.

"I know the truth about mother, but I want to hear it from you. A small thing to ask, I'm sure, as the deed was a trivial one."

When Wellington turned to face him, Arthur's rage vanished. He had done it, and he wanted to be proud. So very, very proud.

"How did you do it?"

I am so proud of you, Wellington.

Arthur tipped his head back, committing to memory the image of Wellington standing there, believing that he was the victor. This was not over. No, this was all—most definitely—far from over.

With pistons pumping and the engine of his motorchair lightly thrumming, Arthur turned his seat away from the decorated, honoured captain, and moved closer to the window.

He heard the footsteps continue down the corridor, pause, and following a brief, muffled conversation with someone — Martins, perhaps? — the soldier was gone.

At least for now.

The wind, silent as well as invisible from his side of the window, pushed through the trees and along the grass, giving his estate the semblance of the ocean. A memory surfaced of a four year-old child in the strong, secure hold of his mother. They had spun about in such a breeze, their laughter audible from where he watched them. He was to have been the heir of the Books Estate, but Arthur had wanted more. He had wanted to leave his mark on the British Empire; and while he had passed his time — on the account of a weak man who had failed him in every way imaginable — he saw a new opportunity at fulfilling a destiny in his son, Wellington Thornhill Books. That epiphany had come to him when he watched his son play and frolic with his mother. When he had heard their laughter, when he saw their bond, he knew what had to be done. Father, mother and son; their path had been set on that fateful day.

It could not — now would not — be allowed end this way.

The soft click of the bookcase dissipated the memory, the faces of wife and son slipping from view as fog burned away by the morning sun. The pair of footsteps walked up behind him, but did not draw as close as Wellington had only moments ago. Perhaps it was the chair that frightened them. The woman did not outwardly show her disdain for his condition, but he could see it in her posture. It lingered in her eyes.

"It is a shame about your son, my Lord," she spoke. "A great loss to the House."

His chair chugged and whirred around again. The woman he found quite stunning, even though at this moment she appeared as a cut-out shadow in the bright daylight of the room. He wondered if the deep crimson eyeliner she wore was some odd intimidation tactic of her order. He found it rather stimulating. A curiosity considering the doctors had told him such carnal urges would be denied once the iron lung was affixed upon his person.

The oaf sent to protect her looked like a caveman wearing a dark mourning suit. Utterly ridiculous.

"Do you believe my work to be lost?" His laugh made her flinch, and her reaction only made his loins ache for her. "My dear child, I spent two decades on that ungrateful whelp. He is more foolish than his dead mother if he believes he can simply walk out of this house without consequences."

"The truth of the matter is your son has, just now, walked away from your influence."

"My influence, even from this infernal chair, is far more reaching than you believe," he snapped. "Do not question that."

"The House of Usher was expecting results from your endeavours, not disappointment." Her voice was tart, with a hint of the school mistress in it.

"I know exactly what your order was expecting. Between my own reports and your visits—" Arthur stopped, and gave a gruff laugh as he looked over them both. "Perhaps I should remind you that I have been issuing these reports to your superiors when you were learning to walk."

"I am here representing the collected interests of the House, Lord Books, not my own. I assure you."

He nodded. She was absolutely right in that respect.

"If you believe I do not have contingencies in place, then you stand double in error," he stated quietly. "So long as my work remains amongst the living, it will always remain under my influence. You have waited for just under two decades. You can wait a few years more."

"You expect me to return to the House with merely your reassurance? Keep calm and carry on, as it were? I think not," she scoffed. She took a step forward, and Arthur allowed himself to settle into his chair. She was quite fetching. "We demand a return on what we have invested into this project."

Arthur smacked his lips silently. He was thirsty. "Do you now?"

The gorilla took a step forward. Very well then. If this was the way she wished to carry out her duties, it is her burden to bear. Not his.

His eyes narrowed on the lumbering man. "Tell me something — can you speak?"

He blinked, looking back at the female for a moment. Was this idiot asking for her permission to reply?

"It is a simple question and one I believe you do not need the graces of your counterpart to answer adequately. Can. You. Speak?" he repeated.

"Of course, my Lord."

Something he genuinely liked about the House of Usher. The gorillas they employed were given a modicum of education and refinement—just enough not to make it tedious dealing with them.

"Excellent."

His middle finger pushed down one of his red buttons. Considering her distance from him and where she stood, this was the better choice of the two. The two leads launched from their concealment just above his head. One drove itself into the curvature of her right breast, the other lodged itself into her wrist. She had no time to reach for either dart before the electricity entered her body. The woman jerked lightly at first, but her quivering grew as a whine rose from the life-granting device around Arthur.

Her guard took one step. "I wouldn't," and he motioned with his eyes to where his ring finger stroked and tapped a second red button.

It was a macabre, bizarre dance of sorts the Usher woman enacted for his pleasure; and as foam seeped from between her beautiful, full ruddy lips, Arthur felt a twitch under his lap blanket.

The electricity continued to pump into her, even after she had fallen to the floor. The twitches only ceased once the generators in his chair silenced. His thumb pressed the yellow button underneath it, and the wires tore free of the woman's pale flesh and retracted back into his chair.

"You will take back to your lords at the House of Usher two missives. The first one, a reminder: Do not make demands of me. Ever. While there has been a marginal investment from your order, I remain the most vested into this creation of mine, and my methodology will remain under my possession until such a time where I will share it. Any further sign of impertinence from your people, I will take as a sign of hostility." He motioned to the dead woman on the floor. "We would not want that, now would we?"

"No, my Lord," he said, nodding so emphatically it seemed like his head might fly off.

Arthur thought for a moment about that possibility, but then dismissed it before continuing. "The House's involvement into my endeavours has been on my sufferance. Testing my patience any further will only yield more disappointments and dangers." Arthur then looked him over. "The other is a recommendation. Elder Goddard is still in your order, yes?"

"Yes, sir, he is."

"Please tell him I sent you with a formal introduction." The middle finger of his left hand pressed the button underneath it. A card popped up from the armrest.

The man started to reach for the ivory-coloured card, but hesitated.

Definitely more than he appeared. "Go on," Arthur spoke, in as soothing a tone as the vocalizer allowed. "Take it."

The man gave Arthur a weak smile, trained his gaze on the card as he slowly leaned in, and quickly snatched the card and withdrew, all in one fluid motion.

"You are an intuitive young man. You should not be condemned to the life of cannon fodder."

"Thank you, my Lord."

He rotated his chair away from the remaining Usher representative. "Now, collect your colleague and leave my estate."

Arthur could hear the man take up the corpse and stomp back through the passage where they had earlier emerged. They would steal away and leave him be, but the House of Usher would not disappear completely. He had absently wondered when that secret society of Goddard's would grow more anxious and perhaps aggressive in their curiosity over his project.

Arthur had been able to manipulate them into doing his bidding on those rare occasions that his own resources were not sufficient. Certainly, there had not been many times he had called upon them, but now they believed themselves to be entitled to something for their involvement—insignificant as it may have been. This new interest of theirs would be something requiring his attention, and something he would have to fortify his estate against. Perhaps even his very person.

There were many options. Arthur ran a finger along the edge of his right handrest. Perhaps a new apparatus was in order. He would need to meet with his clankertons and find out what he could do to make his presence more imposing.

When he watched the grass ripple and sway in the strong summer breeze, he felt an ache—a longing—creep over his skin. His eyes went to the left handrest, and he watched his index finger push the yellow button there.

His legacy to the Empire—whether for its betterment or for its downfall, whomever provided him the better offer—had abandoned him but this was merely a moment's respite. Soon, in a world far from the heat of battle, far from the glory of victory, his son would return and reclaim what Arthur had always planned for him —greatness. From the Books Manor, a new kind of future would arise and it will be from an instrument of his design. Only Arthur understood what was needed and so it would remain until his creation returned home and claimed what would rightfully be his.

You underestimate my son, Lillian taunted from beyond the grave.

The footsteps slowly approached and then Martins stopped at his carefully calculated and customary distance. "You rang, m'Lord?"

"Yes," Arthur began, his nostrils burning lightly as he took in a deep breath, "take me outside. I am in need of proper, fresh air. It always helps me think better."

The Precarious Child

by Pip Ballantine

Hanging by her fingertips from a balcony, was not the situation Verity Fitzroy's father would have hoped his daughter to be in. She knew that and was a little sorry, knowing that he would have been disappointed.

He'd taught Verity about the importance of three points of contact when climbing walls, the proper way of dispatching vipers, and the most efficient method of riding at speed. In fact, she'd learned such etiquette long before most girls were taught how to curl their hair.

With tiny gasp between clenched teeth, she locked her eyes shut hard, and tried not to imagine the stonework giving way fractionally and dropping her to the cobbles four storeys beneath. Also there was the lingering temptation that if she let go, they would finally be together; she missed her parents every day.

The reality was, hanging three storeys above the pavement such surrender would anger Father even more. He would have been proud of her earning a living on the streets of London that didn't involve taking her clothes off. He would have been proud of her surviving a very tough fifteen years in this world.

"Papa," she muttered, "I made a promise, I know, but I miss you." She screwed her eyes even tighter, fighting back tears that formed there. "And I'm scared."

Her surrender, however, would not stand. Not even in the afterlife.

Then her eyes flicked open. *Right then,* she thought, *I've had my tears. Now, time to get myself out of this sticky wicket.*

Mustering all the strength in her arms, Verity swung her lower body until it collided with the main part of the house. Her boots scrambled against the brickwork, and she finally had some luck. The brick of this particular three-storey apartment building was rather rotten and both toes found that third point of contact. She felt relief wash over her as the strain on her shoulders lessened.

Still, Verity felt rather like an insect, with her body hanging wedged between the overhang of the balcony and the wall itself.

The itsey bitsy spider climbed up the waterspout...

She had sung that to the twins this morning. Jeremy and Jonathan were peas in a pod, wise beyond their years, and still they allowed her to mother them just a little. It was sweet of them. Sweet if she didn't know they carried tiny daggers on their person and swore like sailors.

As she clung there, Verity listened for sounds that would signal the intruders into the room she'd been robbing were moving on. It was going to be a close call if her arms and legs could hold out. Clouds overhead were gathering...

Down came the rain and washed the spider out...

"Not bloody likely," she hissed, tightening her handhold on the building as best she could.

She'd come broken into the room at the boarding house with the intention of pillaging it, only to be disturbed by someone else intent on doing the very same thing. The occupant was a very popular man it seemed. He always had been she remembered.

These newcomers were in there now, talking rather intently, but she couldn't make out what they were saying. For now, Verity remained suspended in a summer night of Londontown, hearing her own heartbeat in her ears and contemplating just what had got her into this predicament.

It was simple really...it was Harrison Thorne's fault.

It all traced back to earlier that morning in Kensington.

The problem with Agent Thorne was that he could ask anything of Verity. Hopefully he didn't know that and couldn't read it on her face. Verity sat at one end of the table, staring at the rather blurry photograph of their mark. At the other end was a silent Henry. They often acted like the gang's mother and father, simply because of their age—she fifteen, he nearly seventeen. Verity was however the only one that made any effort with their home.

She attempted to make their little square of Kensington their own: a glass of violets in a cup by the window, a few brightly coloured images on the walls, and a repaired sideboard stacked with clean and tidy but mismatched dishes. As she glanced out of the corner of her eye she hoped Agent Thorne noticed.

He was smiling slightly, standing by the door, and letting his eyes rest on the children sitting very still at the table. Verity shifted a bit and glanced at Henry. Unlike the charming agent, Henry could be really so disagreeable. In fact he was in the process of being so right now. His frown was as thick as a winter storm—but then the appearance of the handsome government agent had this effect.

Verity cleared her throat in embarrassment. "I am sorry, Mr. Thorne, but Henry is always cantankerous before he's eaten."

The eldest of their gang, Henry sometimes took his role a little too seriously. His dark eyes fixed on hers for a moment, glaring out from under a thatch of disarrayed black hair. "I'm just saying, Verity, that it sounds like Mr. Thorne's problem here could be handled some other way by some other folk."

The other children glanced between them—not nervously, but more with the keen interest of spectators at a tennis match at Wimbledon. Verity bit the inside of her cheek, least she snap back. They were the eldest and it wouldn't do to get into a fight with him—that was the thing Henry liked to do most of all: fight.

"It is a small matter," she said evenly, "and even we lowly servants of the Empire have to look out for its welfare."

Mr. Thorne tilted his head. "Modesty does not become you, Miss Fitzroy. While I am a man of the world, I can not find one quarter of the things you are able to in the streets of London. When Clayton was at his hotel in the West End, I was on more-than-familiar territory. But now?" He shook his head. He was embarrassed. "I lost the red-headed cad in the fog and shadows of London. I need your eyes." Thorne motioned to Verity, Henry, and the rest of the children. "All of them."

Colin snatched a piece of bread, and stuffed it into his mouth. "It's no bother, Henry," he chimed in, in a slightly muffled fashion. "We can easily find out where this geezer is hiding—especially with only one leg! That's a dead giveaway!"

"He may seem harmless, but don't let that fool you," Mr. Thorne said, motioning to the photograph underneath her fingertips. "Arthur Clayton is working for some dangerous men. You must take great care not to be seen."

The children nodded solemnly but underneath the table nudged each other. Despite everything they did love a good chase. Also, being paid by Mr. Thorne kept them warm, dry, and out of the workhouse. The less thievery they had to do, the less chance they had of being arrested. Verity very much liked not being arrested.

Another fact she kept to herself was that the Ministry had resources—resources that she could use in her own personal mission. The further they got in good with them the better.

Thinking about the whole dreadful mess of her childhood made her head hurt. No, it wasn't the thinking that was doing it. Something else entirely.

The girl shook her head, but—like all the other times before—the clicking wouldn't stop. Her eyes darted to the strange signet ring the agent wore on his right index finger. Something about it clattered about in the back of her brain. If she concentrated a little harder she'd be able to deduce what it was and what…

"Verity?" Harrison Thorne was looking at her very strangely, and she would hate him to discern her little secret. Even her fellow urchins didn't know the strange workings of her mind.

"Yes," she said softly, shooting a glance at Henry to cut off any further protests, "I think we can help you with whatever you need."

"We are a democracy," Henry interjected, as rose to his feet and looked around at there fellows. "The majority rules. So, who says we should take on this job?"

Every child's hand shot up—except the oldest of them. Instead Henry rolled his eyes. Democracy was apparently not entirely all he wished it were.

"Remember," Verity reminded him, "that Mr. Thorne helped us find this place, and keeps us safe."

Even Henry couldn't argue with that. The streets of London were dangerous for everyone—but most especially children. Thanks to Harrison Thorne, they had the safety of their bolthole. An old mansion owned by the Ministry, but only rarely used as a safe house, Mr. Thorne had shown them a number of secret passages that lead to concealed rooms. For the last two years it had been home, and not a nicer or safer place for orphaned children could be found in any part of Kensington. All of them took great pains that the only adult to ever know they lived here was Mr. Thorne.

"I don't like how he calls us the Ministry's eyes of London," Henry muttered under his breath. "I think it's a rubbish name. We're not in a blimmin' Penny Dreadful and we don't belong to no Ministry."

"It's alright to belong to something," Verity commented, feeling her own slow burning anger rise to the surface. "Besides we can use the coin."

"I can see you are in a bad mood today Henry." Mr. Thorne's deep blue eyes gleamed as he interrupted. "But I suggest you listen to Miss Verity here."

She shifted in her seat again. The agent made her feel very strange, and sent her thoughts winging to other places than where they should have been. It was most certainly nowhere near pursuing her family's killers, or finding her beloved father's collection of antiquities.

Realising this, she leapt to her feet. "Don't mind Henry, we'll find who you want us to."

"Of that I have no doubt. You know how to reach me." Agent Thorne tipped his hat and exited through the concealed staircase.

"You heard the man," Verity snapped. "Let's go find this Clayton gent. If he suspects the Ministry is after him he'll be heading for the lowest bolthole."

Children privileged or impoverished would have thrown a fit at being ordered about like that, but her little group would never question a command from her or Henry. They had only survived this long on the streets by listening to them. Quickly the children were on their feet, sliding on jackets, hats, and pocketing the little devices and nick knacks that gave them a profession.

Watching these urchins carry out preliminary checks of their technological creations gave her a tiny, vain smile. She'd made most of them herself and trained the children in proper care of their arsenal. Modern men of science would have dismissed her compatriots, and even she had her doubts when they first gathered. Happily, her gang had proven her wrong.

Henry came up behind her as she was packing a collection of devices that might come in handy into her jacket and trousers. "I don't like how he orders us about like we're a pack of hounds he can set on a bleedin' fox."

Verity glared at him. "Would you prefer Jonathan and Jeremy pressed into working for an adult gang? Maybe Liam would be happy as a clankerton's tester or a chimneysweep? Or would you see Emma some dirty old man's plaything? The workhouse is always an option, of course."

Henry swallowed and stared abruptly down at his feet.

"I thought not," she continued primly. "Now let's go out and make an honest coin."

The streets of Kensington were well to-do, but like most of London, a street in either direction could lead a person to a different world. Poor, middle-class, prostitute or doctor, they all rubbed shoulders here.

Without needing to consult, the urchins set off to their own favourite haunts in the reeking, deadly city. Henry headed into the East End, where he had distant family members and a reach deep and wide. Jonathan and Jeremy went to the West End, where they mingled with the various children who held horses and ran errands for theatre-goers and actors (when they had coin to spend). Christopher was kind enough to let the doe-eyed Emma tag along with him as he made for Westminster.

That left Verity looking down into the cheeky grins of Liam and Colin. "So where do we start boys?" She knew if she let them run off by themselves not a lot would be achieved except for maybe a few lifted purses. The youngest boys were the easiest to be distracted.

Liam tilted his head. "The Ditch."

"Yeah, plenty of dosses there," Colin chimed in.

Of all the places. "Are you sure?" Verity asked with a little dread. However, they knew this city far more intimately, and she didn't doubt their instincts.

The boys nodded solemnly, and so that was how it had to be.

They caught a ride on the back of a bus, running up alongside as it chuffed away from the stop, and hauling themselves onto the back. It was not the fastest mode of travel, nor the safest if the conductor caught them, but it was fun to watch the world go by and saved their boot leather. Perched like sparrows very near the rear wheel Verity and the boys took in the sights. To keep Liam and Colin mollified, she fished out some toffee she'd acquired two days before and gave it to them.

They passed plenty of fellow urchins—some even waved or called hello. However the three of them were on Ministry business, and so Verity held tight to the boys' sleeves least they make a run for it. The looks they shot her were not exactly delighted.

The boys motioned with their heads, and they jumped as their bus turned a corner. Verity straightened up, squinting through the dust of the afternoon, taking in the less-than-desirable Shoreditch. Verity allowed herself to be lead down an alleyway by the boys who were almost giggling. How they loved to keep her on edge.

One of the difficulties they faced was that in London there was a definite surplus of one-legged men. Wars and industrial accidents had in fact made them as common as dust.

When Liam and Colin finally allowed her to stop, a slow smile spread on Verity's face.

They were standing across the road from Lady Bucket's Hospital for War Veterans. The newly painted sign, clean windows, and smells of food proclaimed that inside could be found a hero's welcome, as well as a hot dinner and warm clothing. Verity chewed her lip and observed for a moment as a group of three well-dressed ladies went in. She knew the type: privileged, looking to do good work in the hopes it would make them better people, or perhaps justify their social shortcomings. Some did it out of appearance, others were genuinely kind hearted. It reminded her distastefully of the workhouse.

"We did good right, Truth?" Colin asked, tugging slightly on her sleeve.

She smiled down at him. The boys liked to seem all posh calling her that—showing that they knew what her name meant in Latin—even if she had told them. "You did, lads. Should have thought of it myself." She attempted to brush any dirt off her half-cloak and trousers. "Now you stay here and keep watch."

They both grumbled a little, but they didn't need telling how much attention two small boys in a place like this would draw. They retreated into the shadows of the alleyway, and Verity quickly crossed the road.

She slipped in with a gaggle of other ladies carrying in large bundles of clothing. They were all too busy being pleased with their charity to notice one extra female among them. She and the charitable women were soon marching into a large room housing the shattered remains of Britain's warriors. While the prim and proper ladies did little to hide their disdain, Verity reminded herself sternly that these men had fought for the Empire. However, it was hard looking at them. Despite her years on the street, these broken souls were pathetic to see. Their wounds were not just physical. It was their eyes; as still and dead as stones.

As the boys had guessed, one-legged men were in abundance here. The lucky ones had articulated prosthetics of varying age, engineering, and effectiveness. The unlucky ones had mere wooden pegs where once limbs had been. They clattered and stumped their way around the hall, which was full of stretcher beds. It could not have been much different than when they'd been in the army, but certainly better than the streets.

Verity's gaze darted around the room, looking for one man Agent Harrison Thorne was after. None stood out as being particularly clean or better fed than the others. What was needed was a distraction so she could sort the wheat from the chaff.

She dipped into her pocket and felt around. She didn't need to see the objects in there to know what they were; she knew everyone of them by touch. A set of lockpicks she'd stolen from a member of the elephant gang, a spool of razor wire, and a hundred other little objects. Her fingers closed on the tiny oval shape of Mickey. A slow smile spread on Verity's lips.

Hiding him behind her back, she carefully wound the key, and dropped the little clockwork rat onto the floor. Gentile ladies come for a little charitable work were not immune to Mickey's particular charm. This was no toy for a pet or a child, but an articulated rat that ran on articulated feet, with a mechanical body covered in a pelt that made it look all too real. Verity has also made her automated rodent rather aggressive. It scuttled across the floor, letting out a high-pitched squeals as it drew close to objects. Objects like feet. In a few moments the room was full of horrified ladies dancing around screaming. Many were pulling up their skirts. Some of those they'd been helping, in turn tried to help the women. Veterans now lashed out at the rat with their prosthetic and otherwise legs.

In the chaos, Verity slipped in the office. She glanced at the clock and focused on its internal workings, making a mental connection between it and Mickey. Her rat's clockwork would soon enough reach their second sequence and send him scuttling for shelter. Until then, she would have the time necessary to get done what she wanted. Her eyes scanned the hospital director's desk. Everyone in power was always ready to make lists—it seemed it was the only way to for them to ever feel important. A brief stint in a workhouse had made Verity deeply distrustful of lists and the large books they were kept in, but they could be useful at times like this.

Only two men had come in the last week, according to this calendar. One old, one young. From Agent Thorne's description she knew this wasn't going to be some codger. He wasn't as simple as to sign in under his name, but thanks to the blessed fernicktyness of the establishment, they took something they called 'identifying features'. Probably the odd person tried to pull one over on the charity…it happened even in the most worthy of places.

"Young then," she whispered. "And red-haired." Her finger traced the name. It was not Arthur Clayton, but John Marlet, listed as 'mobile' and fit for work duty.

In her head, she heard a quick *click* as if gears in both the clock and Mickey were striking together in perfect precision. Verity squeaked a glance out the door before exiting silently. Mickey had disappeared as his sequence commanded and now the laudable ladies were once more at their tasks, but not without a few hairs out of place and nursing caps askew.

Verity took up a pile of newly knitted socks from the table and began arranging them in a deep basket. Giving a quick glance around her, Verity hastily pulled from her pocket a small tin whistle to her lips. Though no discernable sound came out when she blew on it, Mickey soon appeared from a gap in the wall. The rat quickly scuttled to her foot and then went still.

"Good boy," she whispered to him, before replacing him back in her pocket.

Passing the socks out to grateful veterans gave her an excuse to move in amongst the beds, remain useful, and keep an eye out for her prey. She spotted him easily enough, straight from the picture that Harrison had given her — a young man, red hair, his other leg a second-hand McTighe automaton device. He was pushing a broom around in a very sullen manner. Unlike those who had come of the street he looked less than impressed to be here. As Agent Thorne had insinuated, his investigations had forced him out of a very nice West End hotel and bought him here.

Verity's eyes fixed on his prosthetic leg. For the second time that day, she could hear a soft cacophony no one else was privy too. This time, however, the strange echoing tick in her ear seemed out of synchronisation with the workings of the leg. There was a strange syncopated pattern working *against* the anticipated rattle of the leg's flex and bend.

She's never heard anything like that before. Verity knew Agent Thorne would want her to find him, alert him of Arthur Clayton, his alias, and his location, but that the longer she listened to the odd rhythm of Clayton's leg, the more her skin tingled. Mechanical things turned her into quite the magpie; and if she really admitted to her namesake, Verity was curious.

With Agent Thorne's warning ringing in her ears alongside the odd syncopation of Clayton's leg, Verity circled the room, watching and waiting. The *tick-tock* and the clatter of little gears did not leave her head as she watched the man. The longer she watched him, the more he exuded a nervous disposition often found in the streets of London. He kept pulling out his pocket watch and glancing at it.

Verity had just finished fluffing one decorated soldier's pillow when she heard the pattern shift in pitch. She looked across the room just in time to see Clayton walking out into the growing twilight.

Luckily he wasn't able to move terribly fast. Verity kept her distance discrete, even when Colin and Liam ran over to her, a sticky bag of gobstoppers still in the younger lad's hand.

Keeping an eye on the man hobbling up the street, she whispered, "Liam, come with me, Colin get back to the doss and let them know I've found the gent. I'll send word on his location."

Colin's reply was a nod, and then he disappeared into an alley. Liam dropped back, becoming another shadow among lengthening shadows, but far enough from Verity to be unnoticed. Close enough to lend a hand. Just in case.

The chase was on, at it was. The man's prosthetic kept him much slower than other prey, so Verity and Liam only needed to keep him in line of sight.

Five streets over, he turned into an alley. For too quickly for either child's liking. Verity ducked behind a flower seller while Liam stopped before a window, feigning interest in whatever was within. She peered around her cart, catching their mark looking up and down the street before rounding a corner and disappearing into a boarding house.

Gesturing Liam over, she wrapped her arm around him. "Take a message to the dead drop—give Agent Thorne this address."

Liam stared up at her, his expression hard. "Why don't we both do it?"

"Don't think I am silly enough to go in," she replied smartly. "I won't do any such thing, but we need to keep an eye on him. If he leaves for whatever reason, I'll leave Mickey within sight so you can follow him to wherever we stop." Verity turned Liam around. "Now hop to it."

For once he didn't give her any lip, but scarpered off and melted into the growing darkness. It had been a long day, but Verity knew she might have to stay here awhile. She found a corner of the alley, where the shadows were darkest, and wedged herself in behind some abandoned crates from the nearby costermongers. She'd just got herself comfortable when a light appeared above her head. The crates seemed solid enough, so silently she crept up the tower of wood until she was on level with the window. She could just make out Arthur Clayton, but she almost fell when she caught a reflection in the mirror above the fireplace.

Clayton was talking to another man, a man Verity knew.

"Uncle Octavius," she whispered.

Her father's best friend, who had been with them in Africa, Spain and even Egypt — standing there before Clayton, clearly as where she had last seen him as a child. Tall, brooding, with the long line of a scar on his left cheek. She'd been there when he got it.

She'd also been there when her father had got the news that Uncle Octavius had been killed on the Nile.

Yet now, there he was, in much better health than his dearly departed brother, Thomas.

When she looked at her Uncle Octavius in the mirror, though, he was different. There was no smile. No mirth. He was cold. There was something else Verity noticed—the rattle of Clayton's prosthetic leg. There was nothing peculiar about it now.

Verity was about to ease back into her hiding place when Uncle Octavius and Clayton switched places in what she could only assume was a spirited conversation. When she saw her lost relative, the *rat-tat-tat* she originally heard from Clayton was now centred around him.

Prosthetic legs were wonderful devices that could contain armaments, maps, or cavities used to smuggle items you might not want to certain government agencies to find in your possession. Whoever this red-headed one-legged man was, he must be some kind of courier. Whatever he'd had in his leg was now in her uncle's possession.

She watched her uncle gesture sharply at where Clayton stood, more words that sounded like distant shouts. She could just make out Clayton pointing at Uncle Octavius, then it grew still again. He then limped around him and left through the doorway. Verity gave the drainpipe close to her a tug to test its surety. Then she wrapped her fingers around it and leaned forward to risk a wider view.

Uncle Octavius' attention was at the door. He pulled what appeared to be a call for a butler, but the man that appeared look far too menacing for such a refined position. Her eyes grew wide as she watch Uncle Octavius produce from a small table what she recognized from the streets as a garrotte. He handed it to the imposing man, nodded, and watched him leave. Octavius then went to the mirror, straightened his tie, and then retired deeper into the boarding house.

The off balance rattle now filled her ears. She felt it as clearly as her own heartbeat. It rose up through the house, to the top storey. Her eyes fixed on the spot. She swallowed hard, gripped hard the drainpipe, and made up her mind.

Boarding houses were easier to break into since there was always a lot of comings and goings. No one would react to an odd rattling from the drainpipes outside on occasion which they did as she worked her way up to the next ledge. The clockwork curiosity seemingly passed on to a thought-dead uncle now took precedence over Agent Thorne's original charge.

Hugging the ledge as closely as she could, Verity pulled herself up to the darkened window. Thankfully, the housekeeper had tended to the windows well as she gave its frame a slow tug. The pane slid easily, and now she was inside the boarding house. The odd ticking was easy to trace as she crept quietly from darkened room, through a brightly lit corridor, up another flight of stairs, to another room in the far corner of the building.

She leaned into the door and held her breath. Uncle Octavius, apparently, had stepped out for the night.

Quick as a flash, she'd whisked out her lock-picks and soon found herself in the room where the syncopated *rat-tat-tat* was so clear it made the hair on the back of her neck stand. The room, on quick examination was as bare and desolate as one could imagine in a boarding house. Why was her uncle here? How was her uncle *alive?* Her questions coupled with the steady noise made it difficult to concentrate.

It also made it difficult to hear the scrape of another lock pick at the door. All the warning Verity had was the sound of the cylinder tumbling disengaging. There was no wardrobe to hide in. The bed so low to the floor she couldn't swiftly stuff herself under it.

And that was how she found herself in the here and now, hanging precariously on the ledge of a dead uncle's rented apartment. However her arms were weakening, and she was terrified if she inched her feet out of the toe-hold she had, then the arms would give way entirely.

She heard the intruders moving around upstairs, and imagined that whoever was looking for Uncle Octavius and the device would not be happy to see her. The ticking was deep in her head, and it made everything more difficult.

Either way she was going to end up on the cobblestones, now or later. Her mind raced through the possible things she had in her pocket. But again, one hand down meant less ability to hold on and that didn't seem like an option.

Above she heard a shout, furniture being thrown about, a pop that sounded awfully like a gunshot, and then something like a scream. Her imagination was running faster than a March hare, but she still couldn't decide if this was a good sign or not.

Just at that moment her right arm cramped and buckled. Luckily that was also the exact moment when a hand like iron locked onto her upper arm.

"Let go!" Harrison Thorne barked. He was hanging from the balcony, with his legs wedged in the iron work, but he had a good grip on her. Never had a man looked more like an angel. She smiled and with uttermost faith, obeyed.

He pulled her in, and gave her a rough hug that knocked the remaining breath out of her. It was only a moment before he pushed her back just as roughly. "What do you think you were doing young lady? Did you not hear a word I told you?"

He was angry and outraged, and in an instant Verity went from relieved to embarrassed.

"I'm sorry," she stuttered, completely at a loss for an explanation. "I…I just thought…"

He waved an admonishing finger at her. "No Verity Fitzroy, it is perfectly clear that you didn't think at all."

It was the typical attitude from an adult. They always thought a child's head was full of fluff. In this instance however she was not about to disabuse him of the notion.

"I'm sorry," she repeated. "But I think everyone was looking for something…"

By way of explanation she scrambled back into the room. Walking around the it, she tilted her head like a magpie.

"Verity…" Her rescuer trailed in wake, but she held up her hand for silence. Remarkably, he gave it to her.

Locating the point where the sound was the loudest, Verity dropped to her knees and ran her fingers over the floorboards. One stood fractionally prouder than the other. With a small knife from her pocket she was able to prize it open.

Beneath was the device responsible for the ticking that only she could hear. It was a circular device—no bigger than a pocketwatch—yet every tiny gear was visible and moving. It was light in her hand—far lighter than it had any right to be.

"What is that?" Agent Thorne crouched down and leaned over her shoulder.

"I don't know," she whispered, "but I recognise it. It was in my father's collection."

"What is it doing here then?"

She turned it over in her hands, mesmerised by its perpetual motion that seemed to have no winding mechanism. "I have no idea," she murmured.

Harrison Thorne sank back on his heels. "Did he know what it was?"

She shook her head, wrapping her fingers around it tightly. "As far as I am aware he didn't. It was something he found on a dig in Cyprus. I thought it was lost in when our house burned to the ground." Her voice cracked on the last few words, as the emotion she thought she had a grasp on welled up.

Luckily the Ministry agent made no move to take it from her. If he had—even being who he was—she would have fought him. Quickly she wrapped the device in her handkerchief and secreted it in her pocket. Best to get it out of the way and out of his mind.

She look up at him and smiled. "I have found your Mr. Clayton for you. He is in a returned serviceman's establishment not far from here."

"Yes, thank you," Agent Thorne sighed. "We found his body not far from here. He'd been strangled and thrown into an alleyway. That's why Liam bought me here."

"Then you don't need us any more?" She hoped she sounded casual about the whole thing. Locating Clayton was after all, the only thing Agent Thorne had asked her to do. The device was not part of this, and Uncle Octavius she would keep quiet about too. This was her life, her quest, and the Ministry of Peculiar Occurrences did not need to know about it.

Agent Harrison Thorne trusted her, for he slipped the agreed sum into her palm. "No, you have done you part. This is where your job ends and mine begins once more."

As they walked downstairs together she pondered just how wrong the Agent from the Ministry of Peculiar Occurrences was being. It was in fact the end of his mission, and the start of something far more personal for her.

The strange little device's tick-tock was beginning to feel comfortable…like her own heartbeat returned. She felt Father would have been very pleased about that.

Merry Christmas, Verity Fitzroy

by Pip Ballantine

Christmas Eve, 1891

If there was anything that Verity Fitzroy of the Ministry Seven disliked it was snow and sitting still. So having to endure both was a little bit beyond the pale—especially on Christmas Eve. Presently sitting outside a small house in Hampstead, she was getting quite wet with snow falling on her head and thinking longingly of the summer.

Four of her fellow urchins were inside the house, rifling around for the evidence that Agent Harrison Thorne needed to have their owner arrested. It was one of the little duties that kept the orphans solvent and busy. Verity knew full well the problems she would have if the children were not kept entertained.

They had watched the man leave his house, and then scampered across the slowly whitening garden. The only window that wasn't secure was a tiny one that the younger children, Jonathan, Jeremy and Colin could get through—but not Verity. It wasn't that she had gained any girth, but she had grown. Fifteen years old and she might still have some growing left in her.

Verity preferred not to think about it, but her mind did drift to the other issue that was constantly calling to her. It was a question of her past… and quite possibly her future.

The fact that Uncle Octavius, the man her father had held in such high regard, and Verity had thought dead for so many years, had actually become a murderer had proved quite the distraction in her life.

She'd told no one—not even Harrison Thorne of the Ministry of Peculiar Occurrences—what she had seen while perched on a crate outside a Shoreditch boarding house.

Verity replayed the scene over and over again in her head as she sat under the trees, concealed by shadows, to watch for the return of the owner of the house. She had a small tin whistle in her cold fingers. When blown the sound would not be heard by any human ear, but the tiny drum in Colin's pocket would vibrate.

As she sat watching the road, in her other pocket her hand was wrapped around the circular device that she had recovered from her thought-dead uncle's rooms. Its ticking had stopped, but somehow she felt better touching it—complete some how. It stilled her thoughts.

The lights of the city were distant and twinkling in the chill of the night. From this distance London looked like a fairytale kingdom. Verity smiled bitterly to herself, thinking how that fairytales often contained the darkest shadows and the vilest monsters.

She was so engrossed in her brooding that it took her a long moment to comprehend the faintest ticking in the back of her head. Immediately Verity knew that it was not from the device in her pocket. It came from a far more distant source. To her practiced ear it was the slow rattle of mechanism that had not been wound for a long time. She felt it had to be an old machine somewhere, and it was almost calling for help. Verity whipped her head around, looking for the source, but there was no one nearby—and certainly no machinery.

However, the sound was now registering as familiar. She had heard it last while following a man with a clockwork leg, and it was he that had eventually led her to Uncle Octavius. Perhaps this too was something to do with him.

On the wings of those thoughts, she jumped up and left the shadow of the tree to trot to the low wall surrounding the garden. The trees and shrubs were heavy with snow, and everything was as silent as the grave. Silent that was, except for the sound of her own ragged breathing, and the constant rattling tick of a machine nearby, calling to Verity.

She shot a glance back over her shoulder at the house, but there were no lights on or signs of life. The boys were being very professional.

So Verity thought she could afford a little investigation of her own. Cautiously, she moved out onto the quiet road and ventured down away from the house a little. Verity frowned as she squinted down the street. Something was moving at the intersection, a figure that was a patch of grey in the patchwork of shadows and snow. The whirring and ticking was growing so loud in her head, that she could no longer hear her own breathing. It was almost as if she was becoming less and less aware of her own body, and more part of the mechanism racing in her head.

The figure up ahead turned towards her and the suggestion of its head tilted slightly. Something that might have been a bowler hat was tipped in her direction, and as it did so, it moved out from the shadows just a fraction. A puff of steam stained the dark air at its back as Verity's eyes widened.

It was not human, but it was human sized and shaped. It also had no flesh. Verity immediately knew the word for it, an automaton. A human replicant made of cogs, gears, and pistons. Her father had spoken of such things, and the clankertons that made them. Verity still remembered the awe in his voice. Those that she had heard about however had been mindless creations, controlled by their maker. This somehow seemed to radiate *personality*.

What her parents would have given to see such a creation. Her father had been an archaeologist and making had not been quite his forte. Her mother however, had played with machinery like many of the middle-class did. It was not particularly lady-like, but Mother had never been bothered by such things.

All these thoughts darted through her mind, even as she realised the strange piece in her pocket was warm—almost burning. She was caught between terror and delight. Something about the figure was menacing, the way its eyes burned with the internal fires, and yet it was a walking marvel.

Finally, Verity found herself trotting towards it, one hand wrapped around the tiny device her uncle had most likely killed to have, and the other outstretched before her. The falling snow made the whole scene a strange picture postcard.

Then she heard Colin's scream pierce that odd bubble of quiet. Verity shared one strange look with the automaton, and then spun around on her heel. Now the ticking was washed away in a flood of fear.

As Verity ran back the way she had come, she suddenly realised the horrible thing she had done. The one thing that she had promised never to do. She had put her own problems ahead of the children that were hers to protect.

She rounded the corner into the garden of the house and saw the figure of a tall, gangly man with his hand wrapped around Colin's arm. Jonathan and Jeremy were dancing around him, battering at him while he dragged Colin back towards the house.

The knowledge that whoever this man was, he was dangerous, and very unlikely to call the coppers, welled inside her. The path she was racing down was slippery, and she was panicked. Verity slipped and fell, skidding down the path on her side and colliding with the man. For a moment it was a tangle of children and angry squawking man, arms and legs flying.

However, it was the children that were faster and lighter on their feet. Colin and Jeremy got up first, while Verity pulled Jonathan to his feet. They didn't need to discuss the situation—all four of them ran.

She took the lead, half carrying Jonathan, but making sure she didn't outdistance the boys. They ran through the streets of the quiet town with the yells of the man fading only gradually into the background. Verity took them through the back gardens, alleyways, and amongst trees, but she did not do it blindly. The Ministry Seven knew London more intimately than any adult. Even the Elephants of Diamond Dottie's group, couldn't squeeze through gates, and hide as well as they could.

Finally, after a long while, after turning yet another corner, Verity stopped. In the grey light cast by the moon, they all caught their breath. She didn't want to look at them, but eventually she turned her head. Not many children that young could look accusatory, but the children of the seven hadn't been real innocents for years—Jonathan and Jeremy maybe never.

"What happened?" Jonathan whispered, and she couldn't take the bitter tone of his voice.

"What happened?" Colin glared at her, his fists clenched at his side. "She left her lookout. She wandered off like a duffer. Like we didn't matter."

They were three young kids, but in that moment they could have been three judges pronouncing sentence.

"Why?" Jeremy whispered. "Why did you do it, Verity? We could have been killed…or worse!"

"I…I…" Verity replied, her voice catching, and her chest tightening. "I was…" There was no explanation. She hadn't told them about Uncle Octavius, or the little piece of clockwork in her pocket—so nor could she tell them about the strange automaton in the dark. Her parents and their death was danger she had bought to the doorstep of the Ministry Seven.

"We're supposed to look after each other!" Colin went on, staring up at her with eyes brimming with tears. "Without each other, wot have we got?"

"Nothing," she whispered in reply. "Nothing." Her eyes too welled up with tears, and she couldn't recall having felt so utterly useless in her entire life—even when her parents had been killed. Even then Verity had possessed a plan.

However, now the truth could not be ignored. She'd failed the Ministry Seven. She couldn't imagine what Henry and Christopher would say to her. She simply couldn't face them.

"Go home," she said to the boys, her voice coming out in painful gasps. "Go home."

Before they could reply, Verity spun about and ran. They would easily find their way back to the safe house in Kensington, but she didn't want to go back there. She couldn't.

The events of recent months meant that she wasn't any good for them—in fact she was just the opposite. Verity Fitzroy ran through the snow, her tears freezing on her cheeks. Her feet were carrying her somewhere that she didn't really consciously think about. She caught a ride on the back of a steaming bus, heading towards the Thames, and found herself staring up with burning eyes at the sign, 'Miggins Antiquities'.

It was the home of the Ministry. All the children knew where it was, but none had ever been inside. Fresh tears started on her cheeks. It had been an age since she'd cried—probably back in the workhouse. Yet her failure cut deep.

"Child, are you alright?" A female voice made Verity hastily brush away her tears. She didn't like hearing herself called that, but the kindness in the tone soothed her somehow.

A lovely lady, dressed all in black, with a pair of spectacles perched on the end of her nose was standing by the door to the shop. A chink of light was visible behind her as if she had just stepped out from there.

"Yes," Verity stammered out, though it was far from the truth.

"You're one of Agent Thorne's urchins," the woman said with a strangely distant smile.

Verity didn't know Mr. Thorne had shared his use of the Ministry Seven with anyone else in the organization, but she wasn't surprised. A small smile formed on her lips. It was nice to be considered part of the agent's world. Verity nodded slowly.

"Well no one should be standing outside in the snow—especially on Christmas Eve." The woman pushed the door open wider and gestured Verity in.

The girl did not need further incentive. Getting a chance to see inside the Ministry was an impossible treat.

The woman shut the door behind them and guided Verity upstairs. The rows of desks were empty of people, but it looked like many clerks worked on the ground floor.

"I am Doctor Josepha Blackwell," the woman said as they went. "I work in the research laboratory. In fact, I like to think of myself as the research laboratory. Though I have a few helpers."

She paused and spun around. "I have some hot chocolate still warm in the lab…I think you would like that, yes?"

Verity nodded, but stayed silent least she break the spell and be cast out into the snow again. This woman worked in the very place the girl dreamed of. Was she catching a glimpse of her own possible future?

After being ushered into a lift, the doctor pushed the chadburn for up. Her eyes gleamed slightly as she examined Verity. The girl thought she had seldom been under such close scrutiny.

"So," the older woman said, "what brings you to Miggins Antiquities on Christmas Eve, with all those tears on your face?"

Apparently all that Verity had been waiting for was an ear to listen. She found herself blurting out everything to the odd doctor—everything except what exactly had distracted her outside the house. Fresh bitter tears flowed when she got to the angry words she had exchanged with the boys. Finally, she exclaimed, "Maybe it is better that I never joined the Ministry Seven…they would be better off without me! All I do is mess things up!"

"Really?" Josepha Blackwell leaned down and peered into her eyes. "Do you really think so? How interesting…"

They had reached the laboratory, and after the doctor had spun the wheel, so that the massive iron door unsealed itself, she led Verity in. It was another kind of fairyland to the girl. Her gaze darted enviously over the long, wide benches covered with an array of machines, tools, and bubbling liquids. Her fingers itched to grab hold of things, to begin figuring how they worked and what they could do.

The ticking and whirring in her head began again, and for a moment it became such a cacophony that all thoughts were drowned out. While Verity was getting her bearings, Josepha bustled around turning on a Bunsen burner, which did indeed contain a white liquid that had to be milk.

Though the idea of drinking from a flask used in a laboratory was very strange, Verity nonetheless accepted the chocolate when it was offered to her. She warmed her hands on the glass and watched the doctor. The woman even produced a couple of rather flattened marshmallows from her bag and popped them in. When she sat back on her stool, she once again watched Verity with the intensity of a spectacled hawk.

The girl sipped nervously at it, and almost jumped when the doctor spoke. "You say you'd be better to have never met your friends?" She leaned forward, her eyes huge behind her spectacles. "Are you willing to find out if that is the truth?"

Verity thought of Jonathan, Jeremy and Colin's faces, the hurt and resentment there. They would be better. The words choked her throat, so she just nodded.

"Then let's be scientific about it," the doctor said, tugging Verity over to an object in the corner with a large sheet over it. When Josepha yanked it off, it was revealed as a large wire ball standing over six feet at the highest point, and made of a strange metal, that looked like it might be a silver alloy. The doctor let out a sigh. "I've been working on this beauty in my lunch time. Axelrod thinks it will never work, and I've never been able to find anyone willing to give it a try." She turned to Verity with an open face of expectation.

The girl swallowed hard, but her brain was burning with curiosity. "How does it work?" Verity enquired, wondering for an instant if her brain was in danger of frying.

"Oh," Josepha waved her hand. "It is quite on the sharp edge of latest developments. It is patterned on something we like to call the aethergates, but instead cutting through space, this one delves into the majesty of the mind."

Verity stared at her.

"Come, come," the doctor frowned. "Where is your sense of adventure? Surely, those tears and horrible feelings inside you are worth investigating?"

The ticking began again, repetitive, and spurring Verity onwards. Curiosity bought her up to stand next to the doctor. Josepha beamed at her and opened a cunningly contrived lock on the side of the sphere.

Verity stepped in and closed the gate behind her, while the older woman went to a control panel only a few feet away. "I suggest you close your eyes," she said in a very spritely tone. "Things may get a little bit… bright."

In for a penny, in for a pound, Verity thought, and did as she was bid.

Immediately she felt the hum and whir of the ticking replaced by something else, the smell of hot copper, and the caress of electricity on her skin. For a moment she was afraid to open her eyes.

When she cautiously levered them open, it was immediately apparent she was no longer in Miggins Antiquities. She was on the streets of the East End, or rather in an alleyway. The smell was powerful, and she remembered how it had hit her palpably when she first arrived in London.

Grey water trickled under her feet and distant sobbing could be heard nearby. A child's sobbing. Wrapping her arms around herself against the cold, Verity followed the sound. Leaning against a wall was Jeremy, his face smeared where tears had cut through the dirt on his face. He was leaning over his brother, Jonathan, who had his hand clenched on the side that was bleeding. Scarlet blood was pooling on the cobblestones—the only brightness in the drab scene.

Neither of the boys seemed to see her, and when Verity leaned down to touch them, her hand passed right through them.

Josepha's voice reached her, and whispered things she could never have known otherwise. "Remember when you saved Jeremy from the Elephant gang? Without you this is what would have happened. He's not going to make it I am afraid."

Verity felt the clench of despair at the sight of the little boys, but there was nothing she could do, and deep down she knew that there was more to see. The girl trailed on down the alleyway and out onto the street. It looked just as it had on that first day she saw the twins, but a dire knot was forming in her stomach.

She passed another alleyway, and observed a group of man drinking gin. However, they were not all men...some were boys, and two she recognized instantly. Young Christopher was leaning against Henry, his eyes half-lidded a tilted grin on his face. Henry looked pale and grey under the eyes, somehow older than his sixteen years.

"Without you, without meeting Harrison Thorne, which you did, Henry never had a purpose." Josepha's voice sounded almost sad. "So much potential, and he washed it all away with gin."

"I don't want to see more," Verity said, shaking her head, horrified by these images of those she loved. Yes, loved. She understood that now.

The electricity smothered her again, until she was standing once more in the laboratory of the Ministry inside the gleaming wire cage. Josepha's wide eyes were the first things she saw.

"Well?" she enquired softly as she opened the door to the sphere, but her fingers were twitching nervously.

Verity was so glad that it wasn't real, that she hadn't been swept off to some strange other world that she didn't exist in. Yet, neither could she bear to answer questions like some laboratory creature. Instead, she bolted from the room to the lift, and then out of the building altogether.

No ticking was in her brain, no angry thoughts about her own failings. All she thought of was the feel of the snow on her face, and getting back to the safe house in Kensington.

"Verity?" Harrison Thorne stepped out of the shadows, his bowler hat gleaming white with fresh snow. He was locking the door behind him. "Whatever are you doing here?"

Verity spun around, feeling her cheeks blushing hard. "I met a lady called Doctor Josepha Blackwell, she let me in, showed me something horrible and marvelous."

A frown formed on Harrison's handsome face. "Doctor Blackwell? I think you must be mistaken; she left two days ago to meet her family in Jersey. I saw her off on the airship myself."

Verity tilted her head. "I…I must have…well I must have been mistaken." Had she really met Doctor Blackwell, or had it all been a hallucination…or something even wilder?

"Is everything alright, Verity?" the agent enquired, shifting the large package he was carrying to his other hand.

In the end, did it really matter who it was that had let her in and shown her the terrible reality? What mattered was that she'd found the will to return to her loved ones, because she wasn't alone. She did have family.

Verity turned to him, and let out a laugh. "Everything, everything is just topping, Mr. Thorne!" She glanced down at the package he was carrying. "Is that what I think it is?"

He tilted his head. "If you are thinking it is a goose…then indeed you are right."

Somehow she knew exactly what he was up to. "And am I right in presuming that is bound for a house full of ragamuffins in Kensington?"

He tipped his hat. "As always, Miss Fitzroy, you are sharply observational. I was just heading there. Since…well…I have no family of my own to share the Eve with. But tell me…what are you doing here at Miggins?"

Verity thought of her fellow Ministry workers, their sharp little faces, and the many, many good times they had shared. Then she thought of her lost mother and father, and how despite all that she had managed to find herself a family again.

"Why Mr. Thorne, I have come to fetch you to the table." She tucked her arm under the elbow of the startled agent. "No one should be alone on this day of all days."

As they walked down the street, she whispered to herself. "And apologies and forgiveness will hopefully be just as welcome as that goose."

Snow was falling in London town, there was a strange automaton following her, and an even stranger ticking in her head—yet Miss Verity Fitzroy put all those things away from herself. Tomorrow was Christmas, she had family to welcome her, and the days after that would have to look after themselves.

Positively Shocking

by Tee Morris

London, England
Spring, 1893

Constance tapped her fingers against the wooden table, trying not to allow her eyes to scrutinize the room again. It was no different than it had been five minutes ago. And it had not changed in the five minutes before then. Nor the previous five minutes to before that either.

She was still surrounded by the skill of a master mason worker, with the only light entering the room from the high barred windows well out of her reach. Then there was her table, well worn and smooth. The stool she sat upon had not changed in its size nor had it suddenly become 'comfortable' the longer she sat in it. Her heels bobbed up and down as she stared forward, tapping her fingertips together and trying not to case the room.

However, Constance's eyes darted to each corner of the room. Stone walls. Wooden floor. Reinforced bars in the windows. Just as the room had been when the peelers brought her here.

"Bugger," she whispered.

A jangle of keys caused her to start, but she fought the urge to bolt either for the door or for the far wall. She had been quite alone and undisturbed for a time. The last time something like this happened, the peelers that had nabbed her thought they might have a bit of fun having a go with her. It had been a close call, but a well-placed knee to the bullocks, and a door callously left open made for a noisy, clumsy, but still lucky escape.

Hinges groaned as the heavy hatch swung open. The man who walked in was not a blue bottle, but he was a fine dressed gent. The man was your typical high-brow type: fat, thick mustache, but thinning hair at the top. Something in his eyes though was very different.

The man saw Constance. He did more than that — he acknowledged her. She could feel her shoulders drop ever so slightly when they shared the glance. Resting on one hand was a small stack of papers underneath a tray. On the tray were two cups of a steaming tea. A strong, woody kind, Constance recognised. In the other hand was a small wooden box, just slightly larger than his forearm.

He set the case down first, then slid the modest tray onto the tabletop. He gave a nod to the crusher at the door and took his own seat as the heavy door groaned shut.

The fat man picked up one of the two cups and placed it before her. "I was unsure how you took your tea," he began, reaching in his pocket for a small kerchief. When he set it before Constance, it unfolded of its own accord, revealing three sugar cubes and a tin wand no bigger than her finger. "You can use it to stir your tea, if needed. If you unscrew the cylinder, you will find cream in there."

Real. Tea. Constance blushed a bit as her hands went to pick up two cubes. She then began stirring with the wand, as he suggested. "I do enjoy sweet things, but I prefer not to have my tea with milk."

"And I prefer milk only," he said, smiling pleasantly. "Such are God's Creatures; different tastes, part of what makes us unique."

She gave a little giggle, but her laughter caught in her throat as she saw what his eyes were now reading. He had moved the tray aside and was engrossed in the papers that had been underneath it. The current one under the fat man's fingers was written in a particular flourish that could only be from Detective Willows.

"Something wrong with your tea?" he asked without looking up from the paper.

Constance's eyes jumped to the slender wand, still in her cup. She gave the drink another stir, tapped the peculiar bobble gently on the edge of the cup, and then took another tiny sample. She shuddered at its taste.

"Coo, governor," Constance said, a laugh bubbling up from her, "best cup of tea I ever did have."

"We pride ourselves on our little touches of excellence," he said, still reading. "I apologise for not bringing biscuits."

"Never you mind, governor," she said, taking another sip. "A fine cup of brown joy, this is."

It was on her fourth sip when she suddenly remembered what he was reading.

"Governor—"

"Miss Magee, please, I am not a politician. Therefore," he said, and when he looked at her she was strangely compelled to smile back, "call me Doctor, if you please?"

"A doctor?" She set down her tea and held out her left forearm. "I have been feeling quite an ache when I—"

"Not that kind of doctor, Miss Magee," he interjected, as his eyes began to scan the final page about her.

By the time Constance pulled her sleeve back down, the stranger had pushed the papers aside to give her his undivided attention. "You have quite a colourful dossier, Miss Magee. Perhaps society desires you to disappear behind the walls of Scotland Yard, but if my own research on you is correct, I believe there is more to you than you believe. More than you realize."

Constance scoffed. "If'n you don't mind, Doctor, I already heard this talk before—from a man of the cloth—he told me about my potential." She paused, before adding, "The higher his hand went up my leg, the greater my potential grew."

"I assure you, Miss Magee," the Doctor said, reaching into his coat pocket, "my intentions are honourable."

Constance sat back in her stool. "What's your game then?"

"I have come here with something that no one, despite your abilities, is willing to offer." He slid the papers concerning Constance back in front of him. "A second chance."

She barked a laugh. "Oh are you a barrister then, or have you got an ear of the Queen's?"

"I detect a hint of sarcasm in your tone, Miss Magee."

"Can't pull a flam over you then, guv."

Before she could tell him where he could shove his second chance, the unflappable toff added, "But if you must know, my doctorate is not in law but the sciences, and as for the ear of the queen — did you mean via the pneumatic system, wireless, or *ætherspeak*?"

She laughed at his jest…or at least she laughed until he sat there, across the table, quite confident in his brag.

He wasn't joking.

"My organisation possesses all three," he stated. "However, the *ætherspeak* is only for the highest priority emergencies threatening the Empire."

She could recognize a con. She could also recognize a "Bound for Bedlam" look. This gent was wearing an entirely different countenance, one she rarely saw in his type. He was telling the truth.

"My name is Doctor Basil Sound and I represent a hand of Her Majesty's Government that does not exist. We are currently in need of specialists such as yourself."

"I'm sorry, sir," she interrupted, "but special *what?*"

"It's all here," he said, tapping on the papers in front of him. He then flipped a few pages aside and smiled as his eyes fell on one item. "Here's a perfect example — there was a brawl at The Cooper's Loom. You managed to rally a group of six to go into the pub and restore order." Doctor Sound looked up from the paper. "Why?"

Constance thought for a moment, then said with full assurance, "It was the proper thing to do."

"Exactly. The proper thing to do, which, according to this," Sound said, giving another glance over the police report, "meant you were called upon to do some rather improper things."

He looked up from the papers, and even in the dim lighting of the cell, his eyes twinkled.

"All right then." Constance resigned, and laced her fingers together as she propped her arms on the smooth table top. "What do you need?"

"A spirit that believes less in protocol and more of impetuous action. A fearless nature that refuses to calculate odds. A *leader* that prefers a bold introduction as well as a theatrical exit." Doctor Sound gave her a smile that thrilled her to her very core. "I need you to say, 'yes,' to my group of miscreants, misfits, and mis-adventurers, and lead them when called upon to descend into the very mouth of madness. All in the name of the Queen. All in secret."

Constance felt in desperate need of a pint. Did he say he wanted her to be a *leader?* Sure, she was known for gathering the boys around her and charging into a pub to help calm a hallabaloo—the last thing anyone needed were the blue bottles stepping in as it meant freedom to lay the stripes on anyone—but to lead for the Queen? Her?

"Why should I trust you?" she finally blurted out.

"A very good question," Doctor Sound admitted, "and understanding your lot in life, I would have been far more surprised if you blindly accepted my offer." He slid her papers to one side and mirrored her posture, even down to the lacing of his pudgy fingers together. "The team I am assembling is unlike anything found in Her Majesty's Army. Their intent is to hit hard and then disappear into the æther, leaving the opposition wondering exactly who they were and whether or not they will strike again."

"Shock troops, you mean?" Constance had heard the term once before. From what she could gather, it was a fancier and more noble-sounding than the more likely "cannon fodder."

"They could be regarded as such, but that would make them no better than food for a cannon," he said, his eyebrow bowing ever so slightly, "now would they?"

Constance felt the hairs on the back of her neck rise. How did he—

"The shock troops I am assembling, however, will be different in two respects. They will be specialists for one. The other," and again, he paused, considering her with a sharp eye, "is they will be considered valued assets."

She could not believe the next question tumbling free of her mouth. "And you want me to *lead* them?"

"Particularly after tonight's display at the Fox and Hound," he stated. "Yes, most assuredly."

Constance felt her cheeks tingle with embarrassment. She knew, though, that against the blush she wore the tiniest of smiles. She wondered if that pub still burned as her skin did now. That had been quite a masterful righting of a wrong, ending with a display that served as a warning—even if that warning had landed her in jail.

"I don't have much choice in the matter, now do I?"

"Actually, you do." Doctor Sound's demeanour slowly changed, his impish, mischievous nature that had drawn Constance to him like a moth to gaslight slipped away. His look was now quite stern. "Trust me or stay here. If my trust is betrayed, I will show no mercy or consideration. You will be returned here and be processed accordingly. At least here, your fate is quite plain and expected, isn't it?"

"And if I trust you?"

"Then," he said, his smile returning, "we embark on an adventure together. You will not know what lies around the corner, but you will serve at the pleasure of Her Majesty where you and your team are needed."

While it could not feed her, stave off winter's wrath, or offer her a comfortable bed, trust was a valuable commodity, not freely given away and perhaps harder to earn than a handful of shillings. From outward appearances, he understood that. Constance did not know this man any better than a stranger on the street, but he seemed to know everything about her, and for a polished gent he was familiar with the order of the streets.

She had a choice; go with what she knew, bleak as it was, or trust this Doctor. There was no trying to run a game on this man—that much was clear.

"Very well," she said, "I am your humble servant."

He reached underneath the table and brought up the small box that Constance had all but forgotten about. Motioning for her to stand, he flipped its latches back and turned it so that it would reveal its contents to her when opened.

"On behalf of the Ministry of Peculiar Occurrences," he began, lifting the crate's lid, "welcome, Constance Magee, to the Nefarious Explosive Response Faction."

What her eyes took in made the second time Constance's breath locked in her throat since this man took a seat in front of her. How did he get *that* beyond the crushers?

Doctor Sound pushed the box closer to her and then gathered his tea wand and various papers. Constance reached into the open crate. The polished brass was cool to her touch.

His voice made her jump. "Ready, are we?"

Constance's brow furrowed. "Ready? For what?"

He reached behind him and pressed one of the many bricks that made up the far wall. This brick, however, slid an inch into the wall. Constance had no idea how she'd missed that. A rumble of locks and gears tickled her ears, and just in front of Doctor Sound, the stone tiles underfoot began to form stairs that descended down into darkness.

"Your training, of course." Sound took a few steps but paused as he motioned to Constance and her case. "I would not forget that if I were you. You will need it."

Winter, 1894
Kashmir, Southern Asia

Ordnance. Doctor Sound's paramount reason for avoiding fieldwork.

Now, with a barren wasteland all around them, save for the craggy ridge sloping before them, the Director of the Ministry of Peculiar Occurrences and his select team were enjoying their fill of it.

"Well, Director," began Agent Braun, as she reloaded her pistol, "at least your theory of Methuselah's Order operating a hidden base in Kashmir was spot on."

"If you recall in the debriefing, Agent Braun, I thought the base was actually in the Enclosure of Marttand, not in the ridge overlooking it."

"A pity you could not have drawn that conclusion, Director," Agent Campbell said, just before standing up and unleashing a few bullets from his own gun. "It would avoid the rather messy situation we are in at present."

"If this is your idea of a messy situation, Bruce," quipped the masked Agent Smith as he swung his personal Gatling gun around, "I recommend you request more assignments in India." Even with his artificial voice, the enigmatic gentleman was still able to keep his intent light and cavalier. "This is what I would call high tea."

With that, Agent Maulik Smith opened fire, his Gatling roaring alongside the boiler that powered it. Doctor Sound watched as part of the distant ridge disappeared in a puff of smoke and fire.

The quiet their arrival had disturbed returned again, but Agent Smith's finger gently stroked the weapon's trigger.

Eliza peeked over the windowsill. "What do you see, Maulik?"

"Movement along the summit. Their infantry are repositioning themselves."

"Snipers," Bruce grumbled. "Bloody lovely. Just let them pick us off like fish in a barrel."

"Hand a soldier a rifle, and they do not instantly become sharpshooters. No," Agent Smith continued, "these men are soldiers, not snipers."

Bruce's brow furrowed. "How can you be so sure?"

"I'm still standing, am I not?" he asked, his tinted eyes still scanning the ridge. "Any sniper worth their salt would find me a quick and elementary kill. The Order's infantry appear inexperienced at a long range."

"Finally," breathed Agent Braun, "an advantage to our side."

"Wait," Agent Smith said, stepping forward, his fingers splaying around the butt of his Gatling. "Something is moving on the ridge face."

"You mean, someone's moving across the ridge face?" she asked.

"No, Eliza," and Agent Smith's finger wrapped around the trigger, "something is moving on the rid—"

His words immediately stopped as he hoisted the Gatling an inch higher and pulled its trigger, unleashing a maelstrom of bullets. What he said next only Doctor Sound understood as an Indian curse as he stopped firing and immediately ran back behind the cover of a nearby stonewall.

The ruins shook all around them as the cannons opened fire. Outside, parts of the wall disintegrated while one small stone structure disappeared completely. A heartbeat later, enemy gunfire resumed.

"Most economic," Doctor Sound observed. "Have your infantry open fire while you prep your long-range cannons. The Order has picked up a few tricks over the millennia, I suppose."

The stalwart Agent Campbell leapt free of his cover at the moment the bullets paused and continued to fire until he saw the puff of smoke. This time, the shell tore through part of the window from where Campbell had been shooting. Two other explosions rocked the foundations underneath them.

"Bugger it," Campbell swore, "I'm out."

"I've got both my girls here," Braun said, motioning to the pounamu pistols in each of her hands. "Another round for each of them in my belt, then I'm done."

Sound looked at his remaining agent. "Smith?"

"Munitions is not the problem with my Queensbury Rules," he said, hefting the small cannon in his grasp, "but water and pressure are. Both are low. I may have a five-to-ten second burst remaining."

Sound looked at each of them. The gunfire was now more intermittent. Deduction—infantry laid down suppressing fire while the cannons reloaded. Conclusion—it would only be a matter of time.

When he pulled from his pocket the small wireless, Bruce gave a groan.

"No," he spat, "not those bloody punks."

"You have an alternative to offer, Agent Campbell?" asked Doctor Sound mildly.

The blast from the ridge ceased all conversation as they waited for the shell. This time, when their ruin shook, debris scattered and scuttled across the stone floor underneath them.

"With all due respect, Director," Eliza cut in before Campbell could retort, "make the call!"

His glance switched from Braun to Smith. Smith merely nodded in reply.

The button gave a soft click as it was pressed. The party heard the beeping from the blue and yellow light atop the wireless transmitter before another salvo slammed into their crumbling sanctuary.

Constance would see the puff of smoke, then would come the pop a few moments later. Through her binoculars she could observe shells tearing away at the Temple of the Sun.

"Come on, old man," she whispered, sliding the binocular's magnifying lever to full, but there was still no retaliation or movement from the ruins. "We're not here for the weather or the scenery. If you wanted to test our mettle—"

"Commander," called Thompson, her chief communications officer, "we got the call."

"Let's not keep the Director waiting then," she returned. "Let's ride!"

Constance turned to look over her team, a collection of diamonds cut from the same rough as she had been, all of them possessing a variety of talents but sharing one commonality—fearlessness. Theirs, she learned through their training, was not a sense of courage but more of foolhardiness, now possessing a sense of direction. The division of two hundred stood in sharp contrast to their barren surroundings. Against the stark yet textured beige of the Kashmir desert moved an undulating mass of blue, orange, and yellow. Some wore wide vertical stripes while others remained in solids, but their chaotic, gaudy fashion was not to entertain or to amuse as would a clown's attire. No, their intent would be to confound.

At first.

Constance gave the dart between her fingers a kiss with her sunflower-coloured lips and then slid the soft projectile into the twin-barreled creation that Doctor Sound had given to her in that London jail over a year ago. Snapping the "Double-Whammy" shut with a flick of her wrist, she saw her troops crank to life their assortment of motorcars and lococycles.

"Thompson," she called, "are the boilers at full?"

"Maximum pressure, Captain," he said, cranking their ride to life and lowering his goggles down across his face. "The dry air here is also good for the wireless, mum. All signals are in the green."

Green, she thought absently, as she caught a glance of her own skirts of blue and black. *I wonder if that would be too much to add into our colours?*

Constance threw the throttle forward, and her motorcar rumbled to life and led the charge.

She could not hear the gunfire or the cannons any longer, but she could see the white puffs emanating from the ridge overlooking the Temple of the Sun. That would be their target. Constance rapped Thompson on the shoulder, motioned to their comrades holding the line to the left, and then to the others holding to the right. Thompson gave her a thumb's up.

All units reported green. Good to go.

She reached up and yanked down the handle above her head. On hearing the dull thud, she leaned forward and watched the yellow flare soar high above their line, hover, and then begin to fall.

Her engine gave a guttural roar as she turned to the left as the car to her left cut towards her, narrowly missing her front bumper. Immediately she cut to the right, and she heard that same car now cut narrowly behind her. She glanced to either side and watched as her ranks slowly disappeared behind a veil of dust and rock all while executing a similar zig-zag pattern. Within minutes, they would appear as nothing more than a sandstorm closing on the temple ruin.

Constance activated the beacon on the roof of her car, then pulled down from her cabin ceiling the enhanced stereoscope. This little offering from the Ministry, connected to her motocar's roadometer and compass, worked in mission settings where limited visibility was a factor. Whether natural, or—in this instance—man-made.

Constance slipped in the image of Marttand, pushed her goggles down, and leaned into the eye enclosure. The card slowly inched towards her, sliding left and right as she changed course. The mere notion of driving with blinders on would send anyone else into a panic, but these maneuvers rehearsed alongside her comrades-in-arms had been practiced and perfected during their training. The idea, when first presented to Doctor Sound and his military liaison, had been dismissed as lunacy; but Constance and her troops — albeit, at the cost of a few bruises — proved the theory credible. Now it was in practice; and only the sound of her second rumbling dangerously close in front and then behind her, along with the stereoscope's image of Marttand, served as her sole judge of distance. Thompson was manning the wireless, monitoring for any sudden word from the rest of the faction. He remained quiet.

No news had to be good news.

The stereoscope indicated they were less than half a mile from the edge of the ridge. She felt for the beacon switch above her head and threw the lever from the forward to the rear position. This would make the light above her go from a rapid strobe to a steady beam.

"Ten…nine…eight…" she whispered. If this worked, the signal would be passed down the line, and they would emerge as one. "…three…two…one."

Constance pushed the stereoscope away, lifted her goggles with her free hand back over her face, and locked her steering wheel in a neutral position.

Through the wisps of earth and desert, she and her fellow troops appeared as a line of metal and machine, their lococycles and motorcars decorated with a light sheen of Kashmir soil that gave their transports the semblance of smoldering monsters erupting from the gates of Hell itself. Constance removed Double-Whammy free of the holster between her seat and the door, and jerked the wheel hard to the right.

The car was now to Constance as a kite in the skilled hands of a scientist catching wind readings in Hyde Park. She allowed her motorcar to drift across the desert floor so they were now parallel with the ridge, but still closing their distance. Constance extended her shotgun and took aim at the only visible target on the ridge: the long, protruding barrel of the enemy cannon. She followed the darts' thin, pearlescent smoke trails to their point of impact.

"Stopwatch!" she shouted back to Thompson, as four other motorcars drifted to where she remained still. Three of them loosed similar double-barreled attacked while two soldiers leapt free of their rides and began firing their "Rickies" (a nicknamed coined by Constance and her troops). Out of the six shots each of their high-powered pistols provided, she could be certain that at least three darts hit their mark.

"First line, down and reload," she shouted to either side, "Go! Go! Go!"

On the third call to fall back, she slammed her foot down and led the line of motorcars as another line of five cars drifted towards them. They too would come to where she had stopped, but would hold on the assault if the first volley failed.

"Five..." Thompson's voice called over the rumble of their engines, "...six...seven...eight..."

The dart Constance had blessed with a single kiss, on impact with its target, was designed specifically for their Faction from those *clankertons,* Axelrod and Blackwell. Within the dart's foam flowed a variety of agents, harmless in themselves until mixed. On striking a solid object, the foam and agents within activated, their chemical and physical interaction taking roughly ten seconds to create a new compound so unstable at room temperature that critical combustion would occur roughly twenty seconds after impact. In colder settings, the darts would explode thirty seconds after impact with its target.

In a barren desert at high noon? Those conditions had never been tested.

Until now.

Constance thought she heard Thompson call out "Eleven" just before she heard the sharp explosion. A heartbeat later came the shockwave, lifting her motorcar off its back wheels as she sped further and further away, their thick camouflage now nothing more than a sheer, dusty veil across the desert.

She adjusted the magnification in her goggles back on the ridge. Both cannons were gone, but soldiers were still visible along the top of their base. They continued to shoot at Marttand as well as her own troops. By the amount of extra gunfire they were drawing, she and her Response Faction would only have moments before they were fish in a rather nasty barrel.

"Thompson, have we got munitions in this motorcar of ours?"

"Aye, tha' we do," he said, patting on two large crates braced between the transport's frame and his communications equipment. "What you have in mind?"

"Flash the Faction," she said, shoving the gearshift into the reverse position. "New target: Us."

The rear tires kicked dirt and rock in all directions while the piston engine snarled angrily. Their motorcar emerged from its cocoon of thick steam and thin dust, and continued its backward trajectory. Constance craned her neck around as the distance vanished between her and the enemy ridge. She glanced back to her front and watched as the other cars now came about and closed in on her. To her left, two lococycles were closing in and pulling their preferred firearms free of holsters.

Constance could also see the lococycle masters shaking their heads. *I know, lads, but trust me...*

She looked back over her shoulder. They were only seconds away.

Thompson's hands grabbed the overhead rumble bar. Constance knew he was probably swearing up a real summer storm.

Their car rumbled up the side of the ridge and threatened to flip over, end-over-end. The rear wheels came back down against the shifting rock; and unable to gain traction, unable to help them climb, the motorcar continued to dig itself into the side of the mountain. Constance watched their wheels sink deeper and deeper into the earth.

When they no longer sunk any further, Constance shut down the motorcar while tearing herself free of the safety restraints. "Move, Thompson!"

Bullets bounced and pelted their motorcar, but Constance kicked her door open and started sliding down the ridge as the closing lococycles drew their aim.

"Come on, Thompson!" she called over her shoulder.

The figure in the back of her motorcar was slumped forward. He wasn't moving.

"Oh, damn it all!" Constance spat as she scrambled back up the slope, throwing her hand forward to catch the motorcar's frame and pull herself up to the cab.

It could have been the impact against the ridge. It could have been surrendering to the gunshot wound in his shoulder. Alive or dead it did not matter. Constance's own discipline applied to her as it did to those that rallied around her: *Leave not a rack behind.* She knew very little about William Shakespeare, but when she and her troops been given a bit of the books as part of their training, she found herself drawn to this particular play. Doctor Sound had referred to this as the calling of her Muse. Constance just thought the way Mr. Shakespeare weaved the words together were pretty. This particular phrase from Prospero, however, struck something in her heart. It became the Faction's motto. It was her promise to them.

His restraint release had jammed, and it was when her knife slashed through the second strap when she heard the dull ringing of explosive darts against the cab of her car.

"One…two…three…" she groaned as she pulled Thompson out of the motorcar. She could hear bullets whizzing past and skipping off the ground. She couldn't think about that, not even as she hefted her communications officer across her shoulders. She had to keep counting. "Six…seven…eight…"

Her legs burned as she stomped her way further and further towards the rumble and roar of motorcars and lococycles. She was still close enough to hear additional darts strike her stranded vehicle, and already she was at "thirteen." Would that be far enough for her to—

The blast and concussion that picked her up and sent both her and Thompson forward was, for a moment, her reality. The desert disappeared. Thompson, she knew curiously enough, was near. The sounds of battle disappeared. A single, soft ring echoed in her own personal darkness.

⋅⇥◯⇤⋅

They were so far away. She couldn't make out what anyone was saying. *No,* she protested, *I like it here. It's quiet. Just leave me be.* The voices, however, continued to chatter. While she wanted to remain where she felt at peace, whatever world currently disturbing her solitude would not be denied.

The ringing in her ears faded away, replaced by the soft din of an airship. Constance recognised the sickbay right away. She had been here before. Many times. Instead of the Kashmir deserts where she last remembered her being, she was on board the *Blythe Spirit*, a commissioned airship for the Ministry.

"Welcome back, Commander McGee."

It hurt. Everywhere. The light hurt her eyes. Doctor Sound's voice hurt her ears. The mattress, soft and warm as it was, made her spine ache. Why, oh why, did Doctor Sound insist on bringing her back?

"Thompson?" she asked.

"Resting up," responded the female voice. Constance took a moment. Not many female agents in the Ministry, and that accent was unmistakable. Braun. Agent Braun. That was her name. "I seem to be alone in my opinion—but well done. You did what's right."

"What you did," Sound scoffed, "was win a fool's gamble. I am astounded at your resilience, truth be told."

"You should be," she grumbled. "You trained us to be so."

"I thought the Switzerland Sanction was daring," he continued, shaking his head, "but this?"

"Doctor Sound, far be it from me to question your authority," interjected a raspy, mechanised voice. It was that chap from India. The one in the mask. "Commander McGee's faction is why we are on board the *Blythe Spirit* and not buried in Kashmir."

"And her Response Faction could have lost their leader this afternoon on account of her chivalry." He clicked his tongue. "As I have argued previously; the line between chivalry and idiocy is imperceptible. Practically non-existent, if you ask me."

"I don't believe anyone did," Eliza snapped.

Constance blinked a few more times and as the pain subsided, so did her blurriness. She could now see at the foot of her bed a stern looking Ministry director.

"Agent Braun," the Doctor Sound began, a warning within his words, "I will disregard your impertinence as battle fatigue."

"Then perhaps you will also disregard mine as well," returned the masked field agent. "Commander McGee's bravery in rescuing Officer Thompson—"

"Agent Smith, it is not her actions I question so much as her judgment. Had that manoeuvre of turning her motorcar into a bomb failed—"

"But it didn't," Agent Braun insisted. "And it blew a hole big enough for her Faction to breach. We also got what we needed on Methuselah's Order. I fail to see the problem here."

Constance closed her eyes. She really wished she could go back to sleep.

Instead, she spoke her mind. "We're shock troops. Kept in waiting until shock is called for." She took a breath—that hurt too—and then added, "Doctor Sound just didn't anticipate our tactics to be *this* shocking."

The director squared his shoulders and tugged lightly on his waistcoat. He never did like it when she read him in such a fashion. It was a trait Constance honed in the streets. Sound still remained on a whole a confounding, contradictory man, but in this moment, she understood him wholly.

"I wondered if Switzerland and Morocco were isolated incidents, but today only confirmed my suspicions concerning the Nefarious Explosive Response Faction."

Constance and Agent Smith both glanced at Agent Braun who scoffed loudly. Sound, however, consulted his pocket watch, gave a light nod, and then returned his gaze— a touch softer now—to Constance as he took from a small table next to her a syringe. She winced at the pinching in her arm, and watched as he removed the needle. He looked her over one more time.

"We will discuss this matter further once you have rested up, Commander," the Ministry Director stated before turning to leave.

"Doctor Sound," Agent Braun interrupted, "I will not stand idly by and watch you reprimand Commander McGee for bravery in the field."

"Nor I," added Smith. "Perhaps Bruce regards them simply as 'punks' but they show a spirit worthy of Ministry field agents."

He stopped at the door, turned, and now his eyes twinkled as they had when Constance first met.

"Did I mention a reprimand, Agent Braun? Agent Smith?"

She didn't care this time if it hurt. Constance smiled. He was doing it again.

"Rest up, Commander McGee," Sound spoke softly, his eyes looking at the two field agents. "We will talk in London."

The two agents stood there staring at one another for a moment. Constance had no doubt behind Smith's mask was an expression similar to the New Zealander's.

"What the hell was *that* all about?" Braun finally asked.

Constance settled into the pillows of her cot. Not as comfortable as her bedroll in the Faction's barracks, but it would do.

"He does that from time to time," she said, her words slurring ever so slightly. How lovely. Sleep was, indeed, returning. "He's a peculiar one, he is. It's what I like about him."

Darkest Before Darkwater

by Tee Morris

Summer, 1894

Fifteen thousand.
Fourteen thousand.
Thirteen.
Twelve.

Rafe's eyes jumped from the altimeter to the dome above him. A cerulean expanse, almost too brilliant to be believed as sky, remained unmarred.

Dear God, he thought quickly as he undid the buckles of his restraints.

Underneath his feet, a cloud raced towards them. He fought to keep his balance as he began climbing up the control station in the centre of their pod.

"Get back in your seat, man!" a crewmate shouted.

"Look at the altimeter, you git!" Rafe screamed in reply, his eyes fixing on the large pair of handles above them. "We are accelerating!"

His hands gripped the cool brass, and he pulled. Hard. He gave another yank. Nothing moved. Not even the slightest of budges. He flipped himself up, his grip tightening on the handles as he braced his feet against the dome. He was now screaming as he pulled, his eyes focusing on a new expanse revealing itself as the mist now dissipated. The Pacific was much like its heavenly counterpart, only this canvas appeared uneven and textured even from their quickly-disappearing height. Rafe heaved, and the handles remained steadfast.

Over his screams he could hear another crewmember unfastening his restraints. On his fourth pull, he felt massive hands grab his sides.

"Sir," came a deep booming baritone, "let me."

Rafe looked at the crewman, and gave a light start. It was no insult to his own manliness he realized—the man was a giant. His cheeks and chin decorated in crests, swirls, and dots that should have made him appear intimidating but in his dark eyes rested a calm assurance. Rafe knew him from the briefest encounters passing each other below decks, seeing him fighting on the open main deck of the *Guy Fawkes,* or on the odd occasion when his person was called for by the captain. Damned if he could remember the man's name however.

The Maori gently lowered Rafe, so that he felt as if he were a babe being passed from his mother's own hands, and then hefted himself up to the handles. He gave a pull. The second time he gave an grunt that could be heard over the buffeting from the outside world.

The altimeter continued to drop. Five thousand. Four…

Not today, Rafe thought as he looked past his feet, and saw the ocean underneath him drawing closer and closer. Were those white caps he saw? *Not today!*

Rafe realized they would have to work together. He lept up and wrapped his arms around the dark man's thick waist, adding his weight to the handles. Above their heads came a hard, sharp *ca-thunk!* Through the dome, the lifeboat's parachutes could be seen slowly unfurling.

It was the most beautiful sight he'd ever seen, but now they only had seconds.

"Let go," Rafe insisted, releasing his Maori ally. His feet struck the deck with a loud *clang*. "Get to your seat!"

He slipped the leather straps easily over his shoulders, but he had to put a bit of effort in locking the brass clasp across his chest. On the sound of its *click,* Rafe glanced upward to the glass windows just in time to watch the parachutes catch air and bring their wild, unhindered descent to an end. He groaned through clenched teeth as he felt himself suddenly jerked out of his seat and into the restraints.

Slamming back into his seat, the air was quite knocked out of him. He took in a deep breath, then another. Then another. The only sounds he could make out over the thudding in his own head, were the muttered prayers of an Irishman, the gasp of the other crewmembers, and the parachute rigging clanking in the lifeboat's housing. The four chutes overhead were domes of silk, swaying gently in their descent. Rafe looked beyond his feet through the glass floor, and his stomach lurched. An expanse of dark ocean blue reflecting sunlight stretched underneath him, the only disruption being a small landmass that grew steadily closer.

His eyes went to the altimeter. It read two thousand feet, but then suddenly spiked upward.

"What in God's name—" the lone female exclaimed.

"We've caught a current. We're not landing yet."

The ship lurched again, lifting him out of his chair. He examined the altimeter. They were descending again, the air currents carrying them closer to the island.

"We're almost down everyone," Rafe announced. "Just hold on a few more minutes."

He gripped his restraints tightly and resisted the urge to hold his breath. The minutes stretched out, until abruptly the air rushed out of him as the lifeboat hit the water. The shock threw him forward, sending a stab of pain through his right shoulder. The water gobbled them down for a moment, and then sunlight poured into the cabin as they broke the surface. Rafe unbuckled his restraints again and grabbed the railing in front of him, pulling himself up to the central controls of their pod. He began to unscrew various valves underneath the control station. He glanced up at the sound of another safety latch unbuckling.

Rafe gave a bright smile, seeing the Maori had also made it to his seat before the parachutes had fired.

A hissing noise now filled the compartment, drowning out all other sounds. Their lifeboat's wild rocking began to subside until it was nothing more than a gentle swaying.

With a nod to his crewmate, Rafe looked at the controls before him, then glanced to those to his left. Still not what he needed. On the third control panel, he read the odometer, nodded, and then opened the compartment underneath. His fingertips grazed the various scrolls kept here until stopping at the one marked with the number he had been whispering. He slipped it free of its holder and secured it on a plate housed with the station. When a second glass plate snapped tight over the map, this quadrant of the Pacific now had a small grid covering it. Rafe began marking with a black grease pencil where he remembered their vessel had been just before the attack. The scattered and interrupted coastline of Melanesia was his only reference. A glance at the odometer, and then Rafe retraced what should have been their trajectory. His markings ended in the middle of the Pacific Ocean.

"You," Rafe whispered as he looked at the bobbling island through the porthole, and then back to his map, "are not supposed to be there. Now how did you manage—"

"We made it!" One of the crew, the Irishman, said, his head pressed into the cushion behind his head. He gave a guffaw and tried to look out of the porthole closest to him. "God bless us, but we made it."

"Crewman, stand down and hold your tongue!" Rafe snapped, feeling the pod lurched around him, and then once more. "We are far from a point where we can celebrate. Stay in your seats. Landfall is not going to be a gentle experience."

Rafe had just fastened the safety clip, when he felt the lifeboat begin to lean forward, as if it were being reloaded into its escape cannon for a second firing. However the leather harness kept him from falling. Now parallel with the waves he could see through the portholes the darkness of the Pacific. He could observe the occasional fish or two swim up and away from the window. Behind him bright sunlight poured in onto the Maori who screwed his eyes shut, turning away from the glare. They pitched again, and Rafe could make out through the glass a sudden change in colours. They were were drawing closer to land. He caught a glimmer of black. Then another.

He tightened his grip on the harness. "Brace for im—"

Even while the restraints held him to his seat, the jolt rocked his body, causing his teeth the slam into one another. Something lifted their lifeboat up, and Rafe's eyes focused just at the moment their ship dropped.

Through the porthole, he could make out a dark shape growing larger and larger. It shattered through the pod's thick, tempered glass, sending water in all directions. It would not take long, at this rate. Not long at all.

Another hard bump, and Rafe realised they were rocking side to side, no longer moving forward. He struggled with the clasp until it gave way, but his hands kept a grip on the harness as he wriggled free.

"Abandon ship!" he called before dropping into the ankle-deep water beneath him.

The sole woman in their pod managed to keep her head above the rising water. Once free, she and Rafe waded over to the Maori who was now completely submerged. Reaching above him, Rafe yanked free a small knife from the control's storage space. He passed it to her and then took the second kept there for himself. The water, dark and thick with silt, was now to their knees, its surface churning to a white foam as they cut into the man's seat harness. Rafe's arm shot back first, soon followed by the woman's. The crewman burst to the surface, gasping for air, reaching for any sort of purchase.

"Come on, man. Catch your breath on the beach," Rafe said, passing him to the woman. "I'll be out in a moment."

There were two more compartments above him, one he knew held the maps. Those were useless now. The other, from where the knives came from, held two Remington-Elliot Derringers and a small case of rounds. Their compressors were glowing softly green, and each of their housings gave a sharp hissed when the pistols were removed. Both pistols and knife went into a small satchel, also kept within this space. Securing the bag, he leapt to the ladder rung over his head and started the hard climb out.

A sudden burst of sunlight caused him to blink, and the air around him now smelled strongly of salt. He took in a deep breath, discerning the hint of moist vegetation on doing so, and dropped onto the hard packed sand. He combed his hair back with his fingers and took in the sights around him. A narrow beach that curved to the left. Palm trees and ferns swayed gently as a warm tropic breeze pushed through their tops. Miles and miles of the Pacific Ocean. Clear skies in every direction.

Land. They were on dry land.

Giving the satchel a reassuring pat, Rafe joined his fellow castaways in the shade of a small grove. He plopped down into the sand and produced one of the Derringers. He cracked open the housing and began loading in the rounds.

"Weapons?" a crewman, stained with what appeared to be black powder, barked. "What gives you the right?"

"Apart from my rank on the *Fawkes*?" Rafe bit back.

"We're not on the *Fawkes*, now are we?" he retorted.

Rafe cocked an eyebrow as he flicked the three-barrel pistol shut. "And I knew where they were."

The gruff Englishman thrust out a hand. "Fine then. As the ranking Gunner here, I deserves a weapon."

There was a hint of logic there. "Your name, airman?"

"Colin Derbish," he said, tipping his head back as he added, "Gunner's Mate."

Rafe nodded, and looked to the other crewman beside Derbish. "Jonathan Whitestone. Welder."

His eyes jumped to the Maori. He almost looked embarrassed as he introduced himself. "Maaka Montgomery. Airman."

Yes, Maaka, Rafe now recalled. *Bloody giant of a man.*

His thought was interrupted by Colin's snort. Rafe heard him mutter, "Bloody wog."

The insult made their heads turn to him slowly, but it was Rafe that wiped the smirk off Derbish's face. "Remind yourself, Gunner, that this wog saved your hide moments ago."

He held his stare on Derbish for a moment longer, and looked to the young airman next to Maaka. The young man cleared his throat. "Miles Havenshill. Airman."

That left the girl. "Althea Galway, sir. Engineer."

Rafe's brow furrowed. "First Mate?" She shook her head, her eyes shifting to the sand underfoot. "Second?"

Her eyes flicked back up. "Apprentice."

Underneath smudges of grease and grime, large sapphire eyes stared back at him. Her face, stained as it was, could not seem to mar her sweetness, a delightful beauty that believed in tomorrows before her and dreams to become.

Again, it was Derbish who broke the silence. "I should have taken Number Eight when I had the chance."

With a look over all five of them, Rafe nodded and looked back at the lifeboat. "Right then. Our next or—"

"Jus' a moment, mate," Colin said, closing the distance between Rafe and himself by another step. "We still don' have your name, now do we; and seein' as your wantin' to take charge, I'd like to have an idea of what gives ya' the right?"

"I am—" Rafe started, paused, and then chuckled as he corrected himself with "—*was* your Ship's Navigator. Lieutenant Rafael Stringfellow Rafton." He then motioned to the others. "As I am the ranking officer amongst us and the one holding the gun, I welcome to my first command, and your first order: secure the lifeboat."

No one moved.

So it was to be like that, was it? "Gentlemen, lady, that lifeboat may very well be our shelter for the night. We will want to dry out the chutes so we can use them as hammocks or additional shade. There may also be some stores and equipment we can salvage, but we will lose all of that if the tide carries her out to sea."

Maaka and Althea both nodded, but the others looked apprehensive.

"Colin is right," Rafe said, giving the Remington in his grasp a visual assessment. Three rounds. If needed, he could even out his chances. Only if needed. "We are no longer on the *Fawkes*. It's just this rock and the six of us, so," he said, pulling himself to his feet, "I suggest we make the most of the time and secure the pod."

"But, Master Rafton," Miles asked, "shouldn't we set up a signal fire to call for help?"

"To whom, airman? To the *Guy Fawkes*? Considering the condition her Bridge before I was ordered off it, there will be no reunion. And considering our profession of choice, I doubt if Her Majesty would welcome us back into her loving embrace unless of course it is in irons."

"There has to be someone we can call for a pickup," Colin said, motioning to the lifeboat with his knife. "It's not as if we can't offer our services—"

"Would you listen to the man?" Althea snapped, her nerves still sounding frayed after their escape from the ship. "We have few options here."

Colin spun to glare at Althea. "Watch yer tone with me, bitch. I never let no one speak ta me in tha' manner, and I will not—"

"We are in the middle of the Pacific Ocean!" she spat, cutting him off.

He was on her before anyone could step in between them. His slap knocked her off her feet.

"I told you to keep your tongue still," he warned, still advancing on her as she scrambled across the shifting sand. "And may I remind you—"

The sand exploded between the fallen girl and the gunner. They both looked back at Rafe who was now studying the smoke coming out of the top barrel.

"May *I* remind *you*, Derbish, that I have a gun?" he asked. He waited, watching Colin step away from Althea and take a seat next to Jonathan. Jonathan glanced at him, and then scooted a few inches away from him. "Our engineer is quite right — we have few options before us. Our priority is to secure the lifeboat." Rafe stood secured the gun back into his satchel, and then dusted himself free of sand. "Once that is done, we start our first reconnaissance."

Beaching the lifeboat was hardly the effort that Rafe envisioned it to be, once all of the crew pitched in their equal efforts. The inflatables were still full, giving the large metal pod an easier surface to drag across the wet sand. On reaching the drier, uneven sand, the crew deflated the airsacks and made quick work of the chutes, stringing them between palm trees. Rafe walked closer to the breaking waves and turned back to the shore to look at what remained of the *Guy Fawkes*. A crew of six (counting himself), a battered lifeboat with its identifying number 9 now visible from where he stood, and several parachutes billowing gently behind the pod when the steady Pacific breeze ran along their shore.

Rafe looked back into the satchel he had kept secure on his person. He managed to find a small telescope and a compass within the stores. There were also, secure in the pod, rations that would last them for two days. Maybe three. From there, it would be living off the land.

Hopefully, they would be able to.

He was about to return to their modest encampment when he saw it rising over the now visible peak. He produced the telescope from his satchel and followed the smoke trail.

"Master Navigator?" It was the one calling himself Whitestone. He, too, noted the plume of smoke. "Do you think the volcano may be active?"

Rafe gave a long, low sigh, and shook his head. "The smoke appears too dark to be ash. It's black. Something wooden is making that."

"A distress signal, you think?" asked another walking up to them both.

It was the first intelligent thing Colin had said since their introduction.

"Can't say for certain until we investigate." Rafe collapsed the telescope and turned to Colin. "Shall we away?"

Whitestone gave him a customary salute and headed back to shore.

Colin snorted. "We still have an issue. A weapon?"

"Ah yes, of course." Rafe reached into the satchel and produced the sole knife within. Turning the blade handle first to Colin, he gave a slight nod to him. "It's the only knife I have." Rafe then motion back to shore. "After you, Gunner."

Colin held the weapon tightly and, with a final, long look at Rafe, he began walking back to the lifeboat.

He followed the smoke for another moment. Whatever was causing it was still burning. An island that doesn't exist. A thin spire of man-made smoke. And survivors whose loyalty to him wasn't quite certain.

Rafe's optimism was still eluding him, even when he reached his crewmates.

"Now then," he began, producing the Remington and refreshing the earlier-spent round, "as we are outlaws, we have nothing to lose so let us meet this island's tenants, yes? I will take the lead." He produced the second pistol from the satchel and tossed it to Maaka. Colin spluttered for a moment, but fell silent as Rafe said, "Maaka, cover our backs."

The island's vegetation, at least on this side of the mountain, proved easily managed. Rafe had seen far heavier, less hospitable terrain in his days aboard the *Guy Fawkes*. He silently assessed that the island had remained uncharted for a reason. It was a remote spit of sand, vegetation, and volcanic rock, serving well for marooning an uncooperative crew member, but not much good beyond that. The island was dominated by the volcano at its heart; and with a final check to make certain his threadbare crew had proper protection against the jagged rock, he led the ascent to its summit.

The volcano's incline was not too steep, so their climb remained steady.

Rafe paused just shy of what appeared to be the lip. He motioned, palm down, for everyone to stay low. Silently, slowly, the six outlaws crept up to the edge of the rock's mouth. What they found there not only told the story of island itself, but of how this island had remained invisible to air and sea men alike. The volcano appeared to have suffered a massive eruption ages ago, and now the western face was gone and opened the volcano's belly to the Pacific, this formed a lagoon that ended at the source of the fire. This, too, came as a surprise as the source of the fire was in the heart of the volcano—but *not* the volcano itself.

"Master Rafton…" Miles began, but his voice trailed off.

"No," Rafe said, pulling out the telescope from the satchel, "you are not suffering delusions."

"That's a bloody port," Jonathan muttered. He then rapped Rafe's shoulder. "And look — embedded in the rock."

"Now that is an impressive gunport, would you not agree, Whitestone?" The spyglass brought Rafe closer to it. The battery, it appeared, was unmanned. "So it seems someone wanted to keep this place a secret." He ran the scope along the docks, and then collapsed it, switching it for the Remington. "And it looks as if this port is secret no longer. I didn't see any movement, but I would hardly say this means we let our guards down."

Colin blinked and then pointed to the battle-weary docks. "We're going down there?"

"I'm sorry, did you have other appointments to keep today?" Rafe asked.

"Mister Rafton," Miles spoke, "what I think the Gunner's Mate is asking is what we are all concerned about here."

"And to play Miss Galway's parrot, we have few options in front of us." Rafe looked to each of them, and then back to the port. "When night falls, the temperature will drop like a stone. At least there, we will find some sort of shelter from the elements. If we are fortunate, we will find additional weapons as well. If we find weapons, we also find food. Agreed?"

Colin's expression did not change. In fact, Rafe noted it hadn't altered since leaving the beach.

"I'm following you, Master Rafton," came Galway's lone female's voice.

"And I, sir," Maaka added.

Jonathan looked over the docks and then considered the navigator. "Something feels a bit off about this, but I follow you, Master Rafton."

Four sets of eyes turned to Miles Havenshill. He gave the lightest of shrugs. "I really don't fancy the idea of sleeping in the lifeboat."

"Oh fuck all," Colin swore.

"Stay here if you like, but we would fare better with you in our company."

Colin looked at them all, spat, and then gave a reluctant nod.

Rafe checked the Remington's indicators. All green. "Everyone stay close."

They had not traversed the mouth far before coming across an intentional opening in the volcano's lip. Before them was a trail, a well-used one at that, leading to steps carved in rock. Rafe stopped the crew with a single finger pressed to his lips, and then slowly, with the Remington held at the ready, he crept out into the open, looking up and back the trail. A tightness grew in his chest, but he fought the urge to breathe. He took another glance behind him, then ahead.

When his gun dropped, the rest of the crew joined him. All it took was a sharp gesture up the path, and they understood his intention. Maaka followed only a few paces behind as Rafe led them down into the volcano.

The soft crackle of fire reached their ears only a few steps later. Their path underfoot switched from rock to wooden decking to rock again. They found their first corpse at the final platform before the docks. Rafe rolled him over, looking for signs of a bullet hole. He felt a tap on his shoulder. Jonathan motioned to his neck and then parted his fists with a tiny twisting motion.

A broken neck? That meant close quarters combat.

Rafe looked at them all and pointed two fingers to his eyes. Everyone nodded, and they moved on.

The dock seemed big enough to handle two, possibly three small seafaring vessels, but that sort of traffic should have meant a good-sized complement of deckhands present. There was no one to put out the fires, no one to defend whatever could be left here. Rafe looked around him, taking count of the few dead that littered the wood, and then powered down the Remington before placing it back in the bag. Maaka furrowed his brow, keeping his own pistol raised.

"What is it, Rafton?" Colin whispered tersely.

"This area is secure."

"Are you daft, man?" he barked. "How can you be sure?"

Rafe pursed his lips together as he motioned to the isolated fires dotting the docks. "Where are the fire crews to put out these flames? While I'm sure they will soon snuff themselves out, wouldn't you think there would be a fire brigade of some sort wanting to assure that?" He gave a nod to the Maori who lowered his weapon. "Stand down, Maaka. We're safe. Spare the compressor."

"If you don't mind, Master Rafton," Maaka splayed his fingers around the gun's handle. "I'll keep her powered up."

This was a battle not worth fighting at this point. "As you wish, Airman."

Rafe popped his head through open doorway after open doorway as they continued along the length of the pier. All these posts had been cleared. Nothing or no one remained.

The last door, however, made the navigator pause. He waited for the crew to gather before speaking. "Looks like this is the way in."

"What? Down those stairs?" Miles asked.

"Still think this port is secure?" grumbled Colin.

"If I were not a cautious man, Gunner," Rafe said with a smirk, "then I would have taken the weapon from Maaka. He is still armed and watching our back."

He opened the door a bit wider, and found a row of lanterns still hanging on their hooks. Rafe grabbed a pair and lit them both with a piece of debris from the docks. With a flame now inside each lantern, Rafe adjusted the light and then passed one to Maaka.

The acrid scent of smoke was heavier here, and where the staircase diverged was where Rafe and his crew found it harder to breathe. At least, from the stairwell off to the right. The passage to their left, however, offered better air. Rafe motioned with the light, and deeper they all descended into the rock. Sparks popped and fell from above their heads as lights fought to remain functioning. Rafe glanced back to them as the steps continued downward into haze and shadow. He then looked up at one of the flickering lights overhead, and wondered if his crew also asked the same questions buzzing about his own brain. Electricity? Down in the depths of a dead volcano? Where in God's name had Rafe and his crewmates landed?

Their steps ended at a room that looked as if had served, once upon a time, as a Ready Room. Some of its tables had been overturned. Parchments and what appeared to be log books or journals littered the floor. In the far corner of the ready room was a large barrel. Its contents—charred remains of more books—spilled across the wood underfoot.

"Master Navigator," Althea spoke, gently taking his arm. "Something is trying to keep these lights running. If these light are still drawing power, that means a generator—"

"Before you lose me in the language of a *clankerton*, are you saying you can get these lights to work?"

"A power relay should be close by."

Rafe motioned for the Maori. "Maaka, go with her. Let's see if we can get some lights here."

"Aye, sir."

With a quick wink to Althea, he watched the two of them leave through a connected passageway, their light visible for only a moment before the shadows devoured it.

The blow came from behind, not hard enough to knock him out but hard enough to disorient him. It gave the attacker ample time to fish out the remaining Remington from his satchel.

Rafe fought to keep hold on his consciousness, blinking almost in time with the flickering lights above him. He heard the gun arming as he took in a deep breath, the back of his head keeping time with his heartbeat. The crew, Rafe did admit as he pushed back the pain, had followed him far longer than he had anticipated. He had convinced himself the first true play for command would have occurred at the volcano's mouth.

"Now that you're armed," Rafe winced, turning to face his attacker, "what exactly is your plan, Airman?"

Miles gripped the Remington with both hands, his eyes darting back to where Althea and Maaka disappeared. "We find the communications tower here and call for help. If'n that don't we find ourselves a boat and a map."

Rafe gave a soft laugh, shaking his head. "Just like that?"

"This is a port. It has got to have boats. It has got to have maps!"

"So just you, Gunner Derbish, and Welder Whitestone then? Taking a stand against the Pacific?"

"Our chances are better than stayin'—" and those were the last words of Airman Havenshill.

The Remington faltered in his hand, but Colin managed to catch it before it fell completely. He removed the dagger from the young man's neck and gave him a hard shove against the wall. Miles fumbled at the fatal neck wound for a moment, but couldn't do anything to slow the loss of blood. When the lights flickered up to full illumination, he saw a table within reach. He grabbed its corner and went to pull himself back on his feet, but then fell back to where he had landed.

Colin gave the pistol a final look and then presented it to Rafe, handle first.

Rafe considered the gesture, and tipped his head to one side.

"Master Navigator, I will not have a bloody airman speak on my behalf unless he knows it. I do not take ta' that lightly."

"And yet," Rafe began, still looking between the Remington and Colin, "you will take orders from me?"

"Well, sir, you are the ranking officer here, yes? I may not like your orders, but if I mutinied every time I disagreed with an officer, I would have been tossed off the *Guy Fawkes* before today. Probably without a lifeboat."

Rafe took the pistol and gave Colin a nod. "Glad we have an understanding."

"Of sorts, Master Navigator."

The pistol returned to Rafe's satchel just as Maaka and Althea reappeared in the doorway. They paused at seeing Colin and Jonathan so close to Rafe, but Rafe kept Maaka's pistol down with a very subtle shake of his head. On finding Miles sprawled across the floor, the pool of blood slowly spreading around him, they looked to Rafe, silently demanding an answer.

"You missed the excitement," Rafe quipped.

"Actually, sir," Althea said, giving Maaka a glance before motioning to an overturned table. "We all missed the excitement."

Maaka had just righted the table when Althea placed with a resounding *thud* the array of dynamite on top of it. Rafe and the other two men jumped back on seeing the massive bomb, but Althea motioned for them to take a closer look.

"Note the detonator, gentlemen," she said, pointing to the central box nested in the cradle of explosives.

One panel had been removed, revealing a collection of wires and gears. There did not appear to be anything truly telling about the mechanism until Rafe could just make out etched on the central vial of dark glass a single word. The writing was in English.

Althea continued as if she were holding a class lecture. "The device holds a liquid that, on contact with a steady current of electricity, becomes volatile, particularly with dynamite. I've heard of this stuff. It's called 'fluid fuse.' Quickly becoming the ordnance of choice in Her Majesty's Government." She looked each men in the eye before adding, "This device hails from Old Blighty."

"Someone from England? Out here?" Rafe looked around him, and scoffed. "Wherever that is."

"The reason it did not go off, Master Rafton, is the wiring." Althea pointed to the loose wires reaching up form what would have been the top of the detonator. "You see here—corrosion. It can sometimes happen if wiring is exposed to the elements, and there appears to be some kind of salt contamination here. From what I gather, these wires were meant to pull a steady current from the lights, bringing the fluid fuse to its flashpoint."

"That is why the lights were flickering around us," Maaka spoke. "The corrosion prevented a strong enough connection."

"So, no boom?" Rafe asked. Both nodded in reply. "Do you think there's another one of these somewhere?"

"If there were, I think it contributed to whatever happened here. A bomb like this could easily render a port useless. Two of them?"

"Effective?"

"Indulgent, actually. Two bombs like this could easily send a seaport to the bottom of the lagoon."

An interesting notion. Rafe looked over the bomb again and considered the mind behind such a construct. "But let's take into account something else — this is not your average, everyday seaport. This is some sort of facility built within a network of caves inside a dead volcano, and the island is uncharted." He looked back at the stairwell from where they had disappeared to, and asked, "Althea, Maaka, what else is down there?"

"We stopped once we saw this device, sir," Maaka replied. "Miss Galway set to fixing the lights, which she did, and then we returned with this, thinking you would want to know of it."

"Well, now that I do, I think we need to find out exactly what a loyal servant of Her Majesty wanted so desperately to hide. Miss Galway, would you mind carrying the light this time?"

Now numbering five, the castaways descended deeper into the caverns, passing the spot where Althea and Maaka had restored lighting in the operations room. They could discern a constant dripping, and the air around them was no longer tinged with the smell of smoke and fire, but something cleaner. Sea water.

The steps ended at wooden planks, and now they could hear water lapping against both wood and stone. The lantern cast light only a few feet in front of them, the void around them revealing nothing except that this cave felt big. *Very* big. No telling exactly how—

"Master Navigator," Althea spoke, breaking the heavy silence around them, "if you please?" She offered him their lantern.

She positioned Rafe's arm to extend to the closest rock wall, and their sole light managed to reveal a power switch. Whether it had been the shock of the earlier-speculated bomb, or if someone had been in a hurry, the lone switch had been removed from its contacts. Althea took hold of its handle and looked back to Rafe.

"Gentlemen, before Miss Galway satisfies her engineer's curiosity, I would like to offer that reconnecting those leads could very well set off explosives condemning us to a fiery death followed by tons of rock and earth smothering us."

Jonathan, quiet for some time now, asked, "Or?"

"Or," Rafe sighed, "she may turn the lights on."

"Fuck all," Colin said, "as you said on the beach, what options have we got?"

Rafe nodded. Althea, closed her eyes, muttered what Rafe could only assume was a prayer, and brought the level down to the connectors.

The leads popped and crackled lightly when contacting the leads, and then the lights around them slowly grew brighter and brighter. This grotto appeared to be a forge of some sort as Jonathan gave a chuckle on what he recognised as tools of his trade. Rafe caught a glimpse at the man's eyes, and surmised that Jonathan Whitestone would be hard pressed to leave here. These were *advanced* tools of the trade, and they were now his.

"Well, at least one of us has found paradise here," Rafe said.

Althea finally took a breath and looked at Rafe with a bright smile, but the smile soon faded as her eyes darted behind him. The smile did not surrender to any sort of dread, but more of pure awe. Rafe then noticed that both Maaka and Colin, also looking past him, wore similar expressions.

Rafe turned around, took a single step back, and then marvelled at what the grotto's shadows had once hidden.

"Gentlemen, Miss Galway." Hearing his own voice was also a surprise. "I do believe *another* option has presented itself."

A Christmas to Die for

By Pip Ballantine and Tee Morris

Siena, Italy
December, 1894

Even an assassin must go home for Christmas.

Sophia del Morte was not smiling when she stepped down onto the airship's gangway, and looked around at the swells of people within the aeroport; some embracing one another in delight while others familiar counterparts greeted one another in a distinctly chilly manner. There was no need to take survey of the tiny travel centre as Sophia knew it intimately. It was packed with a crowd of bustling travellers, but considering the time of year, this was to be expected.

A quick hairpin into the nape of the neck of those plodding in front of her would move things along, but such initiative would not win Nonna's approval. The matriarch of the del Morte family did not appreciate attracting such attention this close to the family village. Nonna's wrath was not something even Sophia wanted to face.

The town of Siena was pretty, with its caramel coloured buildings, rooftops sprinkled with snow, and the elegant Torre del Mangia towering above the Piazza del Campo, but it was not her final destination. This was merely a waypoint before reaching Monteriggioni, because this was as close as conventional transportation could get her. Her Nonna and relatives would not allow anything as dangerous as an airship to get close to their mountain village. This insistence was well known amongst the local provinces, so much in fact the local government agreed to designate the aerospace above Monteriggioni a "no-fly" zone. It was safer that way.

In light of this, Sophia now faced a day of horseback riding, cross-country to reach Monteriggioni; nothing like an hour testing her thighs' endurance to get into the Christmas spirit.

Picking up her small valise, she strode towards the exit leading to the main street, the pending holiday with her family turning over and over in her head. She kept her hat tilted at a ridiculous angle so it obscured most of her face, but the concealed occulars in the rim allowed her to have proper peripheral vision of the street. It would be most humiliating to be caught unawares so close to her birthplace.

However, to the citizens of Siena she was only a woman in a stylish green dress. Much as it was in the travel centre, there was a throng of people outside. The majority were returning locals like herself, meandering and milling about. This made Sophia's journey to the local stables particularly frustrating, because there another crowd had gathered. More waiting. Lovely.

So she stood in the chill with the rest of the rabble, waiting for her turn to find a suitable horse for the final leg of her journey.

"Sophia!" the voice behind her called.

She spun on her heel, her hand already pulling free her muff pistol, but the grip on its handle immediately slackened.

Mio dio, she swore inwardly. *Why me?*

Ortensia. Sophia had been delayed so late in leaving London that she would be arriving with Ortensia.

The black sheep of the family trotted towards her with a smile so merry and bright, it turned the heads of the men around her. Ortensia had the same dark beauty all women of the del Morte family claimed as their own, even though she did not claim that surname. Unlike the rest of Sophia's family, her cousin Ortensia was not an assassin, a spy, or even a bounty hunter. With the name of their village as her surname, she had undertaken the honourable profession of "surgeon" in Vienna. Thankfully, Sophia only had to see her once a year and could easily avoid her company at this once-a-year-test-of-mettle commonly known as Christmas.

However it appeared, this year would not be as Sophia preferred—a solo journey.

"Sophia!" Ortensia trumpeted again, sending unsuspecting travellers to the ground as she parted the crowd through brute force to wrapped her arms around her cousin. Ortensia smelt of bleach and roses. Her cousin had obviously tried to cover up the odour of her profession in completely the wrong way.

"Ortensia," Sophia muttered, remaining stock still even as her enthusiastic cousin rocked her back and forth, "what a…" She was family. Flesh and blood. Family made Nonna happy. "…delightful surprise. I did not expect to see you here at the travel centre."

When Ortensia let her go, Sophia smiled as best as she could, as her cousin remarked. "You look lovely as always. I wish I knew your secret."

"I keep my distance from formaldehyde."

The laugh—beginning as a cackle, turning into a seal's bark, and ending with a single snort—cut through the din of the crowd, silencing them for a long, terrifying moment. "Oh cousin, I always did find you the wittiest of our clan!"

"It will be so nice to have company on the ride." Sophia might be used to deception on a daily basis for her work, but somehow lying to family, even the rather awkward Ortensia, did not come so easily. It was a mystery to her why it was so difficult, but there it was.

Ortensia nodded, though her eyes didn't meet Sophia's. That was another mystery—why her cousin kept punishing herself by coming back to the village every year. The menfolk of the del Morte clan could pursue what profession struck their interests, as long as it wasn't the family business. The del Morte women, however, were *expected* to follow in their ancestors' footsteps.

Ortensia should have done the decent thing if she wasn't going to do that, and quietly slip away, disappear from sight…

…yet here she was once again.

"We should rent a carriage instead of horses. Less dust, fewer flies to be concerned with, yes?

"Delightful," Sophia replied, adjusting her hat. "I suppose we must be the very last to reach the village."

"Oh yes," Ortensia said with a slight shrug. "Everyone else probably arrived on the 8th for *L'Immacolata Concezione*, but some of us have jobs." She cleared her throat as she straightened her spectacles. "*Proper* jobs."

Sophia's eyes narrowed. Really? *This* discussion? They weren't even at the table yet!

"Yes, well, those of us *upholding the legacy* experience complications from time to time," Sophia stated. "I was not able to get away."

Her cousin glanced at her, sniffing slightly as she took a step before Sophia. At least Ortensia had the good sense not to blurt out anything in front of the rest of those waiting. The time for open discussion was not here.

Just then the stablemaster came out of his office, and scanned the line of people until his eyes fell on the del Morte women. Taking a deep breath that seemed to shake his large frame, he motioned them over, away from the line of those waiting.

"Ladies, I was expecting your arrival. How can I be of assistance?"

"A carriage." Ortensia said, her face seeming to channel the intensity del Morte women would show in the field. The potential she occasionally displayed was, in a way, heartbreaking.

"A carriage?" he asked, quickly running his finger down his clipboard. His skin blanched a bit as he admitted, "Well, there is a couple from Corleonne, but I have two horses left. I suppose they can enjoy a spot of nature before reaching their destination." His smile was somewhat nervous. "Simply meet me around back, and I'll have you on the road in a moment's time." He then gave a meek shrug and added, "Remember me to your Nonna."

Sophia narrowed her eyes and glared at him in an appropriate manner, but Ortensia ruined the effect by paying the man. "Thank you, sir. We certainly will."

It was twenty miles to Monteriggioni, and usually Sophia would have born the discomfort of horseback travel in silence. In the comforts of this luxurious carriage, her cousin would have none of that. Whatever skills she had a surgeon, Ortensia lacked in the ability to read people. For the entirety of the journey Ortensia talked. And talked. *And talked.* There was mention of lives she had saved. Brave soldiers. Heroic aeronauts. People facing potential death sentences on account of another physician's diagnosis. Vienna's Miracle Worker, as Ortensia told her tales. It seemed for every life Sophia had snuffed elegantly and efficiently for a hefty price, Ortensia saved five all in the name of some silly oath she took at medical school.

What cheek!

Sophia gathered her strength under her cousin's endless torrent of stories. Ortensia chattered on about her life in Vienna, the way the men treated—or ignored—her, and why this chance to come home was a breath of fresh air. Sophia remained patient, nodding or shaking her head from time to time, but having no reply apart from that. Her usual methods on silencing anyone prattling as incessantly as Ortensia would have been deadly; but as the doctor was family, she needed to remain patient. If she'd been able to survive three hours of the Count of Tyrol dribbling on about his damn sheep, she would be able survive her own cousin. Nonna always reminded her that family was the most important thing in the world. If she arrived without her cousin, regardless of her "pariah" status, there would be questions. *Many* questions.

Still, it was fun to imagine inflicting her more lethal skills on Ortensia.

Sophia sighed, and focused her gaze on the approaching hilltop. The towers and walls of Monteriggioni seemed like a mirage to her. It had been over a year, last Christmas since she had seen it. However, darkness had settled early, and there was no gaslight to see by. Only the moon, full and kindly, showed them the way to Monteriggioni.

That was when Sophia checked her timepiece. "I suppose we are missing mass," she sighed.

"Oh, I asked the driver not to rush the journey," Ortensia tittered. "A smoother ride and more time for us to get caught up."

Sophia glared at her cousin. Bribing a coachman…to drive slower?

As they reached the road up towards the village, there were some lights flickering in the darkness. Then despite Ortensia still nattering on, Sophia felt her heart lighten as their coach began the winding path towards the Romea Gate. Not even Ortensia could keep the assassin from revelling in nostalgia as they rattled up the street between the small buildings. Suddenly she was eight all over again, riding the horse she had stolen from her aunt, and only reluctantly coming home with nightfall.

Up ahead though she could see candles lighting the Piazza di Roma. The tables were already set out in a circle, enough for the whole del Morte clan, waiting for their arrival.

Sophia's heart sank. "*Cavolo!*" She spat out as she exited the carriage.

"Oh dear," Ortensia sighed. "Perhaps we were late for Mass, but at least we have our choice of seating."

The church of Santa Maria Assunta had to be packed full of the whole family, and one of them would have been counting who wasn't there.

Sophia spun on her cousin. "We *would* have made it if it wasn't for your…" but her voice petered out when she saw her cousin's downcast face. Despite being the black sheep, she was still family.

"I just…" Ortensia began, then shook her head. "I was being selfish."

"Selfish?" Whatever did her babbling cousin mean by that? "It doesn't matter, Ortensia. We can take the time to tidy ourselves up, and see what is cooking."

After collecting their luggage and paying the coachman, the two went to Nonna's house. It smelt as heavenly as ever; garlic, tomatoes and baking. Everything was warm and inviting, ready to be served. Ortensia and Sophia found space in one of the upstairs rooms, and set about making themselves respectable.

Washing the dust of the road off her face, Sophia glanced across as her cousin. "Father Notti can hear our confessions the day after Christmas. Mine may be an all day affair." She looked Ortensia over. "Yours at least won't take long."

Something about being home in Monteriggioni lightened her mood, to the point where even Ortensia was no longer an irritation.

Her doctor-cousin, made a face, but the tension quickly dissipated on hearing a church bell ringing. Running downstairs, Sophia couldn't quite decide if her heart was pounding from fear or delight. Probably both, considering it was her family.

There they were, streaming out of the church, the women and the men talking and laughing. The del Morte family, a proud legacy and generations of problem solvers—provided the price was adequate.

Sophia and Ortensia stood before Nonna's house, politely waiting for them to approach. The men began to take their places at the table, while the women made their way to Nonna's house and the cooking.

He grandmother looked just as she always had: breathtakingly beautiful. In her youth Francesca del Morte had been feted across all of Italy, and had marriage proposals by the hundreds. In the end she had married a simple farmer from Monteriggioni, and brought all her sisters to marry their brothers. They had in a systematic and strategic manner taken over the village, turning the unassuming little corner of Tuscany into what would become a base of operations. The del Morte sisters, and their female offspring, explored their taste for blood and adventure, a pursuit that had continued for generations.

It was only at Christmas that they conformed to any kind of standards the rest of the world imposed.

"There she is!" Nonna exclaimed, immediately followed by a soft chorus of voices from behind her. "Sophia! So good to see you!" Nonna's eyes welled with tears as she hugged her tight. Sophia hated the emotion this woman engendered, but this was her mentor, her centre, her spirit. Nonna smelled of baked bread and lavender—which instantly made Sophia feel like she was that young girl again.

A hint of the intensity that Nonna had passed on to her surfaced when the woman looked at Sophia's cousin. "Ortensia," she stated flatly, "late as usual."

Nonna stared at them with her deep brown eyes and shook her finger at them both. "Missing Mass, I should be angry with you but..." Nonna's tears returned. "The point is you are here. That is what matters." She glanced over her shoulder and sighed. "Guila and Chiara won't be coming home for Christmas any more."

It did happen, but two in one year was unusual. Sophia crossed herself, and glanced at Ortensia who was doing the same. At least she was still capable of paying respects to those that did uphold the family legacy.

Nonna squeezed their arms. "Still we must celebrate! This is the Lord's Day, and a celebration of life, love and family, yes?"

Yes, this was a time of celebration, Sophia decided. Mourning would have its moment.

Soon the women found themselves swept into the midst of the other del Mortes, and away into the kitchen. Perhaps her targets would have been surprised, but Sophia loved to cook, at least in her Nonna's kitchen. Sophia's skill with a blade remained unparalleled, even within her own family, so when handed a bundle of basil and sage, Sophia had the fragrant herbs chopped in moment, much to the applause and approval of her family. She toured around the kitchen, catching kisses from sisters, aunts, cousins, and nieces, all the while tasting from bubbling pots.

Christmas Eve promised a dinner based around fish, but the lack of poultry did not mean a lack of flavour. Sophia took a platter groaning with canapes on one shoulder, while Ortensia bore one full with olives, artichokes, and anchovies. Behind them trailed the rest of the women folk, carrying the rest of the feast.

Sophia settled in a chair at the end of the table with Ortensia at one side, her younger cousin Rosa on the other. Children ran backwards and forwards delivering wine and water, and Sophia ran her eye over them. The next generation looked lively, and she was sure Nonna had already taught them much. Her eyes then turned to the table itself, noting the cutlery. It was sharp enough to cut through the tender fish, but when she picked up her knife, Sophia could feel ball bearings in the handle. Her gaze darted to Ortensia. Chances were in her hilt there was a stone or perhaps some heavy liquid inside its own handle. Something different to throw the potential weapon's balance. The fork could easily pierce pasta and softer meats. Human flesh only with great force. Nonna did not live this long by chance, and family meant everything to her. She took the same precautions with them as she did with meeting new contacts. Besides, they were a large Italian family of assassins, sometimes things could get...heated.

Once the first course had concluded, Sophia began examining the men at the table. Her cousins and aunts sometimes came home pregnant, as it was with Gina and Apellonia, or sometimes took husbands from the surrounding villages. They were the type of men who realised their good fortune at marrying a del Morte woman, or if they did not, they often ended up under the good earth instead of working it. Her gaze stopped on Rosa's apparent escort for the evening. She clutched the hand of this man, whispering into his ear, which evoked a warm, delightful smile to his face.

Sophia raised her glass and sipped delicately at wine within it, all the while watching the man. He was handsome, and knew how to set his carriage off with a fine tailored suit and carefully-coiffed hairstyle; a profitable businessman, or perhaps minor nobility? Rosa preferred that sort of standing in her gentlemen, be they escorts or targets.

Something about the cut of his suit, though, bothered her.

"Where is your man, Sophia?" Nonna suddenly blurted out across the table.

The conversation stilled on the query, all eyes turning to her.

"Well," Sophia began, cursing herself silently. She should have prepared for this. "I have been rather busy of late."

In the corner of her eye, she could see Ravina share a long glance with Evie. Evie gave a wry grin and shook her head slowly.

So I am particular in choosing a mate, Sophia spat inwardly. *At least I didn't open my legs for a husband after my first kill. Please…*

Nonna's *No Weapons at the Dinner Table* policy always made sense to her at this time of year.

"Well, that is your choice," her grandmother said. Was she shaking her head as well? "You are going to be twenty-five before you realise. I would hate to see you an Old Maid."

Sophia returned to her fish, taking a sip of her wine to conceal her expression. She hated disappointing Nonna.

"I've been seeing a delightful gentleman in Vienna, Nonna," Ortensia announced suddenly.

"That's nice," Nonna replied, the civility in her voice rather chilly.

"Is he a physician as well?" Ortensia's sister, Monica, asked.

"Oh no," Ortensia said, waving her hand absently. "That would be a bit much, two doctors in a courtship? It would be one disagreeing opinion after another after another."

"What does he do then?" Evie asked.

"He's a policeman. A special investigator."

Over the clatter of flatware came curses and condemnation from the del Morte clan, all of which came as a shock to the doctor among them.

"Whatever is wrong with courting an officer of the law?" Ortensia protested. "Law enforcement is a *noble* profession."

"You're doing this on purpose, aren't you?" Nonna asked dryly.

From the stories she had told her, Sophia knew Ortensia was brilliant; but the girl was as thick as that clotted cream the British hold in such high regard.

"Really, Ortensia," Monica said, rolling her eyes, "you live to be a disgrace to this family, don't you?"

Sister rivalry was to be expected, but even Sophia thought those words highly inappropriate—especially now when they were all gathered here for Nonna. She could see Ortensia's shoulders drop as her fork pushed pieces of fish and pasta back and forth across her plate.

Hearing her own voice came as a surprise, even to Sophia. "I would not cast stones at your sister's house so freely, Monica," she warned.

"What do you mean by that?" Monica returned, taking up the wine matching the colour of her hair. "Ortensia is a laughing stock and an embarrassment to the family name. Everyone knows it."

"Monica…" Nonna began.

"Is Ortensia a free spirit within our family? Yes. Does that make her an embarrassment? No." Sophia waited for Monica to roll her eyes again—a mannerism of hers that always worked under Sophia's skin—and drink deep of her wine before adding, "Now, the Hamburg Sanction—*that* would be an embarrassment to the family name."

Monica forced her mouthful of wine down quickly, nearly chocking on it in order to fire back at Sophia's claim. Her wine glass clattered by her plate. "I had taken full account of the target's grounds and knew the routine—"

"Monica…" Nonna repeated.

"And how could I have foreseen such terrible weather?" Monica continued, her eyes darting across her plate and silverware. *Admirable,* Sophia thought quickly, but dismissed the passing thought. Monica's ability with a knife? The tart could barely hit the broadside of a villa with her rifle. Throwing a knife? That would merely accomplish in disarming herself. "That storm should have blown over by the time I was ready to make the hit," she insisted.

"That sounds like you did not take everything into consideration," Sophia said, drawing strength from seeing Ortensia's face brighten. "Perhaps a bit more effort on your part was too much to ask for."

"I would have only needed one bullet, one angle, one shot," Monica insisted. "The timing was not right."

"Or perhaps a bit more effort was too much to expect," Sophia bit back.

"*Enough!*" Nonna snapped, her voice sharp as a whip's crack. Even the children at the adjoining table went silent. With all the attention now fixed at the head of the table, Nonna glanced at each del Morte present. Her face was still and fixed, no sense of outrage or anger. Just intense focus, and that terrified Sophia. "We all make our choices in life, and we should be grateful! Guila and Chiara are no longer able to make choices of any kind," and she paused to make the sign of the cross, prompting others at her table to do so, "and you sit here and question—openly or in secret—Ortensia's lot in life? You should count your blessings."

After a long moment of sombre silence, Nonna returned to her meal. The now cowed del Morte children followed suit.

The dinner eventually worked through the tension, although this meant that Ortensia remained quiet, seemingly lost in her own thoughts. Sophia avoided Evie's and Ravina's eyes, lest they both know she had caught their silent judgement following Nonna's questioning, and kept Monica in her peripheral. Yes, she was family; and her family was proud. Sophia had given her cousin's pride a severe bruise.

With the arrival of dessert, Sophia felt a slight pang of sadness. Even with reoccurring lulls in conversation, many of these stumbling, awkward interruptions settled with a glare from Nonna, she didn't want to the meal to end. As she leaned back in her chair and let chatter, gossip, and the warmth of good food and good wine wash over her, she considered for a moment just staying in the village, spending a few months tending to the vineyard while honing her skills.

Then she recalled the conditions for a sabbatical in Monteriggioni: injury or pregnancy. Those were the rules. Babinos, then work in the kitchen next to Nonna, and live out life; or rest and heal after a sanction goes wrong. Like Hamburg. That would mean something went wrong, and disappointing Nonna was not to her liking.

"Sophia?" Her grandmother was standing by her chair, not smiling, so it was time.

The menfolk were still at the table, so open professional talk among the women would not happen just yet, but Nonna always took her working relatives aside to find out a little more.

Linking arms with Nonna, Sophia followed her back into the kitchen. Sophia sat while her grandmother began to slice the pannetone. "How are things with you, *uccellino*?"

Sophia shrugged, picking at the remains of the ziti on the table. "Well enough, Nonna."

Her grandmother's hand slapped out faster than Sophia had guessed it could. Age, she believed, was only making the matriarch faster. "You are getting a name for yourself. Perhaps more successful than your mother was." She reached over and gently pinched Sophia's face. "But you must be careful. She over-reached herself, and I don't want that to happen to you."

A chill ran through Sophia, and for a moment she couldn't find the words. "I won't, Nonna. I promise. My current mark is a delightful change of pace from up-ending a government or eliminating another's competitor. The assignment is—how the English say—a cake walk."

Her grandmother's face twisted, she disliked the English and foreign languages equally. "I don't believe is such things, *uccellino*."

"My target," Sophia said, quickly popping a crumb of the cake into her mouth, "is an archivist."

"You are to kill an archivist?" Nonna snorted. "What? Does he have in his possession the slippers of St. Peter? Or the ring finger of St. Augustine?"

"No, but the client wants him. Alive for a change. Books is his name. Wellington Thornhill Books. I am to romance him, subdue him, and then deliver him. I made contact with him just last week. The man is like a kitten. Hardly much of a problem."

"Do not under estimate anyone," Nonna replied with a wag of her finger. "Remember—when kittens are riled, they go on the attack, and they do have claws." Her eyes narrowed. "Is this a House of Usher contract?"

"Yes." Saying those words filled Sophia with pride. Usher was the best paying employee for an assassin to have, or so she had heard within the network.

Nonna sighed, leaning back against her kitchen bench. In this flickering gaslight she looked older somehow, and very tired. "Tell me they paid up front?"

Sophia's smile faded.

"So I thought." Nonna shook her head ruefully. "Quite the reputation, they have, but reputation is like legends—exaggerated. Our family had dealt with the House before, and they are terrible at paying their bills in a prompt manner. Do not trust them, Sophia. Make sure it is *you* using *them*, and not the other way around."

"I will make sure, Nonna, that I remain in control, be it the House of Usher or some other client."

"Good." Then she held out her arms and her granddaughter went to her. They hugged for a moment, Sophia inhaling the smell and love of her Nonna. "I will not live forever, and I must know she who assume my title of 'Nonna' is worthy of carrying it." Sophia went to protest, but her grandmother waved her off. "I want you to be ready. More ready that Monica was for the Hamburg Sanction," she muttered, shaking her head in disgust.

Sophia gave out a trickle of laughter as Nonna motioned to the dessert. "Now let's get the pannetone out," her grandmother said. "Once the menfolk have eaten we can send them off to tend to the children, and we can talk business as a family."

They returned to the Piazza di Roma, and together passed around slices of cake.

The wine and Nonna's words practically naming her as successor to the matriarchy of the del Mortes had cleared from her head. As she took her seat back down between Rosa and Ortensia, her eyes returned to the man seated on the far side of Rosa, Sophia's mind drifting back in the direction of her profession.

"Rosa," Sophia began, devouring a small bite of the sweet cake, "where did you find this striking gentleman on your arm."

"Madrid," Rosa said, casting a glance to her beau. "It was fate, to be sure."

Fate? Sophia did not believe in fate. Rosa did. Sophia blamed that ridiculous tripe Jane Austen sold as literature.

"James Mantle," he said, and Sophia felt her breath catch in his throat. The man had quite a voice; rich baritone, but with a delightful silky overtone to it. "I am an investment broker. My office is in Manchester, but my work takes me everywhere. London. Paris. Toronto. New York."

"Really?" Sophia asked. She glanced at his hands. Yes, he was certainly not a farmer or working class, but the pale band across one finger did catch her eye. Not that he would be the first married man that Rosa enjoyed favours with. "You investigate investments?"

He nodded, raising his glass to her. "I make certain that investments go in projected directions."

"And what were you doing in Madrid?" Sophia asked.

"Exactly what I said," he chuckled. "Checking on investments."

"Fascinating," Sophia said with a curt nod. "My last assignment, before my current one, was in Madrid."

"Was it now?" he asked.

"Sophia?" she heard Nonna call out from the head of the table.

Not now, Nonna. "Yes. It was a delightful, simple assignment."

"Mind if I ask where you are now?" Mantle asked.

"Your earlier-mentioned London. A rather dirty city, if you not mind my saying."

"Well, London may not be the cleanest jewel in the crown of the Empire," he said with a shrug, "but it is still the centrepiece and remains the driving force of the world, I dare say."

Sophia would have desired talk return to family disappointments and awkward tensions as opposed to this new topic of politics...had Mantle's boast been sincere. It felt forced, if not rehearsed.

"Would you dare?" Sophia asked.

"I would, *Mademoiselle*," he quipped. A strange silence had now fallen over the table, but he remained blissfully unaware as he continued. "Then again, where you are in London is probably not the prettiest part of the City."

"And what part is that?"

"The Industrial Section. I'm guessing Industry Row along the Thames, or somewhere in the East End? Since you mentioned how dirty things were, yes?"

Sophia nodded. "Indeed." She took a sip of wine, then held a finger up as if she suddenly recalled, "Industry Row is, however, a fascinating corner of London."

Mantle sniffed. "I wouldn't know."

"Oh I think you do," she returned, "seeing as the House of Usher has an enemy somewhere in Industry Row."

Rosa furrowed her brow. "The House of Usher? Whatever are you—"

"James here knows all about the House of Usher," Sophia stated, "seeing as he just called me '*Mademoiselle,*' a greeting only my Usher contact uses as a feeble attempt to insult me and keep my attention. Why would such a cultured man dare to use French at an Italian table?" She motioned to Mantle's finger with its pale band across it. "And without your ring to announce the House's presence."

"Is this true?" Rosa snapped, her eyes boring into his.

He raised his hands, inclining his head slightly. "Ladies, I believe the tensions at the table and wine may be contributing to a bit of the suspicion at the table."

"This is the house of del Morte," Nonna stated proudly. "Suspicion is part of what keeps us alive. Trust is not some trinket we drop into a Christmas stocking, but it is a treasure earned." Her steely gaze switched to Rosa. "Do any of those silly books teach you that?"

"Nonna," Rosa protested, "*Sense and Sensibility* is a treasure."

Sophia watched Mantle as he rose from his chair. He froze in his ascent as all the women sat up that much straighter while the menfolk all nervously looked to one another.

"Well now," Giuseppe, Appellonia's husband blurted out, causing Mantle to flinch, "shall we check on the children?"

Mantle remained at the table, the rest of the menfolk all clearing out as he reached his full height.

"My dear Rosa," Mantle said, smiling warmly as his slid away from his spot, "you did warn me that my brashness may get the better of me with your family." He switched his gaze to Sophia and nodded. "My apologies for the coincidental slight. May I refill your glass?"

Sophia tilted her head in reply. So he was preparing his final play? How predictable. Well, perhaps this was slightly more interesting than listening to Monica explain Hamburg. "Please, Signor."

His feet barely made a sound as he made for the table where the bottles of Chianti sat, but he never reached the bottles as he turned on his heel and grabbed Ortensia, holding her fast against his body by her throat while from underneath his jacket sleeve a knife that now rested against Ortensia's throat. From a glance it looked far sharper than Nonna's cutlery.

Much like the sound of reindeer hooves across a rooftop, guns appeared from shadows, the del Morte clan taking aim on the man using their black sheep as a shield between himself and their bullets.

"Let's not do anything we shall regret, yes?" Mantle said, pressing the blade deeper into Ortensia's creamy white skin. The action earned a hiss and a whimper from the family surgeon. "Yes, Rosa, I am sorry but our meeting had been arranged."

Rosa, absent of a gun as she was still seated before her dessert. "You mean, it *wasn't* fate?"

"Afraid not," he sighed. "It was research into our investment. The House wanted to be sure they hired the right individual for this particular job. We cannot afford any cock-up's with Mr. Books, so I was sent to do a bit of background work on Miss Sophia del Morte here."

Sophia splayed her fingers around the handle of her Bodeo-Olivetti revolver. It had been quite difficult to conceal but, considering the present standoff, worthwhile. "And your assessment?"

"The children," Mantle began. "Why not the wife and children? You had been told to eliminate the competition."

"I had been instructed to eliminate the competitor, and I did so," she stated. "If the wife has picked up the business since, that is not my problem. She may lead her husband's investments to ruin, or they may flourish under her care; but that was not within my scope."

"So, *familia*? An all-important work ethic for you, Miss del Morte?" Mantle asked.

"Not completely," came a hard voice from the end of the table. "When was I not clear as crystal—*no weapons at the dinner table!*"

"Sorry, Nonna," the women replied in unison.

"Now, ladies," Mantle began, pulling Ortensia closer to him, "knowing what I know about how much you all value family—even the rejects like this one here—I don't think you will risk a shot lest I cut her throat. So we will simply back away, together, and once I find a suitable place for you all to collect darling Ortensia—"

His words were suddenly exchanged for a howl as Ortensia's arm whipped back and then struck his thigh. Hard. The unexpected shock to the man's body caused him to drop the knife in his grasp, but he did not let go of the surgeon until she twisted her arm once, twice, and then yanked up, tearing the inside leg of his fine Saville Row trousers.

While still night-time, Sophia could make out what was in Ortensia's grasp. It was one of Nonna's innocuous forks.

"*Doctor,*" Ortensia screamed into James Mantle's stunned face. "*Doctor Ortensia Monteriggioni, if you please!* I did not graduate *top of my class* to be reduced to titles such as 'black sheep' and 'darling' so show respect as I have earned it!" When the fork ripped free of the man's leg, the tearing of flesh rang in Sophia's ears. Mantle attempted to press against the wounds in between his cries of agony, but his fingers soon disappeared under liquid blankets of his own blood. "I have just severed your femoral artery—Latin: arteria femoralis—which, if you had even the *slightest* notion of human anatomy, is a large artery in the thigh serving as a main arterial supply to the lower limbs. You can try to stop the bleeding but it will do you no good. It's hard to say how long you have seeing as your heart rate is elevated." He collapsed before her, his moans growing weaker and weaker.

The myriad of pistols all lowered as Ortensia picked up the fine knife Mantle had threatened her with and waved it at him as if it were a scolding finger of Nonna's. "And you were intending to cut my throat but how, I ask you? Across my neck? No! The common carotid artery which, from your vantage point, you would have wanted to sever the left one. Located here!"

She sheathed the knife sheathed in the man's neck, and after a moment of twitching, Mantle went still.

The awkward silence so familiar around the del Morte table returned once more, even as the blood-stained, dishevelled Ortensia took her seat again. Instead of collapsing, she took up her wine glass and polished it off.

A deep breath later and the doctor said, "There is no mercy for those who refuse to indulge in basic research! That *bastado* was ruining Christmas."

"*Caspita!*" Nonna exclaimed. "*Magnifico!*"

The collected women erupted into cheers, their sudden celebration signalling to the menfolk and children it was safe to return. They joined in on the elation and the retelling of how Ortensia finally lived up to her potential.

Sophia clapped her doctor-cousin on the back. "How did you manage to break the skin with one of Nonna's forks?"

Ortensia blinked, and wiped the blood away from her eyes. "In my profession, particularly with autopsies, you build a strength when pulling apart rib cages, even when working with medical technology. I have quite the upper-body strength."

"That you do," Sophia chortled. "So does this mean you will finally take up the family calling?"

During the celebration, which now included music coming from the menfolk and dancing of the various couples there, a bottle of wine had materialised in front of Ortensia. She refilled her glass, staring deep into the blood red libation. "I don't know."

"What do you mean, you don't know?"

"Sophia," Ortensia hissed, her look angry at first, then softening to sorrow, "why do you think I entered the medical profession? You were always my favourite cousin. The one I looked up to. The one I never wanted to disappoint." She took a deep drink of wine and said finally, "I could never be as good as you."

How could Sophia have missed that? The insistence of her company. All the stories. Ortensia simply wanted her to be proud of her cousin in the medical field.

She leaned across and put her hand on Ortensia's. "I am proud of you, but I know you could be more. And I can help you. With your knowledge of medicine, your skill, your reputation, you could be better than me."

"How?"

A wicked smile crossed Sophia's face. "Consider how much closer a doctor of high renown can get to a mark."

Before she could give an answer, Nonna grabbed Ortensia in a fierce hug. "Oh my girl, finally we see the del Morte spirit in you." Her eyes shot across to Sophia. "Don't you agree, mia Sophia? Has not our Ortensia finally embraced her heritage?"

Sophia leaned back in her chair, raised her glass of Chiatini to Ortensia, and smiled. "Yes, I believe she has, and that Nonna I would say, is truly a Christmas miracle."

The Fawlt in Our Stars

by Pip Ballantine and Tee Morris

Torquay, England
Late Fall, 1895

"Are you sure this is the place?" Wellington stared up at the hotel, one eyebrow crooked, the nasty feeling that had been developing in the pit of his stomach in leaving London growing worse on an exponential scale.

Eliza fished the slip of paper she had written up that morning before boarding the train. A frown creased her brow. "The Imperial Turrets Hotel."

Both of them turned their eyes to the spread of buildings, painted white which occupied the top of the hill. The view down to the coast of Torquay might be impressive, but this hotel sprawling before them was most certainly not. Paint peeled from every surface, the crooked roofline promised leaks, and the brick wall at the front leaned. Hardly an advertisement for the builder's skill. The main house stood so alone up here that one might have almost thought that other buildings were embarrassed to be next to it.

"Look at that, Miss Braun," he said with a grumble, "even the letters can't quite bring themselves to stay." The word 'hotel' hung from the 'H' off the end of the sign.

"Perhaps an unhappy guest took their feelings out on it," Eliza replied, her gaze drawing together. "Look Welly, often our business isn't as glamourous as some might think. "

Wellington pressed his lips together. Since that whole Phoenix Society hullabaloo, he found himself lured away more frequently from his precious Archives, and he wasn't entirely happy about that. This might all be part of a grand plan by the formidable, and still unsettlingly alluring, Miss Eliza

D Braun to make his life miserable, or to indulge her far greater calling as a field agent. She was actually starting to get a grasp on the Archives, but Wellington was deeply regretting his revealing of cold cases to her.

Getting dragged to Torquay in the middle of a grey autumnal day wasn't how he might have imagined a life of intrigue and adventure might go. This place was a far cry from the palatial estate of Deveraux Havelocke, but this was where Agent Horacio "Turk" Turkingsdale's investigation had ended abruptly on a series of brutal murders. The queen herself assigned the Ministry to investigate these disappearances, but sadly, the trail got cold here. Dismal as this place seemed on their outside, Wellington did not find it at all surprising that Turkingsdale had in fact resigned his investigation here. This place seemed to be nothing more than a place for things to end. Hamlet's Denmark would be a welcoming holiday spot in comparison to this place.

"Coming in then?" a voice cut through the silence.

The gangly man wore an ugly green tweed suit that almost made him blend in with the creeping ivy behind him. If Wellington did not know any better, he would swear he'd been waiting there for hours just for them.

He was very lucky not to have got shot on the spot by Miss Braun. "I…" she paused and took a breath. "We were having a little discussion before—"

"Well, I can't hold the door open all day," the man barked from under his bristling moustache, though it was notable that he wasn't actually doing any such thing. "Either come inside or be on your way, thank you very much."

Wellington noticed Eliza's hand clenching into a fist, a sign that he had learned in their scant few months together that an intervention was in the offering. He quickly stepped forward before there was blood spilt on the threshold. Taking hold of the door he opened it for his fake wife to stomp through, but with a quick huff of disdain, and one final drag from a cigarette he'd been apparently hiding behind his back, the dreadfully rude guest stepped through the doorway, muttering something about "why he even bothers" and "the decline of sophisticated society" as he made his way to the front desk.

Wellington did not have to look back at Eliza to know his parter was about to erupt like Vesuvius.

Once inside the hotel, the atmosphere changed from dismal to downright depressing. Carpet the colour of algae matched dull brown patterned walls. A large grandfather clock with no discernible movement to it stood opposite the front desk, behind which leaned the proprietor. A middle-aged woman with an impressively styled pile of grey hair, and dressed in a deep plum dress, read a newspaper spread out before her. Above her head a dreary looking sign reading 'Bernard and Sylvia Sunder, proprietors' hung, in desperate need of dusting.

"Guest have arrived, dear," she said in a tone dripping with condescension. She never looked up from the paper.

"Yes, Sylvia, guests have arrived," the rude man snapped, and Wellington broke into a sweat as he watched this curt, crass, radish excuse for an Englishman take a place *behind the front desk*. "But please, do not tear yourself away from whatever pressing matter you are tending to. I have no doubt it is more important than the well being of a potential source of revenue."

"Are you sure we have any room?" Sylvia asked, turning the page of what had to be riveting journalism under her fingertips. "Consider the weekend."

"Consider the bills that we have to pay which only happen with *paying* customers, not the over-privileged snobs that are currently drinking and eating away our profits. Let me handle the reservations this weekend, *if you please,*" with incredible alacrity, the man's tone switched from sheer contempt to a spit-polished veneer of hospitality. "Hello, welcome to Imperial Turrets. Are you interested in a room or perhaps our honeymoon suite?"

Wellington started to answer, but flinched when the woman reading the paper exploded into something of a low cackle that ended with an even lower, guttural gasp.

The man, Bernard Sunder, Wellington surmised, stood there. Stoic.

"We were hoping for a room, yes," Wellington began. "Nothing fancy as we are simply—"

"Yes, yes, the Seaview Suite it is," Bernard cut in, making a note, "luggage?"

Eliza motioned to the two bags on either side of them. "In plain sight, mate?"

Bernard's eyebrows raised slightly. "Ah, a colonial." Through clenched teeth, he added, "How delightful."

The jarring laugh from Sylvia made Eliza flinch this time.

"I know that may sound like someone taking a Gatling gun to a seal, but never you mind, it is only my wife's laugh. Right then, I will have your bags tended to."

Bernard struck a bell. The ring echoed for a bit as Bernard, Wellington, and Eliza stared at each other. Bernard stuck the bell again. Again, they stood there in awkward silence. With a huff and a shake of his head, he turned to the wall behind him, lifted up a panel, and pressed firmly the large red button labelled in block letters "FULL START"…which did nothing to change the return of the awkward silence.

"Miguel!" Bernard bellowed.

An automaton, dressed in a white waiter's uniform buttoned up tight to his throat, chugged and whirred out from the back, the face etched into the metal seemingly frozen in surprise, or confusion. Perhaps both. His illuminated eyes darted side to side as if he was a rabbit and the humans foxes who had surprised him.

"Miguel," Bernard said, continuing to fill out the paperwork for Wellington and Eliza, "take these suitcases to the top floor, Room 2."

The automaton looked at Wellington and Eliza, flinched, before looking back to Bernard, stepping back into a half-crouch. *"¿Qué?"*

Bernard stopped writing and looked up with a glare that even made Eliza tense beside him. *"Toma. El burros. El espacio dos."*

Miguel's head spun completely around its pivot point, before he shrugged. *"No, es imposiblé. No puedo hacer esto."*

Bernard straightened. "What?"

"Burro es…" Miguel paused, and played the recording of a donkey braying angrily.

"For the love of God…" Eliza whispered. *"¿Miguel,"* she began, her accent flawless as she asked, *"por favor, podrías llevar nuestras maletas a la habitación dos?"*

Miguel's eyes blinked happily, *"Ah, tu hablas español!"*

"Un poco, un poco," Eliza replied sweetly.

"No, no, tu hablas muy bien!"

"Gracias, gracias."

Miguel chugged and puffed cheerily over to their suitcases, picked them up, and proceeded to the vertical conveyer-belt that lifted him up into the higher floors of the hotel.

"I don't know why you bought that silly machine, Bernard," chided Sylvia, still engrossed in her publication.

"Because, my dear, you are not aware nor care to make yourself aware of the sciences. That particular model is in a constant state of learning. The more we order it about, the smarter it becomes."

"That particular model is a prototype and originally slated for a hotel in Barcelona." She looked up from her reading and returned Bernard's perpetual glares with one of her own. "You got it cheap because the hotel who ordered it went bankrupt."

"Well, never you mind," and Bernard's disdain turned on Eliza, "perhaps the colonial here and her multi-lingual talents can fix Miguel's processors and reset him to speak proper English, yes?"

Eliza had reached her fill. "Now, look here, mate..."

"We are rather tired and would like to retire for the afternoon," Wellington interjected. "Freshen up a bit as well? I assume dinner is at 6?"

"Quite," Bernard said, slapping a single room key on the desk. He plastered across his face a fake smile and bowed slightly as he said, "Enjoy your stay at Imperial Turrets."

Wellington dared to take a step closer to the desk. He snatched the key quickly and grabbed Eliza. It was not so much to protect her from the hotel purveyor's ire, but to protect him from his protégé's wrath. He led Eliza to the stairs and pulled her close as they ascended in silence.

⋅⇾⇌⇽⋅

"*Sí, sí,*" Miguel insisted. "Is your room!"

No good deed goes unpunished, Eliza seethed as she looked at their delightful room. With only one bed between them. What was it about her and Welly always going undercover and finding hotels that apparently had only rooms with one bed available. It was as if hotel managers everywhere were conspiring to get the two of them knocking boots.

She glanced sideways at Wellington. *Not that it would be a* bad *thing...*

Quickly, she shook the thought free of her mind. Her mind wandering to idle thoughts like that were indication she needed to clock in some field time. Sharpen her skills, stop nurturing outlandish fantasies involving her mentor. "I will take the couch this time, Welly."

"Tosh," he returned, waving his hand dismissively. "I insist you take the bed."

How she wished she did not find that chivalrous streak in him so charming. "Nonsense, I have taken the bed the last three times, and in all previous cases I heard you winging about your back." Wellington started to protest, but Eliza held up a finger. "You are taking the bed this time."

Wellington after a moment's pause, he held his hands up in surrender. Excellent. She preferred it when he did as told. Bless him.

He took a seat on the edge of the suite's bed and flinched. Wellington looked to either side of him, pressed once, then twice, and pursed his lips as his eyes darted to the tiny window opposite of them. "Are you *quite sure* you wouldn't want the bed?"

"Welly," Eliza warned, "what…" Before she could get out the words "up to" she took a seat on the somewhat worn chaise lounge she would be using as her bed for their stay. "No, Wellington, I assure you, you're making out quite well with that bed." Her eyes glanced out of a similar, narrow window opposite her, offering an inch or so view of the ocean in the distance. "Seaside view… technically…" Eliza muttered.

"Hardly the sort of place for the upper classes to holiday," Wellington added, casting wary glances to each corner. "Do you think…?"

"Wellington, if this place did indeed have listening devices of any kind, I would think cheap. Not wireless or æthertechnology." She considered the small painting depicting a farm scene. Possibly costing the detestable man downstairs a haypenny from whatever street-side artist he bought it from. "I mean, cheap. Portrait of a dead relative where you stand behind it, remove the eyes, and spy on the guests."

"You can't be serious," Wellington scoffed.

"You did meet the same purveyor here, yes?"

Wellington paused. "Right, yes, I see it now." He glanced at the end table by their bed. "He may have invested his saving in this rather advanced-looking call system."

Eliza glanced at what Wellington was touching. Set into the chipped wooden surface of the table was a small set of buttons. Three of them, to be precise. He pressed the white one and waited for a few seconds. Another press, this time longer, and he waited. Nothing.

"I'd be shocked if they worked," Eliza grumbled, rubbing her forehead. "It was here where Turk said the trail stopped? This sorry excuse for a bed-and-breakfast?"

"Police found the victim ripped to pieces on the seashore," Wellington said, pulling the dossier from his suitcase. He flipped through the notes. "The murder was similar to a series of killings outside of Manchester. That was what had attracted Agent Turkingsdale's attention. Pockets of horrific mutilations, all occurring in villages outside of larger cities, that would suddenly end."

"Did he believe it to be the work of a single killer?"

"Agent Turkingsdale had initially thought so, but there was a series of deaths in Cheltenham at the same time bodies turned up in a small village up north."

"Where exactly?"

Wellington squinted his eyes. Yes, Turk's handwriting was truly appalling. "Some place called Bagger's End?"

Eliza shuddered. "I'm surprised Turk even bothered to draw a correlation. Word on the street is people drop like flies in Midsommer."

"What caught Agent Turkingsdale's eye was the date. Both murder sprees ended at the same time. The killings appeared coordinated."

"But the trail ends here?" Eliza asked herself. "What is so unique about Imperial Turrets?"

The door knocked making both of them stop cold in their conversation. Eliza gave a nod to Wellington, and he crossed silently to the door. "Yes?"

"Housekeeping," a female voice replied.

Wellington's body relaxed slightly, which made Eliza only more alert. Her hand slipped underneath her waistcoat where she had a small pistol holstered. Her new partner — a term she still considered rather loose — was far too trusting.

The door opened to reveal a young woman, blonde, with delightful rosy cheeks. She was not pretending to be cheery or happy in her work. As a matter of fact, she looked cross. The maid was also tugging lightly at her collar.

"You rang for service?" she asked.

"Oh, is that what the button is for?" Wellington went wide-eyed, looking rather dim and easily impressed. His propensity towards acting, Eliza admitted, was quite apt. "I thought Miguel would appear. Didn't realise this hotel was staffed with corporeal beings as well."

"Very corporeal, yes," the girl returned, still itching at her neck. "One ring will suffice in the future, thank you very much."

"Ah, very well."

"So, you called for service? Is your room in order?"

"Most satisfactory, yes. I take it dinner is in—"

"Half an hour. Will you be joining us?"

"Table for two, please."

The maid curtseyed and disappeared down the hallway.

"I stand corrected," Eliza said as their door shut. "I guess some things do work around here."

"Perhaps that is what makes this place so unique. It's a guessing game at what will and won't work?" Wellington gathered up the file from the bed and slipped it back into his suitcase. "Perhaps we should head down for dinner. You can tell a lot about an establishment by who is staying there."

"*Bon!*" she said. "Let us not dally, tempting as this—" She pressed against the mattress, and her mouth twisted into a grimace. "—well, I dare not call this a bed as that would be an insult to beds everywhere. Follow me, Books."

Eliza waited for him on the landing, taking his arm as they descended the stairs together, presenting a united front. Wellington straightened his waistcoat and adjusted the chain stretching across his vest as they emerged into the now quiet lobby.

That bizarre laugh of Sylvia Sunder echoed from a room behind the front desk.

"Must be the parlour," Wellington said, craning his neck. "Drinks before dinner? Rather festive considering the surroundings."

"Yes, quite," Eliza said as she crossed to the Front Desk and slid the Registrar towards her. "Most fortuitous."

As she began to scan their pages, Wellington kept an eye on the parlour door. "Any names you recognise?" he asked her over his shoulder.

"No, but who uses their actual name in one of these things? A lot of cover assignations in this hell hole of the purely sexual nature, I would think. Mind you," she said, running her finger down the ledger, "there are an awful lot of guests here this weekend. Especially for this place in the off season."

"You mean, for a place of this calibre, don't you?"

She chuckled. "In fact," she said as she checked the previous page, "it looks as if we snatched up the last room." Eliza leaned in. Were her eyes playing tricks on her? "Bugger me..."

"Miss Braun, please."

"I'm only noticing..." She shook her head. "Even out here, if you wanted to keep a tryst secret..."

"What?"

"Titles," and Eliza flipped the page back and slid the ledger to him.

Wellington looked the page up and down, and adjusted his spectacles as he continued to look at the names. He craned his neck to one side as his eyebrows raised slightly. "I'll be buggered too," he whispered.

"May I help you?" came a voice from behind them.

It was the hotel maid who had visited them earlier. She was considering the two of them carefully. Eliza wished she had worn her *pounamu* pistols, but as she was still in trousers, wearing heavy firepower would have raised eyebrows. It would have to be close quarters combat, provided this girl did not have a gun on her. Hard to tell presently.

"We were..." Wellington began, ".... looking for a copy of the menu for dinner."

Her expression never changed. "In the hotel ledger?"

Eliza held up her hands and slowly took a step forward. "I know this may look a bit odd."

The maid countered with a step back. "A bit, yes."

"We're curious as to whom we are sharing accommodations with." Eliza took another step forward...

...and nearly lost her balance on hearing Sylvia Sunders' grating cackle-laugh.

"Odds-bodkins," Eliza seethed, "that woman."

The girl cocked her head to one side. "Wait, you're not with the gathering?"

As much as Doctor Sound hated snap decisions in the field, this was one of those times. It would either mean the next step forward in this cold case investigation, or a hasty retreat from Imperial Turrets. A victory from any perspective.

"What gathering?" Eliza asked.

The woman cast a quick glance to the parlour and beckoned both Eliza and Wellington to follow her. Finally taking in a breath, Eliza followed the maid, confident that wherever they were being led, it would certainly not be a trap, seeing as Sylvia was entertaining, or something along those lines, in the parlour.

They followed her into the kitchen, and from the smells and sights of what promised to be a fine dinner. It was the maid who spoke first. "Are you with the local authorities? Or are you private agents?"

"Bit of both," Eliza offered.

"Then it is a good thing I found you snooping." Her face went completely white in shock. "You don't know what they might do."

"Who are *they*?"

"And more to the point," Wellington interjected. "Who are you?"

"My name's Molly," she said. "You could call me a Jack-of-All-Trades around here."

"Eh, she's bein' modest, our girl here," the cook chortled. "If it weren't for Molly, this place would fall apart at the seams."

Molly offered the chef a crooked smile. "How Gordon can keep his sense of humour with what happens here, I will never know."

"You have us at a loss again, dear," Eliza asked. "What does happen here?"

Molly looked over her shoulder to the Gordon who gave her a nod, and she stepped forward and inclined her head back. The choker she wore, from a distance, looked hardly out of the ordinary until Eliza noted the fabric appeared to be moving. Wellington leaned in even closer, and her mouth twisted into a frown as she noted Wellington completely oblivious to Molly's flinch.

"Well now," he whispered, adjusting his spectacles, "aren't you fascinating?"

"Personal space, Welly," Eliza spoke softly. "It's something of a trend."

"What?" He looked at Molly. He cleared his throat and backed away, "Yes, quite."

"The gears blend so well with the fabric, you honestly don't notice them unless you stare at the choker, and even then…"

"It appears as if it's a pattern in the fabric catching the light." Wellington motioned with his head to the cameo at Molly's throat. "I assume that is its power supply."

"Yes," Molly said, "body heat charges the battery."

"Biomechanic," Wellington said, impressed.

"Bioelectric, rather," Gordon chimed in. "At least, that is what Molly's been going on about."

When the cook had offered his own thoughts, Eliza noticed his bow tie was of the same fashion as Molly's choker. *Makes sense,* Eliza thought. *Men wouldn't wear chokers.*

"We're not the only ones wearing these obedience collars," Molly stated.

Eliza blinked. "Obedience collars?"

"It's perfectly horrid what they are doing to those poor people, and I simply can't leave things like they are. Not anymore."

Wellington cleared his throat. "Pardon, but which poor people are we speaking of?"

Molly frowned most charmingly. "Why, the guests' servants, or have you noticed? Chokers and bow ties, the lot of them. All answering to their masters' and mistress' bidding. These toffs come here every year, bringing their valets and lady's maids with them. All of us, in their keeping," she said, tapping her cameo, "doing what our owners say."

The idea of such a disgusting practice in this day and age, made Eliza's stomach flip over. "You're saying you are slaves here, and that the Sunders are your keepers?"

Molly nodded, making her little maid's hat flip back and forth. " Soon as they perfect these collars, and that is what they are here for, they intend to make them available to anyone with money."

"Righto," and Eliza thrust her arm out. The knife's handle felt good in the palm of her hand. "Let's get that collar off you, love."

Molly stepped back, her hand going to her throat. Even Gordon stepped away from the stove and covered his neck. "You can't!" Eliza's knife lowered. Gordon let out a huge sigh as his hand came down in time with Molly's. "These devices are powered *bio*electrically, remember? These are fastened in such a manner that if they get removed from our skin, they release a lethal charge."

"I thought those Sunder people were awful enough, but this?" Eliza said, her skin prickling with rage.

"Interesting," Wellington muttered.

Eliza looked over to him. "I'm sorry?"

"Well, if you recall, Bernard Sunder had a master switch for Miguel, and there was that call system in our room."

"The red button calls Miguel. Blue is Gordon. White is me." She winced as she rubbed her neck. "I assure you that system is most efficient."

"There you have it," Wellington said, "Bernard Sunder has them tethered to a remote."

"So there should be some sort of 'Off' switch in here?"

"For Imperial Turrets staff, perhaps," Wellington surmised. "For the other guest and their attendants..."

"Slaves," Eliza seethed.

"... a different frequency controls each one, or at least they should be."

"I'm not sure," Molly said, pressing her lips together. "I know that all of them have a control device of some kind. I caught a glimpse of something that Lord Agnew had in his pocket. It was about the size of his palm, and gold coloured."

"Luckily for you," Wellington said, straightening his waistcoat, "my partner and I are adept at securing objects from unwitting subjects."

It was something of a delight watching this Archivist embrace the Field Agent's bravado. *It suits him,* Eliza thought whimsically.

Molly's lips twitched into a smile. "Do you think you could?"

"We'll have you lot freed in no time," Eliza chimed in, always looking out for a moment to cause chaos. She flexed her fingers. "I'll need a distraction..."

"And I can provide one," Wellington said, going to the door. "Let's not dillydally. You stay here, Molly. Wouldn't want you to get in trouble with your employer... he looks rather explosive."

Eliza and Wellington exchanged a look. This hotel was, without question, an odd assortment of circumstances. The unassuming Molly seemed to be something of a small corner of insanity within this loony bin. A breath of fresh air, really.

As they returned to the lobby, the parlour now sounding quite busy, Eliza turned to Wellington. "Right then. A plan?"

"You distract, I procure," Wellington said, cracking his knuckles. "All I need is one of those devices."

"As you said," Eliza said, gently taking his arm, "let's not dillydally."

⁂

A surge of confidence overtook Wellington when Miss Braun took his arm. Perhaps he would never admit it to himself, and most certainly not to her, that a part of him enjoyed this intrigue. A giant awoke in the summer when he got thrown into the matter with the Phoenix Society. He was reminded of the fine dinner amidst other brothers and sisters of the now-defunct nefarious secret order, and once more he found himself mingling with another shadow society. This particular group enjoying the cocktails of Bernard Sunder, now manning the bar, was wealthy enough to afford any number of posh hotels closer to the water, and yet here they were. For a moment, he was rather worried he would go blind from all the jewellery on display. He glanced to his wide-eyed partner. She, too, appeared rather taken aback. It seemed a good portion of the upper crust of London descended on the Imperial Turrets Hotel for the weekend.

They made their way to the bar where they found an inebriated Mrs Sunder, draped over a comely young man dressed in the fashion of a valet, his collar buttoned high in a somewhat old-fashion style though. His face was handsome enough, but concealed mostly by a fine ginger beard and sideburns. Wellington positively identified at least four peers of the realm, and two captains of industry. This was most certainly not the sort of place that these class of people should have been staying.

Bernard made eye contact with the two of them and his grin faltered. "What are you doing here?" He asked them through a completely superficial smile.

"Staying at your hotel, apparently," Eliza quipped. "And now, drinking your booze."

"A glass of scotch, neat, and a sherry, if you please," Wellington asked.

His glare silently ordered them to disappear from existence, but still he served Eliza her sherry while Wellington took a single-malt. Eliza's eyes raked over the surrounding patrons. It wasn't only the wealthy and well-to-do Wellington noted, but also a good amount of servants. Their hang-dog expressions as they hung in the darker parts of the bar were in stark contrast to the aristocrats they served.

Wellington looked around him. Eliza needed to offer up a distraction. The question is what exactly. He took a sip of his drink and winced.

"Is there a problem?" Bernard asked from behind the bar.

The words tumbled out of his mouth. "No, if you don't mind watered down scotch."

It was as if someone threw a switch and cut off all conversation. Bernard was about to explode. He was sure of it. "I beg your pardon."

Wellington looked at his drink, then to Bernard, then back to the drink, then back to Bernard. Dashitall with his impulsive words. "Oh nothing. Nothing-nothing-nothing, I…"

"Are you insinuating I water down my scotch?"

"Well, watered-down may have been a rather strong…"

"I will have you know I keep this bar stocked with only the *finest* spirits from all over the world."

"I'm sure you do," Wellington insisted, "but it's only that…"

"I will not stand here and get insulted by someone of your lot, mate."

"Well, actually, Sunder," an elder gentleman began, lifting his own scotch, "my single malt is a bit bland."

"And I asked for ice with mine," another lord said, lifting up his own glass. "It's practically flavourless now."

"Right then, ya' bloody snobs," Bernard bellowed as he slammed a sturdy glasses before him. He continued to fill it with scotch as he trumpeted, "When I say I keep this bar stocked, I will show you lot. My staff makes certain these spirits are always amply full. If a bottle goes low, my people are always sure it is full again. Watered down? I'll show you!"

Bernard picked up the tumbler, now full to the rim with scotch. He passed it under his nose with an exaggerated sniff and proceeded to kick it back. In five consecutive gulps the scotch disappeared, the tumbler striking the bar with a sharp *bang*. He stood there for a moment, before pressing down a white button. Wellington could hear the screams of Molly as she came running into the parlour, her hand clasped on the side of her neck until Bernard released the button.

"Molly," he began, "who was in charge of restocking the spirits?"

"Well, actually," and Molly hesitated.

"Yes?"

"It was my fault."

"Miguel!" he screamed, tearing out from behind the bar, *"What have you done to my bar?!"*

"One a moment, Mr Sunder…" Molly called out, making chase.

Wellington shared a few glances with the others, but the silence soon yielded to resumed discussions of politics, the state of the Empire, and Sunder's odd—if not entertaining—behaviour. His eyes were now darting about the room as he set his barely touched scotch, coming to rest on Eliza in the doorway, motioning with her head to follow her.

"Excellent distraction," Eliza said, holding up the small gold box before her. "Managed to pick this from a toff considering his own drink. Let's get these people free." She passed it to Wellington and checkers the watch tucked in her waistcoat pocket. "Do this fast enough, and you and I can head back to London on the last train. I would rather not have to spend a night in this awful hotel."

"I am in more than agreement with you on that, Miss Braun," Wellington said, turning the control device in his hands. "I need to pry this o—"

Eliza produced the knife seemingly from thin air and within a quick flash of the blade catching the light, the back of the control device popped open.

"Thank you, Miss Braun." He looked at the wiring for a moment, his fingertips tracing connections between leads. "I have a theory that," Wellington muttered to himself as he pinched a red wire between his finger and thumb and pulled, "if I send out a signal strong enough, it will overload all the other remotes. That should sever the connection between collars and masters." He pulled the blue wire clear and twisted their exposed tips together, which he plugged back into where the red wire originally led to.

"So, how do we test that theory?" asked Eliza

"Like this," and Wellington pressed the little brown button at the top of the device. The low hum slowly ascended in pitch. Higher. Higher. And high enough that both he and Eliza inclined their heads away from the box. A succession of pops followed by screams came from the parlour before the device in Wellington's hand shorted out with a sharp *bang* and a shower of sparks. For a moment, nothing appeared to have changed.

Then a single, solitary howl came from upstairs.

Eliza's eyes locked with his. "Surely not," she gasped out. "It can't be…"

Both of them sprinted back to the doorway of the parlour and froze. Their eyes widened on what they had accomplished. Yes, the unfortunate servants were free, their control collars hanging about the necks. Hands went up to chokers and bow ties and tore them away from their skin, but not with sighs of relief. One by one, the indentured servants cried out with howls. Actual *lupine* howls.

An elder woman Wellington recognised as Lady Annabelle Wyndermere let out a sharp scream as her valet undertook a terrible transformation in front of everyone. Long hairy snouts pushed out of faces, teeth extending into fangs, and body hair growing rapidly into coarse, thick fur covering his body. Underneath the quickly forming coat, muscles rippled and swelled, threatening to tear through the man's skin. Wellington quickly looked to a maid at the back of the room, the butler by Lord Hedforshire, and finally the handsome valet that Sylvia Sunder was attempting to flirt with. All their eyes had transformed to a bright amber colour.

"That's not…" Wellington swallowed and glanced at Eliza. "The servants…"

"Yes," she said, squeezing his elbow, "the servants are werewolves."

Neither of them lingered to watch for a mad rush for the exits by suddenly fleet-footed aristocrats. With their collars removed, now there would be a reckoning.

Wellington and Eliza were about to head back to their room to shelter in place when the towering frame of Bernard Sunder burst out of the stairwell. He reared back his left fist high in the air, but his awkward punch became a pointed finger. "What did you do?!"

"What?" Wellington asked, "What makes you think…?"

"Don't give me that, you git!" Bernard was now coming completely unhinged as his fists balled up even tighter. "You are not here with the CSB, so you have to be responsible for all this!"

"The CSB?" Eliza asked.

"Yes, the Circle of the Silver Bullet," Bernard insisted. "You're not part of the Circle so it is a simple deduction that you're responsible for all this," he bellowed gesturing madly at the pandemonium unfolding around them.

A wolf the size of a small motorcar burst from the parlour, his roar so powerful that two high ladies toppled to the floor. The beast growl stopped abruptly as it sank its fangs into one of the women, her own screams also abruptly stopping.

"Get to the kitchen," Eliza said, grabbing Bernard by the lapels, "NOW!"

Dodging both hotel guests and lycanthropes, the three pushed through the chaos to reach a tenuous—at best—safety in the kitchen. Gordon must have left the dinner in progress to join in the carnage.

"Righto," Eliza said, tossing Bernard against the sink. "Talk."

"I am a member of a secret society," Bernard said, in between catching his breath, "dedicated to keep the werewolf population of England in check. We are everywhere. Yorkshire. The Lake District. Plymouth. And it is our job, as sanctioned by the Queen herself, to make certain these flea-riddled mutts do not overtake the countryside."

Wellington shook his head, "Just a moment, an agent of our Ministry followed a rash of murders to this hotel. You're telling us werewolves were responsible?"

"Wait, Turkington? He's one of your men?"

"You know him?"

"I told that bastard to keep his mouth shut!"

"He did! That's why we're here!"

"Dear God, we're all dead!!!"

Eliza joined in the screaming. *"Well we wouldn't be in this mess if you and Turk had been a bit more forthcoming about the Circle of the Silver Bullet and what it was all about, now would we?!"*

Something about Eliza's faulty reasoning sobered up Bernard as he went still and looked at them both as if for the first time. "Oh, I see. So all this time, instead of holding you responsible for unleashing the lycanthrope apocalypse on us all, it was *my* fault the whole time not telling your man about a *secret* society that HER MAJESTY had decreed be *kept* secret. So this has been my fault the whole time, it's so clear. Well, I should be punished, shouldn't I?" His right hand reared up and began spanking his own backsides as he chided, "You're — a — naughty — boy — Bernard…"

"Get a hold of yourself, man!" Eliza bellowed over Bernard's self-flagellation.

"You must have a contingency plan for this!" Wellington insisted. "If the collars failed, there had to be a redundancy, yes?"

His hand froze in the air, and an idea apparently came to him. "Right, we've got to find Miguel!"

"Miguel?"

"He can emit a frequency that can stun the werewolves. We have to activate the signal before any of these beasties escape."

Wellington snapped his fingers. "Our room. We can call for Miguel from our room."

"Servant's Access," Eliza said, pointing to the narrow stairwell on the opposite end of the kitchen. She took two steps before turning on Bernard. "Wait a moment, what about your wife?"

"Believe me, I'm more worried about what she will do to the werewolves than vice versa," And with that, Bernard spun Eliza about and pushed her to the stairs. "Now come on!"

Wellington struggled to keep his breathing calm as his lightning-quick assessment of the stairwell and its narrow confines brought every survival instinct to a high alert. He could feel the itch to tap into those talents

Eliza had peacefully slumbered through when all hell broke loose at the Havelocke estate, but he reserved that option for his contingency plan.

The three of them emerged on the top floor, and Wellington shoved past them with the key in hand. Gunfire snapped one level below them, both pistols and shotguns. He pressed the red button repeatedly while Eliza flipped open her own suitcase.

"Come on, Miguel," Wellington whispered. He looked to his partner. "Any chance you have silver bullets on you?"

"Back home, safely tucked away," she said, flipping up a panel and producing her gun belt, "but my lads here will give them something to think about." Eliza pulled out a Crackshot, gave the stock a quick flick to check its barrels, and snapped it shut with another jerk of her arm. "This should make them heel."

"No wonder your bag was so bloody heavy," Wellington said.

A knock at their door, and the Crackshot came up. "Halo," came a synthetic voice from the other side. "Is Miguel. You call?"

Bernard nearly tore the door off its hinges. He yanked the automaton into the room, and said through clinched teeth, "Miguel, initiate 'Bad Dog' sequence."

The automaton looked at Wellington and Eliza, flinched, then looked back to Bernard, stepping back into a half-crouch. *"¿Qué?"*

"Oh dear God, Miguel…" He took a deep breath and said without stammer or pause, *"Inicia el perro malo!"*

Miguel's eyes flashed quickly. *"¡Sí! ¡Sí!"* he replied as he stepped back. The top of his head split open, and from his open cranium, an intricate antenna extended. Its metallic array looked as delicate as a spider's web, the lights set within its many branches and relays blinking rapidly. They continued to blink and flicker in sequence until Miguel's eyes went from a quick, blinking amber to a steady red. The multi-coloured lights in his antennae also flared red.

"There," Bernard said, pointing to the automaton, "the signal is being sent!"

Wellington shook his head. "I don't hear anything."

"Of course you don't, you cloth-eared git," snapped Bernard, "you're not a dog are you?! It's a hypersonic signal."

"How did you do that?" Eliza asked.

"Do what?"

"Rattle off Spanish as if you were born there."

"I learned Classical Spanish, not that strange dialect he got programmed with," Bernard returned. "Now, back downstairs, we need to sort out this mess you two idiots hath wrought."

Wellington looked back to Eliza who was grasping the Crackshot in her hands. She was tapping the side of the stock with her trigger finger. She was holding the urge back, he could see it. The twitch in her left eye was also a bit of a tell.

They stepped into the lobby and nearly collided with Bernard Sunder. He was standing stock still.

Behind the front desk stood Molly and Gordon. Molly turned towards them, and that was when Wellington caught sight in her grasp a large wad of cotton.

"I'm afraid," Molly shouted, "I was only able to take care of myself and Gordon before the others were immobilised. I thought Mr Sunder would activate the failsafe when I saw Miguel scuttle past me."

"Bernard!" came a shrill, shrewish cry. A blood-soaked Sylvia Sunder burst from the parlour, a pistol in her hand. "This is the last – time – I have you manage reservations on the Circle's weekend."

Gordon snarled as he leapt for Sylvia. She fired off a round that struck him in the shoulder, but the gunshot did nothing to stop him from landing on top of her. The two of them tumbled back into the parlour. Another shot rang out.

"Now that I have your attention, Mr Sunder," Molly said, stepping out from behind the front desk, her skin darkening with fur on each step, "I would like to tender my resignation."

While transformation to wolf form looked like sheer agony from the valets and maids they had seen tonight, Molly looked aroused by the change from human to a wolf. Even after she landed against the floor on all fours, her transmuted face still managed a smile.

"Now, look here, Molly," Bernard began, "I have been rather good for you. Think of the skills you have picked up while working here!"

Molly's bark rolled into a snarl that settled into a low, rumbling growl.

"Molly," Bernard continued in a somewhat defiant manner, "you had better reconsider this if you want a positive reference for future employers!"

The hell-beast leapt for Bernard Sunder, but even with her newfound power and advanced musculature, Molly could not anticipate the sprinting ability of her long-legged prey. Neither of them paid any attention to Wellington or Eliza as they ran out into the dusk now falling over Torquay. It was impossible to tell if Molly was playing with her potential food or if Sunder just had that incredible of a stride.

"*You will rue this day,*" Sunder shouted over his shoulder, still managing to shake his fist while maintaining a lead, "*you dozy bint!*"

"What do we do, Miss Braun?" Wellington asked, as they stood in the sudden silence of the Torquay.

She pursed her lips and looked back to the hotel. "Well... the enslaved are indeed set free, and there is a certain rightness to that. I don't know ... what to make of any of this."

"What? You mean, of the supernatural?" Wellington spluttered. "Aren't we supposed to stop them rampaging about?"

"I suppose we should call in for a little more help. The Ministry's animal control unit is based in Plymouth. They should be able to get here in an hour or two, depending on traffic. Plenty of time to collect and catalogue our werewolves."

"And what about—?" and Wellington motioned to the diminishing figures of Molly and Bernard who was now weaving left and right across the open field.

Eliza watched him for a moment. It was amazing how Sunder's voice carried, even at his distance.

Wellington narrowed his gaze. "Sometimes I do worry about your sense of justice, Miss Braun."

She shrugged. "Oh now Welly, you've met Sylvia Sunder. Do you really think we're doing Bernard there any favours in rescuing him?"

His mouth opened but he paused. "Alright, I see your point there."

"So," Eliza jerked her head back towards the hotel. "Shall we pack while we wait for the Plymouth Branch?"

Not pausing for his answer, she strolled back into the now empty bar.

As Molly's howls echoed in the hills of Torquay, it wasn't like Wellington had much of a choice in this matter. He followed after her wondering how on earth he would file this particular cold case? He also wondered if the Sunders managed to survive the evening, would they continue disappointing visitors to the area?

The only certainty he did take from this experience — Imperial Turrets would not be receiving a recommendation from him. Bernard Sunder had made some choices in life, he had no doubt, but hotel management was not the wisest. It just didn't suit him.

Maybe Eliza was right. Maybe they were doing him a favour.

Poor bastard.

In the Spirit of Christmas

by Tee Morris

Christmas, 1895

Wellington Thornhill Books, Esquire, had not planned for anything out of the ordinary this Christmas Eve. His agenda called for a candlelight service at his church, a special Christmas treat of goose for Archimedes when he got home, and then to bed, rising the next morning to a day of progress on his current work. He had solved the challenge of thrust. Now it was a matter of control over pitch and yaw. That mystery he planned to solve as a gift for himself. His Christmas plans did not include, in any way, shape, or form, investigation into an occurrence of any kind, peculiar or otherwise.

He now bit his lip hard as he watched the third apparition appear. Not a single confirmed haunting, but a *third*. In the same location. In the same night. Not free floating orbs. Not wisps of mist. Not partial apparitions.

Full.

Body.

Apparitions.

This spirit appeared more imposing than the others. It was tall, wearing tattered, ancient robes that insinuated druidic origins, and while the shadows concealed its face, Wellington could easily make out pale bones protruding from the robes' cuffs.

His eyes immediately darted to the other side of the room. They had already done this twice before in the evening. This third procedure should be effortless.

The old man had dropped to one knee, as they had planned—almost as if he were about to propose marriage. As the other spirits has appeared completely and totally cognizant to verbal and physical communication, it was a strategy to lower the next fantastic creatures' defenses. Unlike the other visitations, this spirit fed on the very life in the room.

Wellington felt despair well up inside him. The temperature in this already cold, dreary place felt as if it had dropped even further.

"I am in the presence of the Ghost of Christmas Yet To Come?" the old man spoke, his earlier confidence seeming dashed and destroyed.

No reply came from the ghost, save for a gesture. The ghost pointed downward, inclining its bony hand towards him.

"You are about to show me shadows of the things that have not happened, but will happen in the time before us," the old man, his words forming as puffs of fog around his mouth, pressed. "Is that so, Spirit?"

The ghost inclined its head. The only answer this bare apartments' sole occupant received.

Amazing, Wellington thought to himself. *It, too, is fully responsive to corporal beings. Never have I seen such* consistent *interaction at one haunting.*

"Ghost of the Future!" the old man exclaimed, "I fear you more than any spectre I have seen. But as I know your purpose is to do me good, and as I hope to live to be another man from what I was, I am prepared to bear you company, and do it with a thankful heart. Will you not speak to me?"

Wellington furrowed his brow. *Laying it on a bit thick, aren't you?*

The specter gave no reply, but extended its hand straight before them.

"Very well." Then the old man stepped back and shouted, *"Get him!"*

Eliza pushed back the curtain that had concealed her and threw back the switch on the Tesla-McTighe-Fitzroy Paraphysical Containment Rifle, or as the three inventors had nicknamed it, the "Phantom Confounder." The dark lenses of her goggles flickered from the tendrils of energy erupting from its bell-shared barrel. The Confounder attempted to ensnare the ghost where it stood, but suddenly the rifle kicked in Eliza's arms and a pop rang out from the weapon's transistor. Several tendrils went wide, destroying two small figurines on the fire's mantelpiece and bouncing off the mirror over the same mantelpiece and striking a small gas lamp on the wall. The wall fixture exploded, making the phantom and old man recoil.

"Bugger!" Eliza spat. "Wellington, we have a problem!"

Dash it all.

Wellington emerged from his hiding place, sliding the small metal plate underneath the spirit. It was stumbling, so the creature was stunned. At present, this could work in their favour.

The plate stopped just behind the ghost. Wellington grabbed the old man and dove. He was thankful that this man enjoyed the indulgence of a luxurious bed.

"Stay here, Mr. Scrooge," he said before rolling away from him and returning to his feet.

He opened the drawer of Scrooge's bed stand, and produced a small control box. Wellington pressed the green button, and the ghost lurched as the plate began to rattle. He felt his throat constrict as he adjusted a pair of dials on the wireless in his grasp. The black specter was still moving too much.

"Eliza!" Wellington called.

"Just a moment, if you please, the generator is still warming up."

The plate rattled louder.

"We don't *have* a few minutes!"

"Just another—" The phantom let out a low, guttural scream. "Close enough."

The Confounder exploded in a brilliant flash, pure energy whipping and wrapping around the Ghost of Christmas Yet to Come. It released another howl as it wrestled against the Confounder.

"Bugger me, he's strong," muttered Eliza.

"Hold him there," Wellington said as he adjusted the settings on his controls, "and I've got him!"

His thumb lifted the guard on the red switch and flipped it to the *"Open"* position. The metal plate spilt, revealing a dark mass that churned and bubbled underneath the ghost. Eliza shut down the Confounded as the shadows reached up, grabbing hold of the phantom. Its struggle now grew frantic, but Wellington knew the portal's pull would not falter. The creature gave one final reach before surrendering to the portal.

Wellington returned the switch to the "Closed" position, and the portal closed. He took a deep breath, and afforded a smile. Three spirits, three captures. Not bad for one evening.

"Apart from a momentary cock-up, that went rather well, I thought," Eliza said, breaking the silence.

"Yes," Wellington replied, motioning to the massive device now resting across her shoulders, "about that?"

"I think it was that second ghost. Did you see the size of him?" She motioned with her head to the Confounder. "I think its calibration might have been thrown off. I'll make sure to check it when we get back to the office."

Her smile, he always thought, was quite disarming. It was made even more so when she lifted her tinted goggles and rested them across her forehead. The soot and grime from the Confounder had darkened and stained her face, save for a small band of pale white skin across her eyes.

He was about to comment when he heard a soft scratching coming from the bed where he had left Ebenezer Scrooge. Wellington turned to find Scrooge muttering something to himself, and then quickly making notations on a small piece of parchment.

"Mr. Scrooge," Wellington began, "are you well?"

"As well as can be expected," Scrooge returned, his eyes noting the parchment as he turned to the two of them, "I would have been asleep hours ago had we not tonight to contend with."

"Well now, Mr. Scrooge, no need to worry," Eliza said. "You can sleep most soundly now thanks to the Ministry."

"Of that, I have no doubt." Scrooge's eyes looked at both of them, his mouth stretching into a thin frown. "Though I still have no inkling exactly what Ministry you serve."

"Our policies unfortunately mean we must remain in shadow."

"So it would seem." He glanced at the parchment and then presented it to Wellington. "And now, your bill."

Wellington and Eliza both gave a start, but the Archivist was still staring at the bill when Eliza replied, "Our what?"

"For damages to my estate." Scrooge motioned to the scorched mirror over the fireplace and the destroyed gas lamp. "And let's not forget the parlour where you ensnared the Ghost of Christmas Present."

Eliza scoffed. "As much as I hate to repeat myself, but did you see the size of him?"

"You claimed this sort of thing to be a specialty. I was unaware that damage to personal property came with your unique services."

Her eyes returned to the paper in Wellington's hand, and then back to Scrooge. "You billed us *for you time?*"

"In my occupation, I must be alert and well-rested. My mind is far more reliable than any difference engine, provided I get enough sleep. As I am presently not asleep and working with you all, my time is therefore billable. And as I anticipate that I will not simply drift off to sleep in the wake of tonight's excitement, this is time billable to your organization as direct consequences to your actions."

"You've got some cheek, mate!" Eliza spat.

"I pay my taxes. And as I mentioned to some rather insistent annoyances earlier this day, my taxes help to support the establishments of our government. They cost enough. My taxes, however, should not be expected to be exempt from damages upon my personal property due to your incompetence."

Now Wellington took offense. "I crave a pardon, sir, but we captured your ghosts."

"All but one," Scrooge said, his tone so sorrowful that it was insulting. "Marley's Ghost is still at large, I am afraid. And did your partner not admit to her own ineptitude when your contraption there failed to capture the final spirit?"

Her voice seemed colder than the apartments themselves. "Tread. Carefully."

Both men looked to Eliza whose fingers were splaying slowly around the butt of the Confounder.

"Mr. Scrooge," Wellington began, clearing his throat lightly, "please consider that your case would have been dismissed as the rantings of a mad old man if our Scotland Yard contact had not happened to relay it to our Ministry. Miss Braun and I happened to be in the office on its arrival, and we dropped everything in order to give your case our attention."

"I applaud your dedication to your civic duty," Scrooge returned. His expression turned dark. "Now unless you wish me to adjust my invoice for the time you are continuing to take without any consideration to me, I suggest you collect your infernal devices and depart. Good evening."

He turned back to his four-poster bed and crawled between the sheets. He went to blow out his candle, but paused on see Wellington and Eliza still standing there.

"The front door has not moved since your arrival." He motioned with his head to his bedroom door. "Good evening."

Eliza's grumbling was the only sound Wellington could hear as they saw themselves out of the dark, dreary apartments. It had just started to snow, meaning that even with their efforts to bundle against the elements, a long, cold walk home stretched before them. Wellington checked his watch and saw it was just past midnight. How these spirits could also alter time would have been something he would have loved to investigate. Could Scrooge's apartments been constructed at some sort of temporal convergence point?

His thoughts were scattered by Eliza, the bulk of her Confounder looking rather odd against her heavy fur coat. "Jolly nice. We have to walk home, I suppose, after carrying out our civic duty?"

"It seems that way," Wellington muttered.

She looked back up to the window that remained lit softly, and then winked into darkness. "Old bugger really needs a taking to task, doesn't he?"

"He does seem a bit cantankerous," Wellington agreed.

They took a few steps further, and Eliza stopped. He turned to look at her in the gaslight. The grime across her face seemed darker now, making the area once protected by her goggles seeming to glow in the night.

"I'm sorry, Wellington."

Tonight was truly a night of surprises. "I'm sorry, Miss Braun."

"Welly, I know you probably had other plans for Christmas. Perhaps a fine dinner with family or some such; but I was quite happy to have this case appear in the pneumatic system when it did."

"Well, of course you did. It was a chance to return to the field— "

"I did not look forward to another Christmas alone."

His brow furrowed. "You? The vivacious Eliza D. Braun, alone, at Christmas?"

"Christmas is a time for family, and my own is…" Her voice trailed off, and now with the pronounced clean skin around her eyes, the tears welling in there were evident.

Wellington felt a warmth swell in his chest. Eliza had been insistent on him joining her on this case, but not to return to the life of a field agent. She wanted to spend Christmas with family. Instead, she chose to spend the holiday with the next best thing.

"I'm flattered, Miss Braun." And he truly was. Tonight has been a delightful Christmas gift.

He then looked around himself and realized, "Oh, dash it all, I forgot the portalplate at Scrooge's."

"Better go get it then," Eliza said, sniffling a bit. "I'll wait here for you."

Wellington took a quick step back to the detestable man's apartments but stopped. He looked over to the wireless controller slung over his shoulder, looked back at Eliza, and then back towards Scrooge's.

"You know, Miss Braun," Wellington said, a smile forming across his face. "wireless telegraphy is an amazing technology of our age. Before it, we would have to be tethered to devices in order to make them work."

Eliza inclined her head to one side. "Yes," she said plainly, "and your point?"

"With wireless advances, we can now operate devices of all sorts," and he flipped the safety up of the portalplate's switch, "from great distances."

His thumb pushed the portalplate's switch to *"Open"* and, only a few seconds later, the window of Scrooge's bedroom exploded with light.

On hearing Scrooge scream, he turned back to his partner. "Mr. Scrooge said his time was valuable," Wellington said, "so now he can take them all at once, and have it over, yes?"

Eliza glanced at the brilliant, frantic display erupting from Scrooge's window, then looked back to Wellington. "Alice will be off for the day, but I know a butcher who usually has a nice bit of New Zealand lamb. If you are available for Christmas dinner, Wellington, would you care to enjoy the holiday with a touch of Aotearoa?"

Wellington smiled. "I would be delighted."

He extended his arm to her, and with his peculiar wireless control slung over his shoulder and her Confounder resting on her shoulder, the two walked into the night, leaving fresh tracks in the gathering snow around them.

Another scream from Scrooge's apartments cut through the night.

"Merry Christmas, Eliza."

"Merry Christmas, Welly."

Silver Linings

by Tee Morris

Winter, 1896
Cairo, Egypt

"Ah, Cairo." Wellington sighed as he stood on the ship's gangway for a moment, taking in the impressive desert vista before him. "The cradle of civilization and human innovation."

"Along with the cradle of oppressive heat, barren wastelands, and flies that you could hitch up to a hansom and use as a cheap alternative to camels," grumbled his junior archivist as she disembarked.

Wellington Books looked down at the diminutive Eliza D. Braun, arching an eyebrow at her as she twirled her parasol in annoyance.

"Miss Braun, come along, are you telling me you do not find Egypt tantalizing in its history, its undiscovered mysteries the foundation of modern language and even the sciences began here"

She bit back, "If I were fond of this kind of heat, I would take holiday in Australia. Hold my parasol." Eliza unwound the veil from around the top of her pith helmet, and then snatched back the parasol.

"And here I thought you were a romantic," he muttered.

"A romantic? Is that why you insisted on taking an airship to the Sudan, and then chugging upriver on this boat?"

"Chugging upriver?" Wellington asked, stunned. "It's the *Nile!*"

"Oh for God's sake," she seethed, giving the horsetail swatter a few swings, "let's get this over with!"

Hefting his huge brown case, Wellington lumbered down the gangplank, ignoring Eliza's protestations to leave it for the porters. It was apparent that his partner was immune to what he had heard described as "Pharaoh Fever" by travel brokers.

Perhaps this would be a brief stay of only a day or two, and then an airship back to London. No need to prolong this little jaunt if he had to share it with one immune to the wonders of Egypt.

"Mr. Books, Miss Braun?" a voice asked.

Wellington and Eliza turned around to see a tanned gentleman, unmistakably English in his features, with disdain etched on his face. Whether that expression was for him or for his colleagues from headquarters remained a mystery.

"Something I do love about being an archivist for our shadowy Ministry," he said, looking as if he was about to burst out into bitter laughter, "we do not stand on ceremony or secrecy—after all, how dangerous is our position, really?"

Eliza snorted. "You'd be surprised, mate."

Wellington did not care one jot for the way this man was sizing up both him and his partner. The man removed his pith helmet and casually fanned himself as he approach them.

"Marcus Donohue, Ministry Archivist, Egypt Branch." He motioned around him. "Welcome to Hell."

"Dunno about that," Eliza replied, "Australia's outback in the summer makes this place look positively welcoming."

"And Cairo is a pleasant change January in London. Dead of winter and all," Wellington added, "so this is quite nice."

"Quite," he said, looking around him as if incredibly inconvenienced. "Shall we proceed then?"

Wellington nodded and motioned to Eliza. Her scowl assured him that her mind had been made up about their visit to Cairo. Perhaps he would save a lecture on the beauty of Egypt for another trip. Between Eliza's demeanour and the local office's reception, brevity was most certainly in order.

⊷≡◦≡⊷

Egypt had never disappointed Eliza. She still remembered her first case here with Harry. While Paris remained a special jewel in previous assignments and the countryside of Beijing offered ancient mysteries that opened her eyes to amazing possibilities, there was something alluring about Egypt. Harry had taken her to the Giza Pyramids shortly after their arrival, a stop that had absolutely nothing to do with the case they were assigned—but her partner had insisted. They had watched the sun set behind the ancient monuments, and that was when he imparted the importance of this diversion.

To solve a case, to unlock the mysteries of what we deal with, he began, still looking in the direction of where the sun had disappeared, *you need to understand the world around you. Not the world on a whole, but the culture, the people, and the history you are in now. That is your first step in closing a case.*

Eliza still remembered her response: *True, but a fist full of dynamite is also quite handy in unlocking mysteries. Stone pyramids, too.*

He was right, of course, damn him. Her time along the banks of the Nile had been far too brief. It was quite kind of Wellington to try and "broaden her view" of their assignment to Egypt, but she could not voice to her mentor how disappointed she felt.

The truth of it was that Eliza would have loved Cairo if she had been a field agent. However, that goal appeared further and further away. Especially now, returning to the field officially to collect the records of previous cases.

How. Thrilling. The Ministry outpost in Egypt was nestled in one of the many tight alleyways of Cairo and blended in easily with the surroundings. As in their London office, the main foyer and open room were dedicated to cataloguing and inspection of various Ancient Egyptian artefact. That common looting of tombs was encouraged by their Ministry's front office did not improve her mood.

At the back of the receiving room, a single staircase led up to a modest room of four desks. Two of these desks, Eliza knew from previous stations in the Empire, were reserved for visiting agents, while the other two were occupied by those agents local to the area. The gentlemen planted there—finely dressed Egyptians—looked her over, and then disappeared back behind their respective newspapers.

Donohue gave a dry laugh as he continued to another stairwell. "Now, now, gents, do extend a courtesy to our from Old Blighty. I'm sure they will let us on to all that we are failing to notice in our sunny part of the world, yes?"

Up the flight of stairs, was another office decorated with fine antiquities, Egyptian rugs, and against the far wall a pneumatic messaging system that was Ministry-issue equipment.

"Please," Donohue said, motioning to a pair of chairs in front of the desk.

With a quick look to Wellington, Eliza took a seat.

"Is this your first time in Cairo?"

"No," they both said together.

Eliza could see in the corner of her eye Wellington staring at her. She kept her eyes on Donohue.

"Well, thankfully it will be brief. A shame, really," he added, giving Wellington a rakish wink, "missing out on what Cairo has to offer."

"You seem to be doing quite well," Wellington said, brushing a small film of sand and dust free of a Bastet statue. "Egyptian Alabaster. Very nice."

"Privileges of being posted here," he replied dismissively, "and wearing many hats when working overseas with the Ministry of Peculiar Occurrences."

Eliza nodded. "Archivist *and* Field Director?"

"But that does not mean I fail to heed the call of our magnanimous leader," Donohue said sliding a paper bearing the Ministry seal across the desk. "A transfer archived material for cataloguing back in Old Blighty?" He chuckled, sliding the order to one side. "How long do you want this process to take?"

Wellington glanced at Marcus askew. "I beg your pardon?"

"Or will you be reporting this as a 'C.F.' as our predecessors have?"

Wellington straightened. "Whatever do you mean by that?"

"You know, a C.F.? A 'collating fiasco'? That chap who was here last—Whitby, I believe his name was—he knew the game. Reported back to Sound that things were dreadfully in disrepair and insisted on extending his stay here." He shrugged, shaking his head. "My predecessors assured me it was the way of things; one quick message via æthermail and you buy more time to enjoy a bit of the local culture and cuisine."

"Well, Whitby was a bit of a git, now wasn't he?" Eliza snipped. "Buggered off without a word to anyone one day, left the Archives to seed. You're not going to find we're cut of the same cloth."

She caught more movement in her peripheral vision. Hopefully, it was Wellington, beaming with pride. Eliza allowed herself a slight grin.

The proclamation of their ethics seemed to roll off Donohue like water off a duck's back. "An official trip it is, then? Very well. While you load up a hired cart, I'll look into bookings for airships." He jotted down a few notes on the Ministry communiqué, paused, and looked them over as he did on meeting them. "As you all are Ministry stalwarts, I will assume Third Class seating should suffice, yes?"

Wellington leaned forward. "If this will help your office, Mister Donohue, why don't you just direct us to your Archives? We will not trouble you any longer than—"

"Turn around," he interjected. He was looking at flight schedules now.

They both spun about to find six crates behind them. Eliza thought she and Wellington brought more luggage than this.

"That," she began, turning on Donohue, "is *ten years* of cases from Cairo?"

"Yes," he replied, still reviewing travel options for the two of them. "I know this may come as a shock to you, Agent Braun, but as the home office tends to stick their fat noses into our business, we remain watching from our post. Or," he said, suddenly looking up at her with a rather chilly gaze, "we carry out the preliminary work while other agents step in and take credit."

That was when Eliza suddenly remembered Marcus Donohue. The face and the attitude clicked into place. "Now just a minute, mate, Harry and I stepped in only because you lot were dragging your feet!"

Donohue sat up, his grin hardly pleasant or jovial. "Expected, coming from the Ministry elite. But now look at us." He gave a snort. "Two peas, aren't we?"

"Well then," Wellington piped up, shattering the palpable tension, "perhaps we should just collect these cases and head back to London as quickly as possible?"

A sudden metallic *crack* made all three of them jump. Wisps of steam were seeping from one of the "Incoming" tubes. Donohue crossed the room and opened the cylinder.

Donohue returned his eyes to the message, then looked over to her and Wellington.

"Well, it would seem that my day with you, Agent Braun, has been cut short. My presence is needed at police headquarters." He waved the paper in his hand. "Marked 'Urgent' so it must be serious." Donohue grabbed his pith helmet and motioned to the modest archives. "If you are the last ones out, please lock up behind you."

Wellington and Eliza both looked at each other, quite stunned at how this branch could still be in operation in light of Donohue's leadership. From the bottom of the stairwell they heard Donohue call out, "Agent Rateb, grab a memo pad. You're with me."

"Charming fellow," Wellington quipped. Her partner removed his coat and unbuttoned his vest. "Well then, let's get cracking. We should try and at least get an idea of how 'well maintained' these collection of cases are..."

Working with Miss Eliza D. Braun when she wanted to be anywhere else was not for the faint of heart. She had quite the grasp on chilly silences marked with exasperated sighs. Rather than respond, Wellington removed his glasses and pressed two fingers on either side of his nose.

Outside the call to prayer was ringing out, and as if on cue his stomach began to rumble. As he glanced across the top of the boxes, he wondered if now was the best time to suggest a beak for a meal. They had been at this for a good portion of the day, so much so that it was now the evening, and they were they only two souls in the office.

However, the expression on Eliza's face as she rummaged through the box he'd assigned her, suggested it was not a good time to suggest anything unless he wanted to feel the wrath of New Zealand. She was muttering to herself under her breath—another bad sign. He caught 'Donohue', 'self-important moron', and other words that would not have been out of place in the mouth of a sailor.

He was just about to take his chances, when steps thundered up the stairwell. An Egyptian, possessing a finely styled beard, sharply-cut cream suit, and a smart boater-style hat common for the region, burst into the office, panting wildly. Wellington observed Eliza's eyes widen and the hint of a dangerous smile pulled at her lips. She was quite ready to escape the mundane, and this was the sort of readiness that often led him directly into the mouth of madness.

"Where is Director Donahue?" the agent blurted out.

"He is still out, answering an emergency call," Eliza said, before Wellington could get a word in.

He looked at them both, then to the desk, and then tossed the legal pad across the office. Wellington's grasp of the man's dialect was a bit rusty, but he knew it well enough to recognise it as similar words to what Eliza had used earlier concerning Director Donohue.

The agent took a breath, turning his dark gaze to Donohue's desk. "Bastard said he was going to meet me here!"

"We saw you earlier. One of our local agents here in Egypt. We're Agents Eliza Braun, and Wellington Books on assignment from London—"

"—sent to collect your archives for proper cataloguing back in the Ministry Archives," Wellington interjected, hoping to disarm the situation.

Well, *he* thought it was a valiant effort. "Perhaps we can help?" Eliza asked, undeterred by Wellington.

The man was not totally foolish, because he raised a brow in response to this. "The matter is of the utmost urgency and involves the Queen's Own Camel Brigade and Lord Alton Rutland himself."

At the mention of military men and the heir to a duchy, Wellington snapped to attention, his gaze narrowing. "Identify yourself then, and let's be about it."

The man straightened immediately in a similar manner. "Agent Khaled Rateb, currently assigned to Lord Alton Rutland's protection."

Wellington was reaching for his coat before he even realised it. "Explain that while we go."

He dimly heard Eliza race up behind them. "The Camel brigade?"

Agent Rateb shot her a glance. "Yes. The Imperial Camel Brigade is a small, experimental force, designed to move fast and silently in the desert. Part of my assignment is embedding myself with the troops."

They secured the office and began to head into the city itself, the chill of the evening already setting in. Offering his arm to Eliza, the two of them shadowed Rateb as he explained his assignment.

"This experiment is the brainchild of Lord Alton and he is getting quite excellent results," Rateb said. "I was assigned to not only investigate any possible incidents but also protect Lord Alton."

"Lord Alton," Eliza continued to press the man, "he's Duke of Rutland's only heir, correct?"

"Indeed, the very one." Rateb peered around another corner before leading them on towards the far less savoury outskirts of Cairo. "He's a very fine young man, with large responsibilities. This brigade of his is also a testament of his innovation."

"Camels though," Eliza shuddered. "I would think they'd be dreadful animals if you came under fire."

Rateb shared a look with Wellington before replying. "Actually they take it much better, and are less prone to running off."

He led them down a series of narrow alleyways, the closeness of the buildings making Wellington tighten his grip on his cane.

"Donohue and I were called by the Duke himself to keep an eye on his heir. There was some concern that his life was in danger."

"That would explain Director Donohue's reaction to the pneumatic tube," Wellington said to Eliza. "He seemed quite inconvenienced by the message."

Rateb shook his head, appearing to bite back an opinion. He paused, then spoke his words, struggling for control. "After we had met with the Duke of Rutland—"

"Wait," Eliza interrupted, "the Duke was here? *In Cairo*?"

"Yes," Rateb replied.

"Then his concerns for his son were sincere," Wellington added.

"Exactly. I thought this threat, even though it had demanded the attention of the Duke of Rutland, may have been unwarranted until..." The agent shook his head slowly. "You will have to see it to believe it."

They reached the barracks of the Imperial Camel Brigade, located on the edge of Cairo's sprawl. Rateb took them up to the postern gate, removed a lozenge-shaped mechanical device from around his neck and pressed it into a matching symbol in the wall. The gate clicked open.

Wellington was duly impressed. "Security has changed dramatically since my days as a solider."

They slipped into the compound, and immediately Wellington grew suspicious, not of what he heard but of what was notably *absent*. Even in the evening, there were usually lots of noises to be heard in a military encampment, and so it had been when they passed by the barracks of the enlisted soldiers. He had heard the expected cacophony of carousing, music, and laughter. Once they entered this section of the camp—a sequestered area Wellington knew would be "Officers Only" on account of its specialized operations—other than the low *whu-whu* of a pharaoh eagle owl in the distance, a heavy silence lingered. Perhaps security had changed since Wellington was in the military, but soldiers most certainly would have not.

Eliza must have felt something off too, for she had her hand inside her jacket, undoubtedly ready to pull out one of her *ponamu* pistols. With the skin on his back feeling as though it were trying to crawl off his body, and a tumbling knot in the centre of his stomach making him feel rather nauseous, Wellington was for once not going to dissuade her. Working for the Ministry usually led to indescribable strangeness, and this felt decidedly otherworldly.

Agent Rateb paused for a moment, as if he too did not want to go any further. He licked his lips. "Lord Alton and the men loved to gamble in the evenings, but as always I was excused at sundown, and I went to prayers. When I left, the barracks had all been locked up for the night—there was nothing extraordinary. I'd gone every evening in the same way..." His voice trailed off as if examining his routine was dreadfully painful. "Except just before I left, Lord Alton's cousin, Seth Taylor, had surprised him with a visit."

"Seth Taylor?" Eliza asked. "Are you certain it was Seth Taylor?"

"Most certainly. Lord Alton himself identified the man. He was quite affable, and came bearing bottles of wine. When I left he was at the card table with the rest of the officers playing, drinking, laughing…"

Wellington and Eliza shared a glance, and he knew. Wrapping his fingers more tightly about his cane, the archivist jerked his head towards the door. "Show us."

Eliza went in first, but when she came to a sudden stop behind the second door, Wellington almost collided with her…until he saw what had made her halt.

The bodies of ten or so men filled the room, spilled at ungainly angles. Already the whole space was buzzing with flies, even though the blood was fresh. A large, round card table had been tipped over under a solider, still in his uniform hanging from the rafters. His shiny boots were swinging back and forth to the accompaniment of a creaking rope.

"Bloody hell," Eliza whispered, stepping over the body of another man who had taken a shot to the head.

The three of them circled the room, and Wellington was able to make a count: three hangings, five shootings, and two who were disembowelled. He glanced over at Rateb, and wordlessly the agent pointed out young man lying under the card table, a sword still protruding out of his belly. Lord Alton had been discovered.

Eliza bent and touched the neck of the nearest body. "Still warm, so it wasn't long ago. But the angle of the hilt and blade —"

"Agent Braun!" Wellington on bending to examine the bodies a little closer saw the problem immediately. He eyed the pistol still in one of the soldier's grips. "This man's head-wound—"

"They all committed suicide." Eliza came to the same conclusion only a beat behind him. She was examining a man with a knife still in his hands and a slit throat. "This poor lad here did himself in…like that."

"So they are all self-inflicted." Wellington stared around the room, which up until very recently ago must have been similar to the barracks he'd been used to when he'd been in the military. "I've never seen anything like it." He turned to Rateb who was standing at the door, his hands tucked behind his back, and his face stern. "Was Lord Alton in poor spirits?"

Rateb shook his head slowly. "No, not at all. When I left he was laughing and joking along with the rest."

Wellington slowly wandered around the carnage, studying the final moments of the officers. "It is not unheard of for men to go mad, from the sun and heat, or isolation—but none of those were a factor here. For a madness such as this to affect all of them at once..."

Eliza looked up at the man hanging above the table. "Could it have been some kind of suicide agreement that you weren't aware of?"

Now Rateb looked more than a little angry. "We are not heathens here, Agent Braun! The Brigade was in good form—at least it was before this happened to our officers..."

"And this cousin of Lord Alton's," Wellington asked, carefully getting down on his knees to examine the chaos of cards and blood on the floor, "is he among the dead?"

Rateb stepped carefully around the room, checking. "No, these are all brigade officers."

Wellington cast a glace around the collected dead, and then bowed his head to whisper a brief prayer. His thoughts scattered, though, when something gleaming caught his gaze. He went to reach for it, but thought better and pulled out a pencil from his top pocket. "Agent Braun," he said, pushing the stained cards aside, "look at this."

She bent down next to him, inclining her head to one side. "It looks like a coin, but what kind of currency is that?"

When she went to reach for it, he grabbed her arm, and yanked it back. "Let's err on the side of caution, Agent Braun, at least when it comes to handling mysterious objects?" Eliza's brow furrowed. "Do I need remind you of your last assignment in Paris with Agent Thorne?"

"But in that situation, Welly, we *knew* what the artefact was."

"Yes, but did you ever wonder about my predecessor? I've always nursed a lingering suspicion that he had not been so diligent, so look more closely, but don't touch it." Wellington could feel the thrill of discovery course through his veins. "This currency is neither British, nor Egyptian. I believe..." He nudged the coin with his pencil into a handkerchief, and held it up closer to her. "Yes, an Antochan stater. See there—it has the head of the Emperor Augustus on it. It dates back to the Roman occupation of Palestine."

"Very odd thing for a bunch of officers to be wagering with," Eliza commented.

"Yes indeed." He turned to Rateb. "Did you say Lord Alton's cousin had been at a dig in Akeldama?"

The Egyptian agent nodded, his eyes remaining fixed on the gleaming coin.

Wellington couldn't help smiling just a fraction. Could it be that he was actually holding a piece of ancient history in his hand? Something that his friends at the British museum would turn green with envy over?

"Welly!" Eliza snapped, "stop smiling like an idiot and tell us what you know!"

As he poked around the currency, he reminded himself that as amazing as this find could possibly be, this was still the site of an atrocity. "Silver coins, Miss Braun, from an ancient site very near Jerusalem." He gave a soft *"Ah"* as he spied three more coins just like the one in the kerchief. "What—has time in the field erased your memories of Sunday morning church?"

She gave a dry laugh. "My father was a publican. We would be getting the pub ready for the congregation's after church fellowship while the vicar held court."

"Akeldama. The Field of Blood." It was Agent Rateb. His voice sounded hollow, haunted. "This is where Judas Iscariot met his fate betraying the prophet."

"Wait, hold on, mate—you're talking about the Judas Iscariot, as in he who betrayed Jesus Christ?"

"Indeed, and he was paid with thirty pieces of silver." Rateb pointed just in front of him. "There is another coin here."

Wellington pushed the coin into the kerchief. For currency thousands of years old, they gleamed as if minted yesterday. "According to Matthew 27, Judas hanged himself out of guilt. Since those thirty pieces of silver was considered blood money, they refused to return it to the temple's treasury. They instead used the money to purchase a patch of land commonly known as the Potter's Field."

"That's according to Matthew, Welly," Eliza offered. "Acts says that Judas himself used the silver to buy Potter's Field himself, where he then committed suicide." She looked at both men and shrugged. "I said we prepared the pub on Sunday morning, didn't mean we never cracked open a bible."

"Scriptures tend to differ on what happened to the thirty pieces," Rateb said, staring at the silver. "Some accounts claim it was melted down, while others claim the silver was buried with Judas."

"And you're saying," Eliza asked as Wellington bunched up the ends of the kerchief and tied them securely, "these five coins are from the thirty Judas Iscariot was paid with for betraying Jesus? That's…"

He raised one finger. "Before you say 'that's impossible' think of the other objects the Ministry has collected over the years."

"But these are only five pieces," Rateb interrupted, "so, where are the rest?"

Eliza glanced over the dead soldiers once, then twice. "The one survivor of tonight's card game—Seth Taylor. I didn't realise he was related to the Alton bloodline." She shook her head, looking at the card in her hand. "I've dealt with him before, once in Barcelona, another time in Lisbon; both times, confrontations involving the House of Usher. We had nothing on him in Spain, but he left quite a trail of evidence in Portugal. Whispers from the House of Lords were hinting that Taylor's uncle was less-than-happy about his nephew's shenanigans."

"And with Lord Alton here dead at his own hand, nothing stands between him and the title." Wellington said, his eyes falling on the gutted aristocrat on the floor. "It's obviously suicide so there's no blood on his hands."

"But there is," Rateb said, his hands clenching into fist. "Lord Alton was a fine young man. He cared about the people of Egypt, he really did, and now…" the agent gestured to the bedlam around them.

"He should pay," Eliza agreed, "and he will."

No sooner were the words out of her mouth, when a hideous commotion broke out in the compound. The wet roars of camels filled the air, and Wellington knew that something had to be terrifying the beasts. Eliza must have come to the same conclusion. She darted out of the room ahead of him.

Wellington managed to grab Eliza just before she stepped in front of a camel bolting for the main gate. Astride it was a lean young man, working the skirmish saddlebags with both hands. Gatling guns on each side of the camel twirled and snarled at the gate. The wood surrendered to the assault, and when the doors collapsed to the sand with a groan, the camel and its rider galloped out into the night. Without so much as a "thank you" Eliza dashed for the camel enclosure, swearing loudly. Apparently her disdain for the ships of the desert was not feigned. Wellington and Rateb ran after her.

"Those coins are deadly," Eliza said, grabbing hold of the bridle of the nearest, outraged camel. "Imagine what the House of Usher could do with them!"

Rateb tapped Wellington on the soldier. "Give me the coins you found. Showing them to Donohue might inspire him to rouse Agent Noujaim and the local authorities."

"Donohue can find us using the ETS rings," he said, handing the cinched kerchief to Rateb.

It took Wellington a moment to remember how; but with the right manipulation of the bridle, he managed to get his chosen mount to flop down on its knees. The skirmish harness each of the brigade camels wore was kept fastened on five camels just in case of raids from the desert tribes. It made the camels harder to handle than usual though.

Eliza let out a little yell as the camel lurched up. "Finishing school never really prepared me for this sort of sport," she said, running her hands over the controls of the saddle's guns. It was a poor joke, since he'd studied her record and Finishing schools had been spared the delight of educating Agent Braun.

"You're never too old for new experiences," Wellington quipped as he mounted the camel and ascended upward.

"I'm liking this side of you, Books, you know that?"

"Yes, and that scares me a bit," and with a cry, Wellington drove his camel into the night with Eliza right behind him.

Eliza was prepared for neither the stride of the camel, nor the exhilaration she experienced upon riding it. The warm Egyptian wind caressed her face as she and Wellington closed in on Taylor and, under the full moon's glow, she took everything back she ever said derogatory about camels.

Cutting through the darkness ahead were an array of torches surrounding the ancient pyramids. It was a safe assumption, based on Taylor's urging of his mount forward, it was not because he wanted to clock in some very late sightseeing.

"Look there!" Wellington shouted above the noise of the camels, pointing to the right of the pyramid.

Eliza squinted, and could just make out running lights of an airship emerging from the star-filled sky. "It has to be the House of Usher picking up their recruit."

"We can't allow him to reach them!" Wellington shouted, his camel now matching hers.

"Right then," Eliza said, shoving her hands inside the levers of the skirmish saddlebags, "let's see what we have here…"

Wellington's warning was lost in the concussive explosion that shot out from the right saddle compartment.

"Found the rocket launcher!"

Two small explosions briefly overpowered the moon's grey-white luminance. Neither Eliza's nor Taylor's mounts seemed bothered by the ordinance.

"Eliza!"

"Change of strategy!" she shouted just before firing projectile.

This time, the ordinance exploded in front of Taylor. Much like a horse, the camel concluded that forward was not a wise direction in which to continue, so it stopped abruptly, dropping to its knees in the sand. From the way his arms and legs flailed as he soared into the darkness, it appeared Taylor was not prepared for that.

Wellington and Eliza had brought their own camels to a halt and returned to ground just as Seth Taylor found his footing again. He was now at a dead run, making his way towards the nearest pyramid.

Eliza drew her ponamu pistols and gave chase. She had lost him in Portugal. *Not here,* she thought. *Not tonight.*

Above her, the drone of the Usher airship grew louder. Eliza could still make out Taylor in front of her, climbing higher and higher up along the face of the pyramid. She replaced one of her pistols and started her own ascent, but paused on hearing a *clickity-clickity-click-clack* higher up.

The airship was running out a rope ladder and dragging it along the pyramid. She would have to take her stand now.

Eliza stopped, pulled the hammer back on her pistol, and watched the man scrambling just above her. Her shot hit something because she heard Taylor scream, and some loose rock tumbled down the pyramid face. She climbed up another pair of stones, but stopped when a grunt came from Taylor's position. Eliza could just make out the rope ladder in the moonlight, swinging back and forth. On its third pass, Taylor gave a sharp cry and the slack ladder went taunt.

"Go on," she whispered as the airship's engines revved.

More loose rock slid down the pyramid as the Usher airship lifted Taylor free of the structure. He swung wide, struggling to hold on to the rung above his head, one leg dangling useless underneath him.

Eliza waited for Taylor to swing back before she fired. He lurched, slipped free of the rope ladder, and slammed into the jagged pyramid face. He rolled down several shelves before coming to a stop, one arm dangling underneath him.

"Bloody good shot, Eliza," Wellington called from below.

Eliza holstered the pistol then looked over shoulder. "Not really, just lucky."

"A lucky shot in the dark?"

"No," she chuckled, "lucky that white is a fashionable colour here in Egypt."

Eliza adjusted her sun-spectacles as she watched the gangplank of the *Ra* being pushed out. While her features had been less than affable on their arrival, she seemed a bit regretful to be leaving Cairo. She picked up her cup and saucer and took a contemplative sip of tea.

"There's still so much we could do, Wellington," she said suddenly.

"Agent Braun," Wellington said, setting down his own cup, "are we going to have this conversation again?"

"Maybe," she replied, grinning wryly.

"This is a dangerous game you're playing, sneaking in field assignments while we're supposed to be fulfilling archival duties."

"Oh come on, confess—you are starting to enjoy yourself when we break the rules."

Wellington gasped. "I am not!"

Eliza leaned in, pointing an accusatory finger in his direction. "Are you going to tell me you did not feel a thrill when you held in your hand the very silver paid to Judas Iscariot?"

He opened his mouth to protest but his throat seized up. Damnable woman. It was just terrible when she's right. "Perhaps," he admitted begrudgingly. "A bit."

"Ah ha! I knew it," she proclaimed looking terribly pleased with herself, but with nowhere to go her smile faded. "However, there is something perplexing about these silver coins. If handling them meant certain death, how could Seth Taylor carry them about without killing himself?"

Wellington leaned forward. "I received an *æthermissive* from the Jerusalem authorities about Taylor's stay there. Seems that before he came to Cairo, there were several unexpected suicides. One of them was a common offender, but the authorities said he seemed genuinely repentant when caught. The other two, pillars of the community. I would posit that the shame of Judas is only felt by those who have morals to begin with."

Eliza grinned. "Damn, I knew being a proper lady was going to get me in trouble one of these days."

"And this is why I insisted you not touch the coins without some sort of barrier," he said. "I still have hope for you."

The waiter placed a third setting at their table, and Agent Khaled Rateb joined then, his smile mirroring that of the Egyptian sunshine. Wellington almost failed to recognise him with his cheerful disposition.

"Mr. Rateb," Eliza said, tilting her head, "you're looking considerably happier?"

"This is my normal state of affairs," he responded, kissing her offered hand. "I'm afraid earlier you caught me at an inopportune moment." He cleared his throat and shrugged.

"No matter," Wellington responded, toasting him with his teacup. "I'm pleased we happened to be present—" and he stopped to return a stare Eliza was giving him, her accompanying smile far too wicked, "—to assist you."

"As am I." Khaled handed Wellington a polished wooden box that fitted neatly in his hand; carved in it was the Ministry coat of arms. "Here you are, the Cursed Silver of Judas Iscariot."

"Excellent," Wellington said, looking the box over. "It will find a safe and secure home in the Archives."

"I have no doubt."

"You will make sure to keep our involvement to a minimum in your official report?" Wellington asked, ignoring the soft groan from Eliza.

"I have a few more details to add, but in my preliminary report I made certain that your names appear only as logistical support for the Egyptian office. Have no fear."

"Excellent."

A horn blared from the *Ra*, making their heads turn in that direction.

"There you are, your voyage home." Khaled pulled out Eliza's chair, then motioned to the airship. "As a token of appreciation, you will be flying First Class."

"Oh, that was not necessary—"

"But we will accept it graciously," Eliza blurted out.

"And eagerly, it would seem," Wellington said with his eyebrow quirking.

"Mister Books. Miss Braun." With a tip of his hat, Khaled downed the dregs of his tea and departed.

"So where to next?" Eliza asked her partner. "Please say the Bahamas. I can honestly say I have not investigated *any* cases peculiar or otherwise there, so it truly would be a warm getaway." She held up a hand. "But with serious Ministry responsibilities our priority, of course."

"Sadly, no." Wellington pulled out the schedule he and Eliza had left England with. Several offices had been already checked off, and now they were due to head to… "Scotland. Edinburgh offices." He gave a smile and whispered. "Yes, the Edinburgh Express."

Eliza raised a single eyebrow. "Welly?"

"What?"

"You have a look in your eye."

"Oh no," he replied quickly, "No-no-no-no, not at all. It's just…" He looked at the schedule again and nodded. "Eliza, have you ever travelled by hypersteam?"

◆═══◆

Khaled Rateb stopped in the street to look up. Through the opening between the row housing of Cairo, against a cerulean blue expanse, the *Ra* climbed to its cruising altitude. He was duly impressed with the two archivists—certainly not the idiots that Donohue had initially described to Noujaim and himself.

Then again, this was Donohue. Hardly a man of honesty. Or ethics.

He continued his way through the streets to Miggins Antiquities, up the first staircase to the four desks of the agents' receiving area. Zeyad Noujiam was at his desk, hidden behind the paper. Khaled felt a tightness well in his throat on reading the headline concerning Lord Alton's death. A tragic suicide, and a blow to the spirits of both Egypt and England.

Khaled took in a deep breath and asked in his mother tongue, *"Is he here?"*

His fellow agent glanced over the top of his paper. *"Upstairs,"* he replied before snapping it back up.

He climbed the staircase to enter the proverbial lion's den that was the director's office. The six crates that had held the past decade of cases, more precisely the ones that had captured the interest of Donohue and his predecessor, were now en route to London with Agents Books and Braun.

"I assume you have a reason to be up here, Rateb?"

Marcus Donohue was looking at what appeared to be a gold statue of an Egyptian queen his latest acquisition from one of the many excavations happening outside of city limits. Fascinating how the British called what they do "archaeology." He thought of those kind of digs as "grave robbing."

"Agents Books and Braun are en route to London, Director."

"I deduced as much on account of the absence of archives." He narrowed his eyes on the inscription etched in the base of the statuette, the magnifying glass seemingly revealing the secrets of its glyphs.

Seconds ticked by. Khaled remained where he was.

"I take it there is something else?" he asked. Khaled noticed the always-present annoyance in his voice sounded more pronounced now.

"Where were you last night?"

That grabbed his attention. "I'm sorry, Agent Rateb, but did you just ask of my whereabouts?"

"Yes, sir. I did."

"And you are asking this because?"

"Yesterday we were on assignment. You assured me last night that you would remain on watch at least until tonight in order to keep watch over Lord Alton."

"Yes, I know," he said, his eyes still on the statuette, not Khaled, "and that didn't work out so well for Alton, now did it?"

"Sir, when you were needed—"

"No, Rateb, no, when *you* were needed," he said matter-of-factly, "you buggered off to pray."

"Director Donohue," Khaled snapped, struggling to keep his composure, "I was given your word that you would be on call. Had it not been for the archivists, I would have been working alone in keeping a dangerous talisman falling in the hands of the House of Usher."

"Yes, I read your report. Had it not been for the archivists, it would have been a lone Egyptian against—now let me see, what was it, ah yes—a lone agent from the House of Usher." He sat back in his desk, interlocking his fingers together as he considered Khaled. "Throw monkey into a suit it's still a monkey." He stood, crossed around his desk, and stood toe-to-toe with Khaled. "Allow me to remind you, Rateb, that if it weren't for the British Empire and our technology you would not be wearing these fine clothes whilst working for the betterment of Her Majesty but rather begging for scraps covered in your own shit!"

Khaled continued to stare forward into space. He did not expect Donohue to raise his voice in such a fashion. Most uncharacteristic of him. Hopefully, Zeyad heard that.

"Never question my intent or actions. Ever."

"Yes, sir," Khaled muttered.

Donohue stepped back. "I believe you're done here."

"Actually, sir, before they left, the archivists did inform me that Ministry Headquarters are expecting increased occurrences on account of recent archaeological digs."

The director laughed bitterly. "Is that so? How melodramatic."

"This is why," and Khaled pulled out from his coat pocket cinched kerchief, "they have seen it fit to raise your pay. This is an advance on it."

Donohue froze. "Really?"

"Yes, sir."

Donohue took the kerchief from Khaled's hand, undid the knot, and loosed the knot. "Good Lord!" he gasped, eagerly taking and holding it underneath the magnifying glass. "This is legitimate currency."

"Quite."

He chuckled. "I suppose they *are* expecting us to be busy, aren't they?"

"I'll be downstairs if you need me, sir."

As Khaled descended the stairs, he glanced at the director's desk. He silently reminded himself to make certain he got a hold of Agent Book's handkerchief before the investigation launched later on.

Home Alone for the Holidays

by Tee Morris

Christmas Eve, 1896

My name is Archimedes. No, not the philosopher, but that is where my name come from. I am not as unusual as one would think. I sleep. I wake. I eat. Just as any creature of God's creation does after a time on Earth. However, things become peculiar—to coin a word—when we get into specific details of my life.

Hunting is my preferred sport. Not entirely unusual.

I enjoy a good nap in the sunlight. Rather particular, but still not unheard of.

Nothing is more satisfying to me as a treat than a finely smoked salmon, unless it is a freshly killed field mouse.

Yes, I—upon deduction and reason—am a cat.

Before you are rather taken aback by this revelation, please allow me to explain. This *heightened* self-awareness is not entirely unusual. Cats are, by nature, sentient creatures. We are aware of our own existence, pursue a flight-or-fight nature, and know who we can and cannot trust. Our vocabulary, I would be the first to admit, is a bit limiting.

Prey.

Kibbles.

Treat.

Nap.

That is about the sum of a cat's life.

Things changed for me, I would estimate, a few years ago when my hooman…

Oh, old habits, please forgive me…

Things changed a few years ago when my *human*—a rather clever gent by the name of Wellington Thornhill Books, Esquire—changed my meal routine.

While the details of my earlier life are a bit sketchy, I do recall moments as a stray. I found myself whisked away by accident to the outskirts of London to the neighbourhood where Master Books resides. I recall rain, finding shelter on his stoop, and I laid my head down to die. It seemed inevitable on account of my own malnutrition. Imagine my surprise, though, when I awoke to a warm fire, a bowl of cream, and a pair of hazel eyes staring at me.

"Don't fret, little one," Books said to me then. *"You have a home, if you wish."*

I was introduced to tuna that night. Quite the dish to me, at the time.

Master Books has always been concerned about my health since that time, but after a few months of struggling to find adequate sustenance, he offered me a new meal, a rather interesting mix of chicken and fish. *"I have been charged to have you try this,"* he said in a tone that I recognise now as "skeptical" to which he added, *"but if I find you dead by your bowl, I will have Axelrod's guts for garters."*

The new food was delightful, far more delightful to my palate than Spratt's Patent Cat Food. It was within a month of dining, though, I noticed the changes. I was aware of my human's words and the overall tenor of them, but it was when he told the rather friendly old lady next door, Miss Penelope Hufflebottom, to keep an eye on his modest home. *"I shan't be gone for more than a week or so."*

In that moment, I felt a flutter of panic until it dawned on me that a "week" was a scant seven days.

The more of the food from this amazing man called "Axelrod" I ate, the more I comprehended the world around me.

While I was unable to verbally or physically communicate with my human, a limitation on account of physical anatomy, I did make it clear in my habits that this was the food I preferred. After I made the deduction—a skill that I truly adored developing—that there was a direct correlation between the kibbles and my growing conscience, I was afraid of losing it. Stubborn as I was about the food, there were times that "Axelrod" could not produce it. Fortunately, after going a spell or two without any of this special recipe, I came to a conclusion that whatever agent resided in it had taken a permanent hold. Thanks to this wonderful "quack" and "crackpot" as my human referred to him as, I had become truly self-aware.

Now, in my present state, I am aware of several things: It is currently Christmas Eve, a cold snap continues tonight over London Town, and Master Books has been away for a rather long time. Miss Hufflebottom has not been derelict in her duties though, tending to both me and the growing collection of correspondences. When left to my own devices I have managed, with great effort on my part, to unfold the newspaper. I have found that keeping up with both local and global affairs of humans gives me a new insight on them. Today's *Daily Telegraph* featured Christmas wishes from Queen Victoria and excitement over something called the Diamond Jubilee. Preparations were underway, promising a grand spectacle. The Duke of Sussex, Peter Lawson, was quoted that *"This Diamond Jubilee would usher in a new age of enlightenment, prosperity, and glory the likes of which the Empire had never seen."*

Humans are quite odd when it comes to their ages of enlightenment, prosperity, and glory. They really have no idea how lucky they are that there were not more felines such as your dear narrator. On an intimate level, we possess the ability to alter schedules to our whims. An entire Empire under the rule of sentient cats?

The thought just makes me purr with delight.

My eyes narrow on another story of a bizarre death in the streets of London. The lady's name struck me as familiar. Deidre Kinkaid. Found buried underneath the floorboards of a recently renovated building in Whitechapel.

"Not now, Archimedes," my human chided as he removed me from his lap. Self-awareness has not changed in any way the truth that my human's lap is still a preferred place to nap. *"I have to finish this spot of research, and I have been warned by Doctor Sound that Miss Deidre Kinkaid is a stickler for details."*

Agent Kinkaid? She was a Ministry agent. Much like some of the other tragic accidents I've read about.

I look to the door, and feel a swell of expectancy. If my human were to appear, I would be at ease, but it has been months. What could he be doing? If he were to leave for a long time, and he knew that was a possibility when he met Agent Eliza Braun as they were undertaking in secret a collection of unsolved cases, he would have said as much.

"Books, are you ready?" she had asked him.

"Just a minute." That was when he turned and looked down at me. *"Now, Archimedes, Miss Braun and I are going away for a weekend in the country. No need for Miss Hufflebottom to check on you. I'll be back before you know I'm gone."*

"*He'll bring you some barramundi for any inconvenience,*" Miss Braun added.

When he returned from that rather long weekend, he was leaning on a cane with a foot bandaged up rather soundly. He told me of his harrowing adventure with this group calling themselves the Phoenix Society, the narrow escape from their manor, and how Miss Braun had closed the Rag & Bone mystery plaguing her and her recently deceased partner, Harrison Thorne. I know he was telling me this as he had no one else to tell, not they he knew of my own enhanced state; but like any faithful cat, I listened, blinked when appropriate, and nudged his hand with my furry head. He was rather shaken by the whole experience, but he did confide in me something quite exciting. "*Archimedes, Miss Braun dragged me into this intrigue under extreme protest, and yet I have never felt more alive. What you make of that?*"

That was when I knew Agent Eliza Braun was a most delightful woman.

Perhaps that was where he was at present. Off on some grand mission for Queen, Country, and Empire. I know the Ministry has been keeping him quite busy, busy enough that Miss Hufflebottom has been here to make certain I have cream, my dry food, and the occasional treat of tuna. I find it rather sweet that Miss Hufflebottom has decorated my human's home for the holidays. She has put in the bay window a small tree, decorating it in silver and gold ornaments. I sometimes sleep under the modest decoration. It is my tradition at this time of year. She also hung holly and gave our home a delightful, Christmas atmosphere.

I did miss Wellington, though. We had spent a few Christmases together, just us men. A rather nice way to enjoy the holidays, but I also knew he was a bit lonely. However, last year, we were joined by Miss Braun. Apparently, there had been a rather unorthodox Christmas Eve for them, but I had never seen my human laugh that way. He was delighted with the company, as was I. She fed me a bit off her plate. Watching my human and this lady together made me purr that much louder, something Miss Braun made note of.

If they were together, maybe then my human would be safe. So nothing to fear. I returned to my paper and saucer of milk. Hopefully, I wouldn't find any other alarming stories of calamity befalling a Ministry agent.

The scratching at the door snatched my attention. Had my human returned finally after months in the field?

Anticipation turned to dread on seeing two men, wearing what could only be described as a ghastly pattern of tweed, crouched by the main lock. They were attempting a break-in.

What cads!

My ears twitched at the sound of the lock disengaging.

"Right then, Turkish," one of these ill-dressed lummoxes began, "you got that barking-iron of yours close?"

I did not care for the sound of compressors priming as the human called "Turkish" brought into the light a modified Bulldog. "Yeah, Tommy, and it's loaded, so let's make quick work of this little caper."

"Well, keep them eyes peeled. This is the Archivist we're talking about."

Turkish dropped his weapon. "Now what makes you think the Archivist would be daft enough to come home? After all this time?"

"It's reasoning, it is," Tommy insisted. "Think about it—the Department been on the lookout all this time, an' no sign of 'em for months. That Books character's a smart one, so he lays low, then decides after a time 'Right, the Department's looking all over the place for me, but I can come home, get a few baubles, and then be on my merry way.' because this would be the last place we look for him."

"You come up with that all on your own?" asked Turkish.

The shorter human shrugged. "Spent some time reading that Arthur Conan Doyle bloke. Been working on my skills of deductible reasoning."

Deductible reasoning? Why God chose humans over cats in gracing them with opposable thumbs and advanced motor skills sometimes baffled me.

Turkish shook his head and lifted up his weapon once more. "Just shout if you see anything."

I only knew of certain nefarious organisations on account of Master Books. House of Usher, the Illuminati, the Phoenix Society. However, I knew nothing of this "department" other than they were invading his home.

Right then, time for countermeasures.

I tried to cross the room as quietly as possible, but I was long overdue in trimming my own claws. They were not only longer than I preferred, but rather noisy across the wooden floor.

"Tommy," Turkish whispered tersely, "you hear that?"

Looking behind me, I could hear floorboards creaking. Apparently, it was Turkish who decided to follow me towards the kitchen. I hopped up to the countertop and gently scratched against the red button set in the wall. The control panel revealed itself with a soft, low hum that the human may have heard, but he would not have known what it pertained to. Had Turkish done so, he would have called out to Tommy and strongly urged him to flee our house. I hooked my paw around the switch labelled "Kitchen Corridor" and tugged.

Springs activated above Turkish's head, and I watched the wood panel over him slide back. The kettlebell dropped and continued to swing forward, catching Turkish square in the nose and knocking him backward.

"Turk!" called Tommy as he thundered down the stairs. "Turk!"

"Why don't ya call louder," he grumbled, covering his nose as he slowly pulled himself up. "Don't think the neighbours heard you!"

"I think your nose is broken."

"Well, set it!"

"Alright, alright, alright…" I watched the shadows against the wall of Tommy holstering his own side arm and straddling Turkish. He should have been gently placing fingers on either side of his nose if he knew what he was doing. "This is going to hurt, mate."

The soft *crunch* of bone and Turk's howl of pain served as cue for me to hook my paw on the second switch marked *"Teacher's Tool"* and pull. The pneumatic spring underneath Tommy shot the floorboard up into him posterior, and sent him forward, head first.

Into Turk's nose, which crunched on impact with Tommy's head.

"What the bleedin' hell?!" swore Tommy over Turk's groans. "Blimey, mate! Let me fix ya…"

"Ya' don' enough, Tommy," Turkish growled. "Jus' gimme a minute."

Hearing that *crunch* once more was most assuring. While listening to Turk groan yet a second time in just a few minutes, I went to bop with my head the button that would hide the kitchen's control panel; but paused. I had to reach another set of countermeasures, but I would need to give myself a moment's lead.

I flipped the switch marked *"Christmas at Hyde Park"* before bopping the button and scampering for the back door.

I could hear the rush of water through the pipes as I slipped through the smaller cat door. The water began to sprinkle against the stairs and stoop just as I leapt for the ledge. I carefully managed my way along the windowsill and then hopped to the other. Reaching the lattice should not be a problem, provided…

"Pipe down, mate," Tommy barked. "Didya hear that? It came from the kitchen. Someone's in here." Even from where I sat outside, the man's footsteps thundered to the back door. "Yeah, the hatch is swinging here." The door opened as he called, "Come on out, Books!"

It was a real credit to the man he managed to get that out before his foot stepped into the fresh ice. His body seemed to hang in the air for a moment—maybe two—before his body landed hard against the stoop.

Actually that is not quite right. As the threshold was a few inches elevated from the stoop, only the lower half of him landed there. The upper-half, at least from his lower back up to his head, landed on the kitchen floor. I wondered what hurt more—the feel of his head when it impacted with the floor, or the pain of his back as it connected awkwardly with the small step at the threshold.

"Tommy?" Turk called. From the sounds of his footsteps, he was at a full run. "You see 'im?"

"Stay… back…" Tommy managed to groan. For naught.

Turkish cleared the threshold and his foot landed at the far edge of the stoop. On account of his centre of gravity, his foot quickly slipped from under him. Fortunately, he was clear of the doorway so there was no chance of him racking his back against the threshold. However, this meant he would feel the icy stoop fully against his back on landing.

"Bloody hell," Turk groaned, slowly turning on his side. "What kind of ballyhoo is this?

Tommy had come to a sitting position, his voice sounding strained. The poor sod was in a lot of pain, apparently, even as he was reaching up to help his partner. "I'm thinking this whole place has traps around it."

"Really, Tommy?" he asked, taking his hand rather firmly. Did he not see his mate was in pain? "Whatever gave you that notion?"

The two struggled for a moment against the fresh ice and each other, finally coming to rest in the doorway. I returned my attention to the lattice and my own climb up to the second floor. My tail quickly shifted from one side to another as I ascended to the ledge.

Oh, this is the part I always loathe. Even before I became aware. Making the jump from lattice to ledge.

A quick glance up and another to the ledge, and then I pushed. Feeling the bricks underpaw was most satisfying. I crept along to the second level entryway Wellington had built for me. The hatch was an embodiment of his concern in light of my predisposition to walk along the house's narrow ledge. Slipping through the small access hatch, I looked around the modest room.

This was my human's workroom. One of them anyway. He creates incredible feats of scientific engineering here, far smaller than the ones he creates in the basement. I prefer it when he works here as the mishaps are better contained than others. In one of the boxes lining the side of his desk is where I find what I need. My nose twitches at the smell of what I believe my human calls *sulphur*. Yes, this is exactly what is required. I stick my head into the box, hook my teeth into the ornate design of the small sphere's casing, and adjust my balance on account of the object in my mouth. How I walk from this point must be quite deliberate, and most careful. Otherwise, I may literally lose my head over this.

Desktop. Chair. Floor. The sphere shudders in my mouth lightly, but once the vibration subsides, I pad my way to the door.

"There's no one on this floor," I hear from downstairs. Turk. "How about we go and take a look topside?"

"Hold on," and the distinct sound of a large-calibre pistol caused my ears to perk up.

"What in the blue blazes, Tommy?" Turk asked.

"Enfield Mark VI. Added velocity to the bullets via multiple compressors. Optional chamber for shells that'll explode on impact." Tommy sniffed. "Thought it might come in handy seein' as we was coming for the archivist."

"Oh yeah, Tommy, then once we bag the bookworm, we put you out front Department headquarters so you can stand guard… *before ze Germans come.*"

Tommy snorted. "Get off. Ya' can't blame a bloke for being prepared."

"Fine then. You take the lead."

I quietly set the sphere on the floor and crept over to the small control panel similar to the one in the kitchen. Wellington had apparently designed this room to serve as a last stand against intruders such as the ruffians who were now invading our home. He would have stood in this doorway, armed with an offensive weapon of some description while launching countermeasures from the control panel that would have been at foot level for a human. Just under eye level for me. I heard a floorboard creak. Tommy was at the fourth step. My eyes returned to the six switches, and I rubbed my chin against the one farthest to the right. I believe that was the correct one.

At the very least, the switch felt good against my chin. Oh, how I do love a good chin rub!

The switch gave way, and I heard the panel in the stairwell slide back, releasing the nine-pound wooden bowling ball my human had secured to a strong section of hemp. The ball I heard cut through the air.

"Eyes up, Tommy!" Turk shouted.

"Wha—" was all that Tommy managed before the bowling ball connected with his face. I looked into the hallway just in time to catch the moment of impact which lifted Tommy off the stair and sent him flying past his partner. From the sound of his impact against the floor, Tommy would have quite the sore back in the morning.

Turk, however, had somehow manage to stay in the stairwell. Whether it was pressing himself against a wall or merely ducking under Tommy, I could not be certain but I could hear feet pounding against the steps as he shouted, "Give yourself up, Books! Ya' just make it worse."

Oh dear. I leapt up on my back legs briefly and drove my right paw into the second switch. With a click, gears and cogs clattered from beneath me, the second floor hallway, and the staircase.

Turk had managed to reach the last step before the stairs underneath him disappeared. His chin connected hard with the landing just before he slid down a smooth ramp and landed clumsily on top of Tommy. I used my snout to flip the switch back to the neutral position, and with a rapid clamour from underneath the floor, the steps reappeared.

That was when I nudged the small sphere down the hallway to the top of the staircase.

"Tommy," Turk groaned, "you still with me?"

"Not if you keep laying here," Tommy groaned back.

Humans are a funny lot.

With just the slightest of nudges, the small sphere began a slow bounce down the staircase. On each impact against the wooden tread, the volatile gel within it began to glow brighter. If I understood Wellington—and I believe I did—I would have enough time to hide in the master bedroom.

"What is that?" came Tommy.

"I don't know," Turk insisted. "It's coming from the—oh bugger!"

The flash from downstairs cast my furry shadow against my human's door for an instant. Then I heard the intruders moan.

"Christ, Turk, I'm blind!"

"You're not blind, ya' cloth-eared git! It was a flash bomb!" I peered around the corner to see the two rapscallions struggling to get back to their feet. "I don't know if it's Books or someone else, but we're not alone in this house!"

No, you are certainly not.

I padded down the steps, intending to slip beyond Tommy and Turk. So far, I had carried out countermeasures Alpha and Beta. Perhaps it was time to enact Gamma. These last set of countermeasures, I recall my human telling me, would be the final straw that would break a camel's back if intruders were to weather the storms of the previous two.

What? You find it odd that my human would talk to me about such things? Tell me you never talk to your cat about many strange aspects of your life. Cat. Dog. Bird. Even something as exotic as a tarantula. Yes… we are paying attention, as it turns out.

Now, where was I? Oh yes—Countermeasures Gamma…

My plan should have been a flawless operation. Temporarily blind the intruders. Slink past immobilised said-intruders. Make for the parlour where the third set of countermeasures would be. As I had the advantage of four legs and low centre of gravity, this should have been a doddle.

What I had not anticipated was Turk managing to shield his eyes before the blast. His hand grabbed for me, and while my human's countermeasures made both he and Tommy out to be bumbling dolts, Turk's reflexes were hardly clumsy. He managed to grab my back right leg and pull.

"Gotcha!" Turk barked.

I let out a howl. The only warning he would get from me. Just because I was somewhat round in shape, did not mean any of it was jelly.

While I am a furry cat, I am rather toned under my coat, due in part to Axelrod's dry food. I twisted in my captor's grasp and sank my fangs into the first piece of flesh I could find. What I had found was the thick, meaty muscle around his thumb. I tasted the human's blood—and no, not a pleasant flavour at all. I much prefer sparrow or field mouse to humans which, I can assume, is good for humans. I must have really thrown a lot into this bite as I felt my back end swing free. Turk had let me go.

I, on the other hand, had not.

"This bloody monster!" he screamed, lifting his arm up, and me along with it.

As much as I would have loved to deal a bit more damage, I could not afford to take a chance and have Turk hurl me against a wall. I wrenched myself free and fell awkwardly against the wood floor. My limbs scrambled for purchase, but for a moment all I heard were the sounds of my claws scratching against the floor.

When I finally felt myself upright and sprinting, Turk was back on his feet. "It's a bleedin' pussycat! We're being bamboozled by a cat!"

The countermeasures were just around the corner. My greatest concern—which countermeasures? Should I trigger "Newton's Folly" or perhaps "Close Shave" was needed?

I came around the corner, but Turk was standing before me. He must have cut through the library to reach the parlour.

"Ya'see him, Tommy?" Turk called out.

"Yeah, I see him," and I glanced over to my left. Tommy was standing once again, blinking madly. If I didn't know about the flash bomb, I would have taken his odd tick as being his insistence of trust in me. "Bleedin' furball ain't getting past me!"

The floorboard creaking whipped my gaze back to Turk. "Here, kitty-kitty…"

Kitty-kitty? Dear Lord, humans can really be trite at times.

"Don't run, you precious, furry bastard," he cooed. "Just gotta catch ya' and turn you into a muff so you don't make our job any more complicated."

I started to creep back, my eyes darting between the two men. I could make it back to the kitchen, but that would leave these men in my human's house. *Our home.* That was unacceptable.

"Tommy…shoot it!"

What?

"What?"

Turk finally took his eyes off me. "You heard me—shoot the cat!"

"You're joking, you are."

I started to turn my head to Tommy, but sudden kissing noises from Turk grabbed my attention. Damned instincts. No matter how keen my intelligence, the instincts will always be there.

"Tommy, I'm keeping kitty-kitty here distracted. I suggest you shoot him."

"I ain't shootin' no cat!"

Very good, Tommy. Stand by your morals.

"Tommy, now is not the time to take some high ground."

"What sort of monster shoot a cat?" Tommy said with a huff. "That's just wrong!"

Turk's shoulders dropped. "Fine. Then you shoot Books when we find him," he said as he drew from his coat the earlier mentioned Bulldog pistol.

"Fair enough, if you can live with yourself."

I heard the gun click as Turk pulled its hammer back. "I'll sleep just fine tonight."

Oh dear…

Both Turk and I gave a start when the front door blew free of its hinges. I should have bolted as Turk did, now running back through the parlour and library, but I felt the instincts—the curiosity ones—keeping me rooted to the spot. Something fired, but I could not be sure it was a firearm as it sounded more like an object launched from some sort of air compressor. Whatever whipped through the air caught Tommy off-guard and, on hearing his body hit the floor, off-balance.

"Tommy?" Turk called out.

"I think I broke my nose...again!" Tommy said.

Turk's gun fired, and then came the low thrum of focused energy displacement, a rather odd sensation when such a wave runs the length of your pelt. I think the last time I experienced such a thing, I did not set foot in Wellington's basement laboratory for well on a month. The floor underpaw shuddered, so I could assume that whatever the blast was it had effectively immobilized Turk.

I slowly crept forward, my own silence matching the one that had befallen our home. The quiet did not last, sadly.

"Turk?" called Tommy. He was lying in the main hallway, tied up by what appeared to be South American bolas. As his arms were secured tightly to his sides, he failed to get back to his feet. He seemed to be unable to even reach a sitting position. "Turk? What's going—"

The gloved hand whipped off Tommy's cap and buried itself into his hair. With a quick snap, Tommy's head went back and then into the hardwood floor. He was knocked unconscious at the moment of impact.

I stepped back again as my gaze slowly went from prone intruder to triumphant saviour.

Her smile was kind, just as I remembered it. "Quite the evening, wouldn't you say, Archimedes?"

Miss Hufflebottom?

She set down what I instantly recognised as a carrier. "You probably won't like this but—"

Without a second thought, I darted towards her and disappeared into the large box.

"Well now," she said as she closed the carrier's door. I crept next to the mesh and saw her reach up to a small device secured to her shoulder. Pressing down the device's arm created a bright blue-white spark that she spoke into. "Control, this is Ministry Auxiliary Agent 7825. Situation neutralised. Over."

The device went dark until the spark returned, this time with a voice coming from it. "Acknowledged, 7825. Rendezvous at coordinates. Maintain radio silence. Over."

"Acknowledged, Control. Over, and out." She gave a slight sigh and then peered into my carrier. "Well now, Archimedes, we have quite the journey ahead of us. Not that I expect you to know about Hebden Bridge, but I think the country will suit your disposition just fine." I then felt the world lurch slightly as she stood, carrying me to the door. "I just hope you will not mind riding for so long with Victoria."

Victoria? Well now, this evening is getting grander by the moment. Victoria was Miss Hufflebottom's feline companion. A rather fetching ginger-coloured Siberian.

We were in the foyer, and she showed no signs of slowing.

The volume and tenor of my meow stopped her abruptly. "What? Are you hurt, Archimedes?"

Oh, this would be tricky. I had only one chance to do this. If I recall, it was a prolonged coo with a long meow. Not a howl, but a rather pronounced meow.

"Dashitall," she swore, "Agent Books did say you were a rather particular eater."

My crate was set down and I watched through the door window as Miss Hufflebottom hustled back to the kitchen and reappeared a moment later carrying the bag of Axelrod's cat food. I cooed in approval.

"Yes, yes, yes," she said, scooping up my crate, "now let's not dally any longer. We have quite the journey ahead of us."

My prolonged purr rolled into a very strong meow.

"Once we get moving," she insisted.

We crossed the empty street and I heard a small latch disengage and the squeak of what sounded like a tiny door opening. Before I could find out any more, my carrier opened and I dropped into a larger crate.

In the darkness, a pair of golden eyes stared at me. *Oh. It's you.* She was in a coy mood tonight. Perhaps Victoria did not travel well.

Good evening, Victoria, I said pleasantly.

Now while I did say earlier I lacked the ability to communicate with humans, I discovered my communication with other cats had evolved quite quickly. I found that reading another cat's thoughts was rather simple. Child's play, really. However, to hold conversations, that was not to be. Unless, of course…

"There you are," Miss Hufflebottom said, as she placed a bowl of Axelrod's kibble between us. "I hope you don't mind sharing with Victoria."

Not at all.

Victoria was immediately into the food. I don't think it was out of hunger. More out of pleasure as the food was incredibly satisfying. In so many ways.

And how is this batch of Axelrod's food? I purred. Just a tiny aural nudge. I think she found it charming. *Is it to your liking?*

Victoria looked at me, her eyes narrowing. *It is adequate. I have very particular tastes.*

I have no doubt, Victoria.

Our crate shuddered as a rumble rose from underneath where we were.

Victoria's eyes went even wider. *What is that infernal noise?*

I do believe we are in a motorcar.

"Ready are we, my darlings?" Miss Hufflebottom asked. "Next stop: Hebden Bridge! If we make good time, we may reach the rendezvous before Christmas dinner."

I do think it is rather adorable, I began, drawing close to my fellow feline, *how our humans talk to us. I wonder how they would react if we were to reply one day?*

They have their uses, Victoria said with just a hint of disdain.

All an act, I knew. I have seen her cuddle several times with Miss Hufflebottom. Her attempts at superiority I found rather delightful.

We are off on an adventure, it would seem, I offered.

Victoria huffed. *My fur will be ruffled.*

I tucked myself into the corner of our crate and began to purr. *Tosh, Victoria, this will provide us with a new experience and time together. Now, do come and join me.*

She looked at the kibble, then back to me. With one last huff, she crept over to where I had made myself comfortable and nuzzled next to me. It had been quite a day, as Miss Hufflebottom had observed so Victoria was in no danger of any amorous intentions on my part. Then again, I had no idea how long of a voyage lay ahead of us. Her purr taunted me, and it made me wonder. If she were also enjoying the benefits of Axelrod's kibble, would our *kittens* enjoy it as well; or would they be born with such gifts as what we shared? And what if this ability to share thoughts were to evolve beyond the two of us, or even our family? How would my human react if we were to share an actual conversation?

Perhaps we would find out on reaching this place called Hebden Bridge. Something told me this adventure had many more days ahead…

And treats. Treats, most assuredly.

The Evil that Befell Sampson

by Pip Ballantine

"We all know you are the best person to deal with peculiar things," Mrs. Kate Sheppard smiled at the younger woman standing before her, "And quite frankly what has been going on is most peculiar indeed."

Though she was asking for help from Eliza D Braun, Field Agent in the South Pacific Branch of the Ministry of Peculiar Occurrences her tone was warm and friendly. However, even though they had known each other for a long time, more than a quarter of Eliza's life, she still did not feel entirely comfortable around the older woman. Hero worship would do that to pretty much anyone who entertained it. Even more so, when that very same heroine is was one that Eliza hoped could be her mother-in-law given time.

So the younger woman had tried to shake it off many times, but it stubbornly clung to her psyche. Mrs. Sheppard was everything the Agent strove to be: brave, kind and gentile. The first Eliza had easily mastered, the second she managed on occasion, but the third often eluded her.

Kate sat on a walnut parlour chair upholstered in emerald green in the sunshine, her fine white-blond hair fairly gleaming, and her hands folded on her lap. At her side, a small doily-covered table held a steaming teapot, two cups, and a selection of little biscuits. Mrs. Sheppard's posture was erect and firm. She could have taught it in a finishing school.

A more graceful example of Victorian womanhood could not have been found, and yet Eliza was aware that many in New Zealand thought of her as the most dangerous person in the country. She peddled radical ideas, would not be silenced, and encouraged others to rally around her. In other words, she was the pre-eminent suffragist in the nation.

Eliza was both fascinated and terrified of her. Though she worked for the Ministry, she was still a suffragist, and proud to wear the white camellia.

She cleared her throat. "I'm glad to be of assistance, Mrs. Sheppard. However I hope Douglas told you I am the most junior field agent in the Ministry. I should caution that I might find nothing at all."

The suffragist's remarkable blue eyes fixed on the young woman, examining her with the intensity of a hawk. "You've shown a lot of promise, Eliza, and my son has nothing but good things to say about you—not to mention you are one of the few female agents in the Ministry. All that makes you rather special."

"I try, Mrs. Sheppard," Eliza murmured, not quite sure what to do with this unexpected compliment.

"Since we are to be working together you need to stop calling me that. I insist you call me Kate." She turned and began to pour the tea from the blue and white pot. "Milk? Sugar?"

"Both please." Eliza was grateful of the moment this little ritual afforded her, since she was not quite sure how to broach the next subject. So she did what she always did, ploughed forward.

As she took the cup from Kate, she ventured her real concern. "The trouble is that the Ministry has had no cases from Dunedin in the last six months. So I couldn't really tell them what I am doing here. I had to make up some excuse about a sick aunt."

Kate's lips twitched. "I am happy to play that role if it means you can help the movement." She leaned forward. "You see, the reason that it hasn't been passed to the Ministry, is because all the men do not find it peculiar at all."

The tea really was a most excellent Darjeeling. Eliza took another long sip before replying. "Then I have an advantage over them. Please tell me what has been going on?"

"The men call it women coming to their senses." Kate stirred her second cup of tea, concentrating deeply on doing so; the annoyance her voice gave away was consequently slight. "I am sure you know we have had a tradition of many strong and stalwart supporters in this town. The women of Dunedin have in fact weathered many attacks by that cad Henry Smith Fish."

"I had heard he was starting his own petition against the female franchise."

"Yes, by herding up drunken men while they are in the public houses." Kate's smile was sharp. "Everyone saw right through that tactic though, and I am afraid the new names people invented for him were rather…cutting."

Eliza had heard that too, and smiled right along with her hero. "'The talking fish', 'flapping fish head' and 'fish out of water'? It is all really too easy with his last name."

Kate tiled her head. "Yes, well despite all that humour, Mr. Fish is a dreadful opponent, and we were all keeping an eye on him. What we were not expecting was our own ladies to turn on us."

"Pardon?" Eliza froze in place. She was well acquainted with the ladies of the suffrage movement, and the idea that they would abandon that cause was unbelievable. She would have almost expected Mr. Fish to wear the white camellia before that would happen.

"I am afraid so." Kate stared down into her cup. "Our strongest supporters, those with the most influence and money, have begun wearing the red camellia." She picked her own white flower from her buttonhole and glanced at it. "Even Miss Burgess, who is nearly seventy and has been committed to the cause her whole life. Even she has changed coat, and will no longer receive my calls."

It was impossible to know what to say, so instead Eliza got to her feet. "She will not however refuse a visit from a government official! I shall see to this at once."

The older woman rose too. "Thank you, Eliza. I am dreadfully busy with getting the petition to parliament, but this has been worrying me. I really can't understand it at all."

The agent dipped her eyes away, her heart swelling with the opportunity to shine before Douglas and his mother. "Leave it with me," she paused, "Kate."

The suffragist saw her to the front door. "Mabel is an old lady, Eliza. If you can find out why without using any of your more…extreme methods that would be best."

Eliza gave her a crooked smile. "I promise not to blow anything up, just to prove a point."

The suffragist laughed as she held the door open. "I know you will do your best—but I shall not expect miracles."

The house of Miss Mabel Burgess was far more impressive than that of Mrs. Sheppard. It towered on top of the hill, looking down the valley at less fortunate and deserving houses. Miss Burgess had apparently been born to money as well as the suffrage movement. Quite the potent combination!

Eliza rang the doorbell, was admitted, and dropped her calling card onto the tray offered to her by a rather elderly maidservant.

She was shown into the library while the card was delivered, and only had to wait a few moments before the maid returned at quite a lively pace. She was then ushered into the receiving parlour of Miss Burgess.

Eliza had never had the honour of meeting such a prominent and wealthy member of the movement. For some reason it was as if they thought she couldn't be trusted to behave around such ladies. On consideration, it probably because of an incident with the Mayoress of Palmerston North—but that woman was certainly no lady. However today was different. Today Eliza was on her best behaviour.

Miss Burgess sat in a sea of lace and faded beauty on a rose coloured chaise longue. Her smile was so soft and kindly that it was hard to imagine she had any bitterness towards her lot in life. Money would do that—make up for a lot of difficulties. Yet, Eliza had heard the stories. She knew that in her time Miss Burgess had been a powerful and committed suffragist. She'd broken windows, and even flown an ornithopter to the top of the Houses of Parliament in Westminster, to hang a gaily coloured pennant from the rooftops. It had proudly proclaimed, 'Same life, same rights!'

Now that she was supposedly in her dotage, she had been no less ardent in New Zealand—doing her bit and flummoxing men.

Yet, three weeks ago she had withdrawn her considerable personal and financial support from the movement, stopped replying to missives from the Council and shut herself away. She rose to greet Eliza and smiled endearingly. "Miss Braun, is it? I hear you are working for the Ministry of Public Health…my goodness what a job for a lady!"

Eliza could not have been more surprised if Miss Burgess had jumped up and done the can-can on her sideboard. Kate was right—there was something seriously wrong here.

Still, she managed to not let any of her shock show on her face. Instead, she took the offered seat and tried to imagine herself into a role in which the prime danger was from paper-cuts. Flicking open her leather case, Eliza rummaged through it and pulled out a piece that she had only typed up this morning.

"Miss Burgess," she put on her most stern voice, borrowed from her mother, "I have come to enquire as to your contact with Mr. Henry Smith Fish."

"Pardon?" the old lady looked positively white at questioning before even one cup of tea had been drunk. "How did you—"

"Find out you had entertained him?" Eliza smiled, glad that her hunch had paid off. In Dunedin if there was anything anti-suffragist going on, Mr. Fish was at the bottom of it. She fixed the lady of the house with a steely gaze, and quite wished she had found a pair of spectacles to peer over. "This is a small town you know, and people do talk?"

"But why would the Ministry of Public Health be interested in..." Miss Burgess paused, and then clenched her fingers around the arm of her chair. "Oh my..." she breathed, and then shook her head. "No, I can't possibly think that of Mr. Fish." The elderly lady was being far too kind—Fish was known throughout the town as quite the reprobate.

Eliza was smiling on the inside. She didn't care a jot if Henry Smith Fish's reputation was sullied—besides in its current state that was rather unlikely. "Well, I can't really say, Miss Burgess—but I need to know the details of his visit. It puzzles me you see, since you used to be such an ardent suffragist that you would let him cross your threshold."

Her host folded her hands on her lap. "Yes, I used to be. I recall not being entirely happy when he turned up on my doorstep." She frowned. "But I eventually called for tea and listened to him. He was quite pleasant talking about a purchase he had made for his wife."

"That was all you talked about?" Eliza frowned, her hands tightening on the fake piece of paper. "Not about your interest in the suffrage movement?"

Miss Burgess' head jerked upright. "Why on earth would we talk about *that*?" Her lip actually curled. "No, he had a tinker make this very strange, but rather beautiful bracelet for Edna."

That Henry Smith Fish, renowned cad and dilettante should have done any such thing, let alone made a point of showing it to Miss Burgess of all people, set Eliza's instincts buzzing. "If you don't mind me asking, what did this bracelet look like?"

The old lady's eyes seemed to cloud over. "It was quite lovely; all brass surrounding these stunning cobalt blue pieces of glass. It was quite strange, but Mr. Fish put it on his own wrist to show me better how it glowed. There was even this very strange noise..."

Eliza swallowed hard. The Ministry had been wondering what happened to the circlet of Delilah. The pieces of the shattered enamelled diadem had been on loan to the British museum from the Ministry Archives simply because the circlet had been so broken that its manipulative powers had been ended. It seemed Mr Fish had found a way to use a bit of modern technology to get them back.

Looking into the clouded eyes of Miss Burgess, Eliza knew what she had to do, and it involved slugging Mr Henry Smith Fish in the jaw before he could turn it on her. It was now of the utmost importance.

✦⇒ ⇐✦

"He wasn't home?" Douglas, Kate's son, and the love of Eliza's life stood by the chugging loco-motor and stared down at her in bemusement. "Are you telling me, that my little pepperpot can't find her man?" He grinned at her, and Eliza felt her ire rising.

As much as she loved Douglas, sometimes he could be a little condescending—especially when it came to her work. "I didn't just go to his house, Douglas—I scoured all of bloody Dunedin! For such a blowhard he's lying very low."

"Well, we can't be concerned about that little weasel now." Kate Sheppard appeared on the doorstep, pulling on her driving gloves, and with a pair of goggles hanging from around her neck. She was dressed warmly, because even in Spring in an open topped vehicle would be chilly. "We have to get the petition to Wellington by Monday, before parliament is dismissed for the season. Mr. John Hall has to present it before they close the doors. If he does not then the next parliament is guaranteed to be only more toxic to the cause."

The chugging of the loco-motor hardly seemed reassuring. Eliza glanced at it. "Then why are you not taking an airship? You could be there tomorrow morning instead of all this fuss and bother…"

Kate slipped her goggles over her eyes and adjusted them, "Because, my dear girl, both commercial fleets are owned by men unhappy with what we are trying to do. Simply put, they have informed all their offices not to sell tickets to us. We may even have a kind of wanted poster out. Very American. So it is this or Shanks' pony."

The Agent did some quick calculations. With two nights in hand they should be able to reach Picton and the ferry on Saturday night, and the capital by Sunday.

"And it's just the two of you?" Eliza didn't mean to sound dismissive, but Kate and Douglas Sheppard did not seem like a lot to protect the petition, which had taken nearly a year to assemble and would be impossible to replace in time should anything befall it.

Douglas flicked open the lid of the trunk already strapped to the back of the loco. "Don't worry, she's in good hands."

Eliza peered in and got a real thrill to see the huge roll of paper tucked in the case. Thousands upon thousands of woman's signatures were all in there, demanding the same rights as the men of the country for themselves. It was more than a year's work, and the voice of an unheard majority.

"I was up rather late last night pasting the final pages together," Kate whispered over her shoulder, before stepping up into the driving seat of the loco-motor. "I think it will be far more impressive to have John unfurl it across the floor of the debating chamber." Legions of women in all their different districts had worked long and hard to get these signatures, and then sent all the pages to Kate—Monday would see the culmination of their bravery and determination.

The idea of it unfurling before all those flabbergasted men was quite monumental—yet Eliza knew in the pit of her stomach that Henry Smith Fish had not suddenly disappeared by coincidence. If this petition reached Wellington then he would have failed.

Her mind was thus made up. She spun around. "I want to be there to see that, and I want to make sure it gets there." The weight of her ponamu handled pistols in the small of her back, under her jacket made her feel a little more comfortable.

Douglas took her hands in his. "I am not sure that is appropriate, Eliza, since we are not yet married—"

"Stuff and nonsense," Kate interrupted. "I can think of no better guardian of the petition than Miss Eliza D Braun—and I shall do my best to protect her innocence from you, Douglas." She wagged her finger at him with a grin, before holding out her hand to Eliza. "Climb up my dear."

The Agent smiled right back at her, before taking her place behind the Sheppards. Kate took a deep breath, as though just about to fling herself off an extremely tall cliff, then shoved the levers forward, and they were off. Eliza could only hope that they were leaving Mr. Henry Smith Fish behind them in a cloud of steam.

⋅=⋅

They reached Oamaru late on the first day, having thankfully seen very little traffic on the road. Mind you, with the state of it, Eliza was not surprised. Most sensible people took airships these days—and for good reason. She felt as though all her teeth had been in danger of being shaken loose.

At about ten o'clock in the evening they all climbed down, with sore muscles and aching ears, and entered the Valiant Hotel. Light beamed from every window, and a kindly landlady who had kept some bread and cheese for their supper waited on them.

First though, Douglas took charge of the dragging the trunk upstairs to his mother's room. Eliza had to order a room of her own, since she didn't dare share one with Douglas in front of Kate. She was brave—but she wasn't quite *that* brave.

The journey had definitely exhausted all of them, and with promises of an early start, they headed to their separate accommodations to rest as best they could.

Eliza took a bath in her room, soaking out the aches with a healthy dosing of Epson Salts in the water, but with her pistols nonetheless in close proximity. Loco-motors might be new, exciting and speedy, but one thing were not was comfortable. Damn those rich bastards preventing them taking an airship north.

She dare not soak too long, and far too quickly she got out, dried herself off, and slipped into some clothes Kate had loaned her for the trip. They were of a similar size and height, so it wasn't as inconvenient as it could have been.

However getting dressed seemed to take the last of Eliza's energy, and as she sat on her bed, and despite her best efforts, the warmth of the bath and the exhaustion of travel caught up with her. Eliza's eyes drooped and for a brief moment she dreamed of derry doings, fire, and a man with hazel eyes.

Luckily, she was a very light sleeper. One little bang on her door—more of a scrape than a knock—and Eliza was bolt upright her bed, her pistols in her hands. Carefully, she padded to the door and listened.

Someone was moving outside, footsteps going away from her door and towards Kate. The agent's hand slipped into her pocket. There she found the aural-defenders.

Something that the delightful Miss Burgess mentioned had stirred Eliza to caution, and she'd been careful to take one item in particular from the Ministry's agent issued devices.

It was not the first time she or her counterparts had been forced to face mind manipulation devices in their line of work, so the clankertons had come up with some damn fine counter measures—unfortunately there was only one kind that were anywhere near portable to stick in your pocket. She slipped them over the top of her ear and tightened the clamp to hold them in place. They mimicked the shape of the human ear, but were heavy, and dampened her own natural hearing. However they were also only defence against mind control—which she suspected Fish had. After flicking the tiny lever behind her ear, she could immediately hear the whirring of the clockwork, and a faint grinding sound like a music box run amok. It was distracting, but then it was meant to be.

Then, cocking her gun, she levered open her door, and immediately had to step over Douglas. Her training held, so that she didn't panic.

He was crumpled on the floor, his face pressed to the worn carpet, his eyes closed. Eliza felt for a pulse and was damn relieved to find one. He was down, but not dead. Unfortunately she had no time to stop and revive him.

Kate and the petition were in peril, so it was up to the junior agent to help them. Abandoning stealth, she ran towards the suffragist's room. The door was swinging slightly. The lock had been kicked in and broken in the frame. Eliza darted a look around the jamb.

"You can come in, Miss Braun," Henry Smith Fish shouted. "Come in and let's talk."

Her glance had told her one thing, Kate was being held in a choke-hold and very close to the cad—any kind of subtly was done with. Smith was behind Kate, one arm around her throat, as they stood backed against the window. Eliza's eyes darted to the trunk that was pulled out from under the bed, and only feet away from the man who hated it so.

Eliza kept her pistols down, yet did not give them up entirely and stepped into the room. "So let's make a deal; you let go of Mrs. Sheppard and I don't shoot you in the head." She said it in a kindly tone—but meant every word of it.

Smith adjusted the still struggling Kate. Mrs. Sheppard was a martial artist of no little metal, so Smith must have caught her while she slept. So he was living up to his reputation of being a right bastard.

Eliza considered. The shot was a hard one, especially if he moved. "How about instead," he purred, "you put down the gun and then run out into the street to wait for a carriage to run you over?"

The buzz in the air fairly pulsed against her skin. The aural-defenders rattled and chattered in Eliza's ears, and thankfully she did not feel the urge to obey him. "I don't think so," she hissed back.

His hateful face twisted; horrified that she was not obeying and mystified as to why not. After all her hair was loose and he couldn't really see her earlobes properly.

Fish's hand clenched around Kate's throat, and the bracelet flared bright blue. "Or I could tell the delightful Mrs. Sheppard here to stand up in parliament on Monday and convince everyone this petition is forged."

The two women shared a look. Kate was wide-eyed, horrified and frightened—no doubt seeing all she worked for in deadly peril. Her jaw tightened, and then she mouthed, "Shoot it!"

It was no easy shot, but the pistols were as accurate as the agent's aim. Eliza nodded, raised her weapon and obeyed. It was the only thing to do.

Her weapons roared in the tiny room and both of her shots hit home. The brass wiring that held the bracelet together hummed, while the second round shattered some of the glass.

Now the sound was pressing down on them all, like the rumble before the lightning crashed. It seemed to have an actual physical presence.

"The petition!" Kate screamed, twisting away, even as the light grew to blinding strength, destroying all shape and form, and confusing the eye. Eliza had only a moment to make her decision, and she chose to do as asked. She could not let all those women's efforts come to naught.

Throwing herself forward and down, she dove across the floor, smacking into the trunk, and sliding with it through the wardrobe door.

Behind was a sound that resembled what she imagined a dragon's roar might have been like. Eliza felt the air get sucked out of her lungs and everything rang as if they were inside a great bell. Behind her in the bedroom proper, she heard Fish and Kate howl together.

Twisting around, Eliza staggered upright back the way she had come, yelling Kate's name. The carnage she saw there said immediately that the bracelet and Mr. Henry Fish Smith would not be bothering them. Both were in pieces.

Kate lay a short distance off. It looked like at the last moment she'd been able to jerk at least partly free of her attacker—but not quite far enough. Fitful flames were already engulfing the bed and curtains and smoke beginning to fill the room.

Kate's clothing was torn, and there was blood everywhere coming from a devastating head injury. The suffragist's eye was gone in a bloody mess.

Eliza's hands fluttered around the wound not knowing what to do. This couldn't be happening. Only hours before they'd been joking in the loco-motor, and now she was kneeling in the blood of her heroine, screaming for Douglas.

He came and gathered up his mother, and then everyone was evacuating the hotel. Eliza only had enough sense in her to take the travelling case containing the petition with her. Nothing else seemed to matter.

<hr>

"You'll be glad to know Mrs. Sheppard made it through the night." The Goliath of a man standing on the other side of the oak desk did not sound like he was very pleased. His name was King Dick, and never had a man been better named. He looked powerful, he sounded powerful, and as Prime Minister of New Zealand he was. Luckily for Miss Braun, he was not the Minister in charge of the Ministry of Peculiar Occurrences.

Eliza found she didn't have the energy to respond as she should have. She had changed her clothes, but hadn't had a chance to have bath since Oamaru. Her hair still smelt of smoke and blood.

A government airship had been sent to evacuate Kate to Wellington, and after that it had been a bit of a blur. Luckily for the suffragist it would have reflected badly to have the government leave a prominent lady such as herself to die in a tiny town after such an event.

Douglas had accompanied his mother to hospital, while Eliza numbly went to meet Mr. John Hall with the petition in the trunk. She'd barely said two sentences to him, and though he had called after her, she had no reply to give him.

The summons by the Prime Minister would have usually engendered at least some nervousness, but all she could think of was Kate's face covered in blood.

Richard Seddon, not used to being so ignored, cleared his throat again, leaning over the desk. "I don't think, Agent Braun, you realise how much trouble you are in. Not only did you pursue a case without permission from your superior at the Ministry of Peculiar Occurrences, but you also killed a member of Parliament, and caused a fire in a boarding establishment!"

She knew what he wasn't going to say was the real reason he was so angry with her was that she had succeeded in getting the petition to Wellington, and that come Monday morning he would have to deal with that in parliament. King Dick was not known for his appreciation of Kate Sheppard's efforts.

"Even more unfortunately," Seddon said easing himself into his chair, while Eliza remained standing, "I can do nothing about it, since the Ministry of Peculiar Occurrences is directed from London and not from New Zealand." He grunted at that, again making his opinion known without a word.

At that moment, Eliza didn't care. She loved what she did, but she could not shake the recollection of Douglas' face as he followed the stretcher into the hospital. She knew what he had to be thinking. Eliza had said she would protect them, and now his mother hovered on the brink of death. Her job, which he had always seen as a silly fancy, had suddenly become much more serious.

The Prime Minister waited for a moment, for some reaction. When there was none, he slammed his fist on the desk. Eliza did jump at that.

"Damnit woman, I can't get you demoted, but there is one thing I can do. You have to leave immediately!"

"Pardon?" She shook her head as if emerging from a London fog.

King Dick grinned, with an expression that would have looked better on a crocodile. "You have to leave, and by Jove, I'll do everything to make sure you never set foot in this country again. We don't need your sort of feminine derry doing here."

"But..." Eliza was wondering if this nightmare was never going to end, "This is my home!"

"Not anymore." He pulled a sheef of papers in front of him. "You're being reassigned to the London office of the Ministry. And if you ever come back to our fair shores, Miss Eliza D Braun, you will be arrested as a public menace, the murderer of Mr. Henry Smith Fish, and arsonist of the Valiant Hotel."

She had never pleaded for anything in her life, but suddenly she understood how much she loved New Zealand—just as it was about to be snatched away. "Please, sir," she gasped out. "My family are here, the man I love—I can't leave forever. I just can't!"

His look was as cold as an Antarctic winter. "Then don't. Spend your time in a prison here for the rest of your life."

The grim reality began to settle over her. She had won, but she had lost. She could not disgrace her family, Douglas or the Ministry. It had to be London then.

However she was not going to leave without getting a last word in. Now it was her turn to lean over the desk. "I'll go then—but I hope one day Richard Seddon, you learn how painful it is to lose all you love—including your country! Think of me when that day comes!"

With that she turned on her heel and marched out of the Prime Minister's office. She would go and find Douglas, and send word to her family what had happened. It was going to be hard indeed to be parted from them and him—but what other choice did she have? None. None but to be the scapegoat for others rage.

She comforted herself that maybe things would alter, maybe the suffragists would change things, and it would not be men in charge forever. Maybe one day there would be a woman in King Dick's place.

That thought and one other warmed her as she strode out of the parliament buildings. Monday was not yet here, and the petition would be presented. She would stay that long at least, book passage north once it was over. She wanted to see the faces of all those menfolk when Kate and the suffragists' success was revealed.

It would make the leaving easier—or if not, at least worthwhile.

A Very Southern Christmas

by Pip Ballantine

Eliza D Braun stepped down off the airship gangplank and looked around. She'd got a good view of Cooktown coming in from under the clouds, and the greenness had surprised her. In her imaginings Australia was always burnt orange and dusty. This was as green as home though instead of the ferns of New Zealand there was the lush foliage of the tropics. The north of Queensland was quite the eye-opener.

The moist heat wrapped its around her as soon as her foot touched the ground, and she was glad to have dressed in khaki for the occasion. It wasn't really Christmasy, but those that worked for the Ministry of Peculiar Occurrences didn't get to choose the timing of their assignments. When the strange called it couldn't be simply put off. Though she would miss her mother's Christmas pudding, that was the sacrifice she had signed up to make.

Still she would have quite liked a look around if possible, but she was here to help not act the tourist, and a voice calling out her name reminded her of that fact.

"Miss Braun!" She whirled around and peered through the crowd of disembarking passengers to see who it was. She knew a few people from the Australian office of the Ministry of Peculiar Occurrences since they often worked in tandem with them, but the tall man striding in her direction was a stranger.

He parted the crowd like a ship under full steam and towered over most of them while he did so. Dressed as if ready to depart on safari, in dark brown breeches, beige shirt open at the neck, and a wide hat that kept the sun off his face.

His face was certainly worth seeing, and Eliza's skin grew a little hotter than even Australia's climate warranted. As a junior agent she hadn't quite got past the most awful blushes. She shifted her valise to the other hand, so she could hold out one to the man.

"Eliza D Braun from the New Zealand office."

He glanced at her hand for a moment, sighed and then shook it. "You're all they could send?"

A little taken a back, Eliza tried to imagine the poor man was just overly tired and hot. "Regional Director Murphy said I needed experience in the Australian office, so when your request came in—"

"Alright then," he said, snatching her valise out of her hand, "follow me."

It was a good thing she had decided on trousers this morning because Agent Campbell didn't slow down one jot. She concentrated on the large sweat stain on his shirt as she hurried to keep up.

Outside the aeroport he strode towards a large white horse tied up at one of the station's hitches. It was a mode of transport that made Eliza's eyebrows shoot up; she would never have imagined that an agent of the Ministry would have such an antiquated way of getting around. Usually her colleagues embraced the newest technology, or even tinkered about with their own.

Campbell got up onto the tall stallion without any effort, hung her valise on one side of his saddle, and then held out his hand.

Her staring up at him for a moment must have irritated him somehow because he shook his finger near to her face. "Come on, don't tell me you can't ride?"

Normally getting up behind a handsome devil like Agent Campbell would have been an attractive proposition, but the humidity of Cooktown would mean by the time they arrived, they would be stuck together. She wanted to make a good impression in the Australian office and arriving covered in sweat and horseflies wasn't her idea of that.

"I do," she admitted, "but surely the office can't be far away, I could just walk..."

Campbell tilted his hat and glanced down the road. "If you want to stretch your legs, then sure, the office is above the general store on Charlotte Street." Then he clicked his tongue, and the horse sprang away... with her valise bobbing against its side.

"Charlotte Street?" she said to herself, trying not to get upset at being abandoned on the side of the road. After all she had mentioned it.

It turned out that Cooktown was a small enough town that it was but three miles walk. The aeroport was close to the ocean, and the town was on the river.

It would have been a pleasant stroll if not for the heat, but she arrived at the store, and it was a relief to see Campbell's horse tied up outside. Her valise still intact on his saddle.

Maybe Cooktown was a fine place, but she didn't want all of her things stolen, she unhooked her luggage and went inside. The balding shop keeper directed her upstairs, and there she found Campbell. He'd seated himself by the window so a cool breeze could waft through his fine dark hair. A table in front of him was covered in maps, drawings and a couple of newspapers as well. It didn't look like much of an office though.

He gestured before him as if they were nothing but gold. "Here you go Lizzie, all the particulars you need to absorb before we get going."

Dropping her valise, and ignoring what had to be some kind of Australian informality, Eliza bent to examine the particulars of the case.

"Two children gone missing?" she asked, glancing up.

"Since last week," he replied, smoothing his moustache and staring for a moment out the window. "This town survives on the tin industry. Hard working folk, and these were children that didn't just run off. All were in locked houses in upstairs rooms, and no sign of a break in."

The sketches of the scenes of the crime were precise, and she saw that Agent Campbell was right. All the children were taken from second story rooms.

"And trackers?"

Bruce's eyes narrowed. "A couple of Gungarde lads came in to assist the local constabulary, and they did find signs of something passing. Couldn't identify them, but definitely not human they said."

With one finger he moved another sketch over. It was a strange long footprint the like of which she had never seen before.

"Some sort of wild animal?"

"Well actually, no because there was no blood. It wasn't a dingo or any other wild animal that took them." He punched the image with the side of his fist. "This is a bloody automaton."

Eliza frowned. While there were many fantastic devices being built all over the world, an automaton didn't seem like the most likely. Cooktown was small, concentrated on mining which used large drilling machines not human-like automatons.

"So you think this is for the purposes of kidnapping?" she asked, pushing her hair off her face as she looked up.

Bruce leaned forward. "Does that make sense? I said there were hard working folk in this town, but I sure as shit didn't say they were rich."

She recognised what he was doing; throwing down some earthly language to assert his dominance. That just showed he had not read her personnel file. She'd been pulling pints and scrubbing floors in her father's pub for most of her life. They didn't get much earthier than that.

It wasn't like this was the first man to try to put her in her place, and she didn't judge him by it... not yet at least. "So if not for ransom, then why?"

As soon as the words left her mouth, she knew. Children were a target the world over for nefarious purposes; sexual, for work, or as small test subjects for experiments.

"They are calling him Father Christmas around here."

"That's awful!"

Bruce nodded. "Yeah, it is, but word is that he took one naughty boy and one sweet little girl."

"I am sure that is a coincidence." Picking up the image of the tracks she asked, "Where exactly did this tracks lead?"

"That's where you come in," Bruce said, standing up and stretching. "The Gungarde trackers gave up once they started to head to the Black Mountain."

Now it was time for her ignorance to show. "And what is that?"

Putting his hands on the table he leaned closer with a grin, "It's what everyone steers clear of around here."

"Is that why you called me in?" she asked in an even tone.

Bruce crossed his arms. "A copper went missing back in '84 when he was hunting some bush rangers. Now I can't get even the bloody constabulary to follow me out there." His eyes swept her up and down. "I was hoping they would send a big strapping bloke."

Eliza looked into his clear blue eyes and began to see past his handsome exterior. "I assure you, Agent Campbell, while I am not strapping, I have completed all the physical tests the Ministry requires. I am also a fine shot if it should get to that."

He let out a snort. "Well as long as you can ride and aren't afraid of tight spaces, you'll do."

On the map, he pointed to a strange dark elevation among the green indicating jungle. "This here is the Black Mountain, also called Kalkajaka by the local Aborigines. They refuse to go near the place and say its full of evil spirits, or some such."

His voice dripped with dismissal, and that surprised Eliza. Even in her short time of working for the Ministry she'd seen more unbelievable things than she could have reckoned; a Maori chief come back to life, a cursed music box, and the ghost of one of New Zealand's most famous politicians. It was strange then that Agent Campbell who had worked in the same business for so much longer would dismiss the possibility that the native people were right.

Still she wasn't comfortable enough to ask why this was, instead she nodded in what she hoped was a sage manner and stared at the ominous dark stain on the map. "When do we head in?"

He scratched his impressive chin. "A day there and back. It'd be good to get the children back to their families on Christmas Eve."

"It would make the holidays bright," she replied. "So we set off in the morning?"

Now he laughed. "Lizzie, if you ain't noticed this place is full of sun and sweat during the day. Evening and early morning is the best time to travel. I'll go get you a horse and we'll set out towards sundown, and you best pack that valise down into something smaller."

Striding over to the far side of the room, he lifted a hidden latch and swung a portion of the wall back. Behind it was a small arsenal.

"Is all this yours?" she asked, finding herself drawn over to it. She had never seen such a fine display of weaponry in all her life. Even the Ministry armoury in New Zealand didn't have such a gathering of unusual looking rifles and pistols.

"Sure are," he said, running his hand over the nearest gunstock. "I got back from London last month and brought as many of their R&D lads experimentals as they would let me get away with."

Eliza couldn't help but picking up a fine and gleaming pistol with a clear tube on the top. It sparkled green as if a bit of lightning was trapped there.

Bruce leapt forward and carefully guided it out of her hands. "Careful there, Lizzie. Not quite sure what some of these even do, but they warned about the side effects though."

"Still, we should go in as best armed as we can. If we don't have man power, we can at least have fire power."

Bruce tilted his head, and when his smile came it was blinding. "You know, I like the direction of your thinking."

Eliza straightened up and grinned back. Even if he was calling her Lizzie—like her annoying younger brother, Gerald was want to do—he was still a good man. New Zealand and Australia were like brothers, her father had told her, always squabbling but built on the same ideals. She'd never pointed out the convict part of Australian history, and she decided to avoid doing it now to Bruce.

Especially when he allowed her to pick two rifles and three pistols to take with her. Warned off the one with the green vial, she chose two conventional Lee-Metford rifles as well as a nameless experimental and three regular pistols.

She put one in her holster under her jacket and another in the small of her back. The rest of their armaments went into a rifle bag.

Bruce then left her to pack essentials only into a small saddle bag. By the time she finished the relentless sun was creeping towards the horizon.

Shortly after rain started to fall. Bruce appeared with a small brown mare and stared down for a moment, possibly hoping she might have turned into that big strapping bloke while he was away.

"Best get on with it then," he said, dropping the reins in her general direction.

Eliza wasn't much for keeping a stiff upper lip, but she was one for showing her mettle to change people's minds. This wasn't the first person who had doubted her abilities in the Ministry, it was just that back in New Zealand she'd had Director Aroha Murphy's support.

Well, she thought, time I learned how to do without that.

She mounted up and followed after Agent Campbell. He didn't look back, but she didn't worry about that. She was sure by the time they had found this nefarious kidnapper he'd have a better opinion of her. He rode very well, she noted, and cut a fine figure in his saddle.

The sun soon gave way to the moon which hung, huge and looming, but provided enough light to see by. Eliza had heard tell of moonlight goggles being developed at the legendary Ministry R&D department in London, which would have made things much easier, but it would be awhile until such wonders filtered south of the equator.

They followed a road west out of town, Eliza trailing behind Campbell and choosing to remain silent. Instead she watched the surrounding jungle, hearing the whirr of unknown insects, and the rustle of leaves. Australia, unlike New Zealand had native creatures aside from birds. Kangaroos, dingoes, and wombats seemed tolerable, but Eliza harboured a little worry about snakes. Her homeland had none of those, and she couldn't help but peering into the undergrowth.

As if reading her thoughts, Bruce called over his shoulder. "Keep to the track, Braun. Plenty of taipans in this sort of bush country."

Swallowing hard, she rode her mare a little closer.

Bruce chuckled. "Course, one of the legends is that Black Mountain has giant pythons living all over it, so maybe a taipan wouldn't be so bad."

Eliza swallowed hard and decided not to comment on that, least her voice break into a squeak.

Her hand went reflexively to her pistol, and her horse let out a snort.

They travelled most of the night on the road, and when Campbell called for them to make camp, it must have been on the other side of midnight. It had been a while since Eliza had spent so long in the saddle, but after all the talk of snakes, she was quite content to stay there.

Campbell didn't take any notice, tying up his stallion, taking down his bedroll, and setting about making a fire.

"Come on, Braun," he called. "You get the billy on and you'll feel much better."

He handed her the little battered, tin pot and watched as she set about making the tea. She hoped he had brought her along for more than this. Still a cuppa did steady her nerves.

They sat silent around the fire, and she sipped her drink from a mug that looked like it had seen plenty of its own adventures.

"First time in Queensland?" Bruce asked, his smile quite disarming.

She nodded. "Yes, but I have been to Australia before."

"Sydney?"

When she nodded, he gave out a little snort. "Sydney's not really Australia. Just another little big city trying to be London." He gestured around them. "This is the real Australia. The place of bunyips, wild crocs, and bushrangers like Ned Kelly."

"Were you involved in that?" Eliza couldn't help but lean forward.

Bruce shrugged. "He was a damn fine clankerton, but unfortunately bit before my time."

"Oh." She stared into her tea.

He threw the last bit of his tea off into the undergrowth. "Anyway, try to get some sleep. We'll be up early. We'll ride for a good few more miles, but the Black Mountain isn't a place to take a horse." He didn't explain any further and so she wrapped herself in her blanket, tried not to think about taipans crawling in with her, and went to sleep.

They were up again after what felt like only an hour or so. The jungle turned more to bush, with light undergrowth, and just for a while Eliza was happy about that. It was only when they reached the base of the mountain her mood changed back.

As they pulled their horses up just beyond the reach of the trees, Eliza started to understand why the local tribe avoided this place.

Black Mountain did not present a friendly face to visitors. From the green of the bush, it was startling barren, and pitch black. The red earth gave way to uncountable thousands upon thousands of black boulders piled upon each other. They formed a looming presence high above the tops of the trees, with few plants daring to make a home on its slope.

As the wind blew over the rock a low ominous whistle filled the air, making their horses twist their ears this way and that. Eliza's mare pranced sideways, eyes rolling. She didn't blame her one bit.

Looking up at the mountain, she had to fight back the urge to turn around and head away from it. Her throat grew dry. Was the mountain staring back at her?

Bruce tilted his hat. "Yeah, she makes an impression doesn't she."

Why he would give anything like this edifice, a female moniker she didn't know. "Not a good one."

"No, the native people hold this as sacred ground, but they won't go near it." Bruce dismounted and tied up his stallion. Once she was down, he pulled a wrapped bundle from his saddlebag. It was a brass contraption, with gears and levers, that Eliza was dying to examine more closely. He fitted it around his arm and fiddled with the controls.

"That looks interesting," she dared. "Looks like it uses aether to—"

"Well actually it maps underground spaces." He made a face and tapped it. "The clankertons in Brisbane knocked it up for me. I'm going to head in and try to map the underground caves. Place is riddled with them."

Eliza pressed her lips together, wondering if he would ever let her show him she did have some idea what she was talking about. Instead she just said, "I'll watch your back."

He patted her on the shoulder. "Nah, you won't. I have to concentrate on this, and I can't nurse maid you."

"Nurse maid?" Eliza stared at him for a moment hardly believing what he said, before blurting out, "Then why did you bring me with you?"

"Well a strapping bloke would have been helpful, but honestly since all I have is you, the best thing is for you to wait here, and if I don't return by nightfall, head back to Cooktown for help."

She stared at him, barely believing what he was saying. A well-trained dog could have done the same.

Crossing her arms in front of her, she tried to make this handsome man see she was more than just a fail-safe. "Agent Campbell, I am fully trained and I assure..."

He patted her again, this time on the head. "I didn't mean to make it sound like this was optional, Lizzie. I meant, this is an order."

She screwed her mouth tight so hard she wondered her jaw didn't pop off. No one called her Lizzie and got away with it, not even Gerald. Still, this was an order, and she wanted to make the right impression.

"Righto then." Agent Bruce Campbell walked away from her and towards the mountain without looking back. She watched him scramble up through the field of black boulders, picking his way higher and higher, and stopping now and then to fiddle with his underground map maker. He hadn't even given it a decent name. All the while she got hotter and hotter and once again it had nothing to do with the Australian climate.

Eliza did as ordered though. She waited, passing the time by watching wildlife, cleaning her weaponry, and kicking rocks at the base of the mountain.

The weird moans and groans the wind playing with the boulders made didn't make the time pass any quicker. She thought of the million other things she could be doing rather than being stuck here. Even though she loved the Ministry spending Christmas with her family was special. Mum would be heating up the Christmas pudding, while Dad saw to the goose, and her siblings bickered in the parlour.

She almost drifted off under a tree thinking about what she was missing. Only Aroha Murphy's reminder kept her alert. *Constant vigilance is required of an agent.*

So leaning on her elbow, she sat up and scanned the mountain. Bruce had long gone, and nothing moved on the expanse of boulders. It was almost as if they had swallowed him up.

She ate a little bread from her saddlebag at about noon and paced back and forth near the base of the pile of boulders. By the time that the sun began its crawl behind the mountain, she had already had enough.

Agent Campbell might have given her a direct order, but she did not want to be stumbling around on that treacherous ground in the dark. If she was going to go after him then it would be now. Yes, she was going against a direct order, but sometimes an agent had to think for themselves, and she thought Campbell had to be in trouble.

Leaving the horses tied up, she set her foot on the first boulder, and shivered. It wasn't just the eerie sound of the wind, there was a something else; something primal—telling her to go in the other direction.

Hoisting her rifle over her shoulder, she pushed on. It wasn't a huge mountain in the scheme of things, Eliza had climbed Mount Cook back home after all, but there was a something exhausting about this place. The boulders meant you had to climb around them to move forward, and there was no simple place to put her foot. Each step was risking a broken ankle.

Following the direction that Campbell had gone, she scanned about for signs. It wasn't going to be like there would be footprints. A couple of times her leg nearly disappeared as smaller boulders rolled out her way. His warning about giant pythons whispered in her ear. She climbed on, sweating and nervous. The wind was the only sound up here, and she had to fight herself not to turn around.

The sun was going to leave her soon, and then she would have to rely on her lantern. Alone on this strange mountain and with limited visibility.

Though there was no sign of Campbell, she didn't want to call out his name, just in case something terrible replied instead.

She was about to resign herself to endless boulders and silence when she nearly plunged into a ravine. Stones skittered under her feet as she caught herself with the palm of her hands, and she caught a glimpse of a tuft of cotton on one of the rocks. She couldn't say if it was Campbell's, but it was the only sign of humanity she'd found so far. She half-climbed, half-slid down into the break in the mountain.

Now regardless of the sun she would have to rely on her lantern. Lighting it, she held it up before her and ventured in.

Several of the boulders here were different to those of the surface. They were crushed as if smashed by a large hammer. They rattled together, and she stepped through them, and just off to one side of that she found Campbell's cowboy hat.

Bending, she picked it up and put it on. Then she shuttered her lamp to its smallest aperture and took hold of her pistol. Her heart was thundering so hard she wouldn't have been surprised if it didn't echo through the boulder ravine. The black stone absorbed most of her light as she crept forward, placing each foot as carefully as she could. The sweat of her palm on the grip of her weapon made her worry she would drop it.

After about ten minutes of creeping, she saw that her light was no longer the only one in this ravine. Up ahead something was shining. That didn't comfort her, but it at least told her she was going in the right direction.

As she got even closer, she could make out the sound of gears whirring and the occasional puff of steam. Something mechanical was ahead and after another moment she realised it was actually singing a tune. *We Wish You a Merry Christmas*, but tooted out with clanks and jets of steam.

It was the kind of thing she had heard from an organ grinder on the waterfront in Auckland, but on a much grander scale. Eliza was careful not to fall into making assumptions about the kindness of the creation making the music, but she couldn't help smiling a little.

When she peeked over the large boulder in a bend in the ravine, it was to quite a sight; an automaton that stood at least ten feet tall, was bent over a large workbench, its back to her.

A boy of about eleven, and a red-haired girl of about eight were off to the right of the mechanical man, playing with what could only be toys. The gangly boy played with a pile of brass cubes, poking them around with a stick, and occasionally glancing up at the automaton. It was easy to see the concern in his young face. The girl crouched under the table, her arms full of tiny brass dolls. She looked like she was about to cry but was only just holding it back.

Then to top it all off, there was Agent Campbell's crumpled form off to the right of the bench. His satchel and crushed lantern lay a few feet further on. It was hard to figure if he was dead or alive until he let out a little groan.

Quick as a thought the automaton spun around and slammed its large, metallic foot down on Bruce's chest. The agent let out a grunt, so Eliza knew he was alive, but offered no resistance as the machine wrapped him up tight in what looked like coloured string.

"Bad Man," it grumbled, and its voice was far more high pitched than the size would have suggested. "You shall get coal this year." The automaton removed a bag under the table and tucked a piece of charcoal under Bruce's chin. It also opened its own chest and threw a piece or two for good measure.

Eliza got an excellent view of the interior workings; jerking pistons and a red-hot boiler. It was exquisite workmanship.

The little red-haired girl dared to peek out from under the table. "Can we go home soon... Santa?"

"Never, no never," the automaton replied in a cheery tone. "You are my good Christmas helpers and I shall keep you safe in my workshop."

Seeing Campbell get stomped must have taken out the natural prickliness of the red-head, because she retreated under the bench, her eyes filling with tears. Living in a granite ravine in a desolate mountain probably wouldn't be good for the long-term health of the children.

Eliza had never seen an automaton acting like this, nor even heard of one. They were simple creations, who did laundry and carried heavy objects. This one was interacting with human children and maintaining that it was Santa Claus all at the same time.

"I failed to keep a little boy safe once," the automaton said, turning its cylindrical head to stare at the comatose Campbell. "I won't make that mistake again." The voice coming from the automaton quavered.

There is always a story you don't know about, Aroha had told her. Campbell had blown into the ravine, not knowing the story, and the automaton had overpowered him. Brute force was not going to be the answer here—as much as she liked that. Eliza was going to have to be smarter since she had no chance of being stronger than this behemoth.

Tucking away her pistol under her shirt, she instead unsheathed a knife and hid it in her sleeve.

When she stepped out from behind the safety of the boulder, sweat was running down her neck, and her breathing caught in her throat. Nevertheless she managed to squeak out, "There you are Santa."

The automaton was on her in a few large strides. When he snatched her up, she felt sure he would crush her. As it raised her up to its gleaming eyes, she noted as impressive as the brass machine was, there was a touch of the unfinished about it. The face was only the impression of a human, and its arms were two different lengths.

It tilted its head from side to side as she smiled. "It's me, your elf Eliza," she said, trying to hang as limp as possible. "I finally found you."

It examined her like she was a bug, swinging her around. If it decided to close its fist tight, then it would be a short day for her. "Elf?" it said uncertainly.

"Yes, Eliza. I'm here to help you silly."

Thin streams of steam oozed from behind its chest plate as it considered her fate. After a panic inducing moment, it set her down on the table. The children stared at her, their faces frozen in uncertain expressions.

"I am having trouble with these bows," the automaton said after a long pause made of click-clacks and puffs of steam. "David always said bows on everything." He pointed off to the far end of the cavern.

Turning to follow his gaze. Eliza spotted two sets of bones, most definitely human, laid out neatly. One was large, and one was heartbreakingly small. She swallowed hard.

As she set about tying a large bow around the box the Santautomaton indicated, she cleared her throat. "And... what happened to David?"

The large cylindrical head swivelled in her direction. "His father brought him here to keep him safe, but they both got sick and died." Leaning over it patted the little girl on the head. "I won't let that happen to anymore boys and girls. They'll stay safe in Santa's workshop."

More curls of steam broke free of its chest cavity. The story was terrible, but she began to understand. A scientist had come to this hidden spot to try to save his child, but along the way he had somehow created an automaton with more than a few cogs mis-aligned.

With their death the Santautomaton had looked for other children to care for. It was so big it could have easily snatched them out of top floor windows. If it wasn't so terrifying, it might have been quite sweet. Oh yes, and it had stomped on Campbell.

"I can see you're doing a good job," she said, wriggling around to fiddle with the bows. When the automaton turned to pick up a spanner, she dropped the knife onto the ground, right next to Bruce. She did not dare to look down to see if he got the hint.

Instead, she tilted her head closer to the Santautomaton's chest; there was a strange noise that accompanied the steam. Out in this wilderness by himself, not quite finished, the machine seemed to be running off kilter.

Keep them talking, Aroha's lessons had shown her the worth of that. Suspects often hung themselves with their own words, and maybe that applied to automatons too.

"So why these children?" she asked, sliding closer to the machine. Only a few more inches and she'd be able to get her hand inside. It wouldn't take much to yank one of those pistons loose.

Santautomaton turned his brass head, and that was when the wave of blue light hit him from behind. The machine cried out.

The two children darted for cover under the bench, even as Eliza held out her hand. "No!" she screamed out, but it was too late. The energy from Campbell's rifle blew every screw from the automaton's chest and sent cogs and pistons flying from inside.

"Davidddddd..." the wail cut off before the tumble of metal and gears crashed to the ground.

Agent Bruce Campbell, a wash of blood obscuring the right side of his face, took the rifle down from his shoulder with a grim smile.

Eliza looked at him, her face contorted with horror. "He hadn't done anyone any harm!"

Bruce tilted his head, the corner of his mouth twitching. "Nah, he was Lizzie... it was a kidnapper of children. A bloody insane machine."

The Santautomaton was a crazed wreck, pieces melted together, and everything blown apart. She was sure no one would be able to make heads nor tails of these remains, but she did know Campbell had wrecked a unique creation.

She stared back at him, seeing his black and white world reflected in his eyes. "Just because he got one up on you didn't mean you had to destroy him just like that. I was very close to simply shutting him down. Imagine what we could have learned."

He shook his head. "You've got to harden up, Lizzie girl. You're going to have to make decisions in a snap, like I just did."

Climbing down from the bench she glared at him. "Not exactly the spirit of the season, Bruce, and not even a thank you for saving your bacon when I should have high tailed it back to town."

His dark brows furrowed at the impertinent use of his first name. "Well actually, you know you could have saved me a stomping or two?"

Eliza's blood was now getting up to boiling point. She'd had enough of his snide comments. "You know where a jackass go to get a nice cool drink, Bruce?"

He frowned at her. "…. from a stream?"

Her hands clenched into fists. "… no from a 'well actually.'"

He didn't understand, and he never would.

The two children glanced between them.

"Are you married?" The little girl asked, crossing her arms in front of her.

Eliza snorted and picked her up. "We are most certainly not, but guess what, we can get you back to your parents."

When the girl pointed down, the boy handed her one of the exquisitely jointed brass dolls she'd been playing.

"He did make good toys," the boy said, shoving his hands into his pockets.

"Yes, yes he did." She ruffled his hair. "Just as long as you understand that wasn't the real Santa Claus. Bruce here didn't destroy the real Santa."

"Oh I know that," the little girl replied. "No jackass could ever kill Santa."

So with Bruce fuming in their wake, the three of them headed back towards town, and a proper Christmas.

photo by Bruce F. Press Photography

New Zealand-born fantasy writer and podcaster **Philippa (Pip) Ballantine** is the author of the *Books of the Order* series, and has appeared in collections such as *Steampunk World* and *Clockwork Fairy Tales*. She is also the co-author with her husband, **Tee Morris,** of *Social Media for Writers*. Tee penned *Twitch for Dummies* and *Discord for Dummies*, co-authored *Podcasting for Dummies,* and has contributed articles and stories for numerous anthologies including *Farscape Forever!, Tales of a Tesla Ranger,* and *A Cosmic Christmas 2 You.*

Together, they are the creators of the Ministry of Peculiar Occurrences. Both the series and its companion podcast, *Tales from the Archives,* have won numerous awards including the 2011 Airship Award for Best in Steampunk Literature, the 2013 Parsec Award for Best Podcast Anthology, and RT Reviewers' Choice for Best Steampunk of 2014.

The two reside in Manassas, Virginia with their daughter and a mighty clowder of cats. You can find out more about them and explore more of the Ministry at **ministryofpeculiaroccurrences.com**